Twice IN A BLUE MOON

CHRISTINA LAUREN

piatkus

PIATKUS

First published in the US in 2019 by Gallery Books,
an imprint of Simon & Schuster, Inc.
First published in Great Britain in 2019 by Piatkus

1 3 5 7 9 10 8 6 4 2

Copyright © 2019 by Christina Hobbs and Lauren Billings

Interior design by Lewelin Polanco

A CIP catalogue record for this book
is available from the British Library.

TPB ISBN 978-0-349-42275-6

Printed and bound in Great Britain by Clays Ltd, Elcograf S.p.A.

Papers used by Piatkus are from well-managed forests
and other responsible sources.

Piatkus
An imprint of
Little, Brown Book Group
Carmelite House
50 Victoria Embankment
London EC4Y 0DZ

An Hachette UK Company
www.hachette.co.uk

www.littlebrown.co.uk

The item should be returned or renewed by the last date stamped below.

Dylid dychwelyd neu adnewyddu'r eitem erbyn y dyddiad olaf sydd wedi'i stampio isod

Ringland Library

To renew visit / Adnewyddwch ar
www.newport.gov.uk/libraries

ALSO BY

Christina Lauren

Dating You / Hating You
Roomies
Love and Other Words
Josh and Hazel's Guide to Not Dating
My Favorite Half-Night Stand
The Unhoneymooners

THE BEAUTIFUL SERIES

Beautiful Bastard
Beautiful Stranger
Beautiful Bitch
Beautiful Bombshell
Beautiful Player
Beautiful Beginning
Beautiful Beloved
Beautiful Secret
Beautiful Boss
Beautiful

THE WILD SEASONS SERIES

Sweet Filthy Boy
Dirty Rowdy Thing
Dark Wild Night
Wicked Sexy Liar

YOUNG ADULT

The House
Sublime
Autoboyography

one

JUNE
Fourteen Years Ago

NANA TURNED TO INSPECT the hotel room. Behind her, the curtains drifted closed with a whisper. With her dark, sharp eyes, she surveyed the cream and red decor, the generic paintings, and the television she no doubt found gaudily perched on the otherwise beautiful dresser. Never in my life had I been in a room this fancy, but her gaze, as it touched everything, read *Given the cost, I expected more.*

Mom had always described this expression as *pruney*. It fit. My grandmother—only sixty-one—totally looked like a piece of soft dried fruit when she got mad.

As if on cue, she grimaced like she'd just smelled something sour. "Our view is the *street*. If I wanted to stare at a city street I could have driven to San Francisco." She blinked away from the dresser to the telephone on the desk, moving toward it with purpose. "We aren't even on the right side of the building."

Oakland, to New York, to London, landing just over an

hour ago. For the longest leg, our seats were in the middle of a group of five, on the bulkhead row, where we were flanked on one side by a frail older man who immediately fell asleep on Nana's shoulder and on the other by a mother with an infant. By the time we were finally situated in the hotel room, I just wanted a meal, and a nap, and a tiny patch of quiet away from Nana the Prune.

Mom and I had lived with Nana since I was eight. I knew she had it in her to be a good sport; I'd seen it every day for the past ten years. But right then we were far from home, way out of our comfort zone, and Nana—owner of a small-town café—detested spending her hard-earned money and not getting exactly what she was promised.

I nodded to the window as a very European black taxi zoomed by. "It *is* a pretty great street, though."

"I paid for a view of the *Thames*." She ran a blunt fingertip down the list of hotel extensions, and my stomach clenched into a ball of guilt at the reminder that this vacation was way more lavish than anything we'd ever done. "*And* Big Ben." The tremble of her hand told me exactly how quickly she was calculating what she could have done with that money if we'd stayed somewhere cheaper.

Out of habit, I tugged at a string on the hem of my shirt, wrapping it around my finger until the tip pulsed. Nana batted my hand away before she sat at the desk, heaving an impatient breath as she lifted the phone from its cradle.

"Yes. Hello," she said. "I'm in room 1288 and I have brought my granddaughter all the way here from—yes, that's correct, I am Judith Houriet."

I looked up at her. She'd said Judith, not Jude. *Jude* Houriet baked pies, served the same regular customers she'd had since she opened her café at nineteen, and never made a fuss when someone couldn't afford their meal. *Judith* Houriet was apparently much fancier: she traveled to London with her granddaughter and certainly deserved the view of Big Ben she'd been promised.

"As I was saying," she continued, "we are here to celebrate her eighteenth birthday, and I specifically booked a room with a view of Big Ben and the Tham—yes." She turned to me, stage-whispering, "Now I'm on *hold*."

Judith didn't even sound like my nana. Was this what happened when we left the cocoon of our town? This woman in front of me had the same soft curves and stout worker's hands, but wore a structured black jacket I knew Jude could barely afford, and was missing her ubiquitous yellow gingham apron. Jude wore her hair in a bun with a pencil dug through it; Judith wore her hair blown out and tidy.

When whoever was on the other end returned, I could tell it wasn't with good news. Nana's "Well that's unacceptable," and "I can *assure* you I am going to complain," and "I expect a refund of the difference in room rates," told me we were out of luck.

She hung up and exhaled long and slow, the way she did when it had been raining for days, I was bored and testy, and she was at her wits' end with me. At least this time I knew I wasn't the reason behind her mood.

"I can't tell you how grateful I am," I said quietly. "Even in this room."

She blew out another breath and looked over at me, softening only slightly. "Well. We'll see what we can do about it."

Two weeks with Nana in a tiny hotel room, where she was sure to complain about the poor water pressure or the too-soft mattress or how much everything cost.

But two weeks in *London*. Two weeks of exploring, of adventure, of cramming in as much experience as I could before my life got small again. Two weeks seeing sights I'd only ever read about in books, or seen on TV. Two weeks watching some of the best theater productions anywhere in the world.

Two weeks of not being in Guerneville.

Dealing with a little pruney was worth it. Standing, I lifted my suitcase onto my bed and began unpacking.

★ ★

After a surreal walk across Westminster Bridge and past the towering Big Ben—I could actually *feel* the chimes through the center of my chest—we ducked into the darkness of a small pub called The Red Lion. Inside, it smelled of stale beer, old grease, and leather. Nana peeked in her purse, making sure she'd converted enough cash for dinner.

A few figures lurked near the bar, yelling at the television, but the only other people there for a meal at five in the evening were a couple of guys seated near the window.

When Nana spoke—strong voice, clear American accent saying, "A table for two, please. Near the window."—the older of the two men stood abruptly, sending the table screeching toward his companion.

"Across the pond as well?" he called out. He was around Nana's age, tall and broad, black with a shock of salt-and-pepper hair and a thick mustache. "We just ordered. Please, come join us."

Nana's dread over having to socialize with anyone tonight was apparent; it settled across her shoulders in a gentle curve.

She waved away the host, taking the menus from his hand and leading us both to their table by the window.

"Luther Hill." The older man stretched out his hand to Nana. "This is my grandson, Sam Brandis."

Nana gingerly shook his hand. "I'm Jude. This is my granddaughter, Tate."

Luther moved to shake my hand next, but I was hardly paying attention. Sam stood at his side, and just looking at him sent an earthquake rattling down my spine, the way the chimes of Big Ben had reverberated along my bones earlier. If Luther was tall, Sam was a redwood, a skyscraper, wide as a road.

He ducked a little to pull my attention from the expanse of his chest, giving me a smile that I imagined must be cultivated to reassure people that he wasn't going to break their hand when he shook it.

He pressed his palm to mine and squeezed, carefully. "Hi, Tate."

He was gorgeous, but just imperfect enough to seem . . . perfect. His nose had been broken at some point, and healed with a small bump near the bridge. He had a scar through one of his eyebrows and one on his chin—a tiny, indented comma below his lip. But there was something about the shadow he cast, the solid weight of him, and the way he came together—his soft brown hair, wide-set green-brown eyes, and full, smooth mouth—that made my pulse seem to echo in my throat. I felt like I could stare and stare at his face for the rest of the night and still find something new in the morning.

"Hi, Sam."

Nana's chair screeched dissonantly across the wooden floor, and I snapped my gaze to where Luther was helping her into her seat. Only two weeks prior, I had ended a three-year relationship with Jesse—the only boy in Guerneville I'd ever considered worthy of affection. Boys were the last thing on my mind.

Weren't they?

London wasn't supposed to be about boys. It was about being in a place with museums, and history, and people who were raised in a city rather than in a tiny, damp, redwood-lined river town. It was meant to be about doing every last thing Nana had ever dreamed of doing here. It was about having one fancy adventure before I ducked back into the shadows and began college in Sonoma.

But it seemed Sam didn't get the mental memo that London wasn't about him, because although I'd looked away, I could feel the way he was still watching me. And was still holding my hand. In unison, we looked down. His hand felt heavy, like a rock, around mine. Slowly he let go.

We sat together at the cramped table—Nana across from me, Sam to my right. Nana smoothed the linen table-cloth with an inspecting hand, pursing her lips; I could tell she was still mad about the view and barely containing the need to voice it to someone else, to hear them confirm that she was right to be up in arms over this injustice.

In my peripheral vision, I caught Sam's long fingers as they reached out and engulfed his water glass.

"Well now." Luther leaned in, pulling a whistling breath in through his nose. "How long have you been in town?"

"We just landed, actually," I said.

He looked at me, smiling beneath his bushy old-man pornstache. "Where you all from?"

"Guerneville," I said, clarifying, "about an hour north of San Francisco."

He dropped a hand on the table so heavily that Nana startled and his water rippled inside the glass. "San Francisco!" Luther's smile grew wider, flashing a collection of uneven teeth. "I've got a friend out there. Ever met a Doug Gilbert?"

Nana hesitated, brows tucking down before saying, "We . . . no. We've not met him."

"Unless he drives up north for the best blackberry pie in California, we probably haven't crossed paths." I said it proudly, but Nana frowned at me like I'd just given them some scandalously identifying information.

Sam's eyes gleamed with amusement. "I hear San Francisco is a pretty big city, Grandpa."

"True, true." Luther laughed at this, at himself. "We have a small farm in Eden, Vermont, just north of Montpelier. Everyone knows everyone there, I suppose."

"We sure know how that is," Nana said politely before surreptitiously peeking down at the dinner menu.

I struggled to find something to say, to make us seem as friendly as they were. "What do you farm?"

"Dairy," Luther told me, his smile encouraging and bright. "And since everyone does it, we also do a bit of sweet corn and apples. We're here celebrating Sam's twenty-first birthday, just three days ago." Luther reached across the table, clutching Sam's hand. "Time is flying by, I tell you that."

Nana finally looked back up. "My Tate just graduated from high school." A tight cringe worked its way down my spine at the way she emphasized my age, glancing pointedly at Sam. He might have been twice my size, but twenty-one is only three years older than eighteen. Going by her expression, you'd think he'd been practically middle-aged. "She's starting college in the fall."

Luther coughed wetly into his napkin. "Whereabouts?"

"Sonoma State," I said.

He seemed to be working on a follow-up question, but Nana impatiently flagged down the waiter. "I'll have the fish and chips," she ordered, without waiting for him to come to a full stop at the table. "But if you could put them on separate plates, I'd appreciate it. And a side salad, no tomatoes. Carrots only if they aren't shredded."

I caught Sam's eye and registered the sympathetic amusement there. I wanted to explain that she owns a restaurant but hates eating out. She's picky enough to make her food perfect, but never trusts anyone else to do the same. After he gave me a small smile, we both looked away.

Nana held up a hand to keep the waiter's attention from turning to me yet. "And dressing on the side. Also, I'll have a glass of chardonnay and an ice water. *With ice.*" She lowered her voice to explain to me—but not so quietly that everyone else didn't hear it too: "Europeans have a thing about ice. I'll never understand it."

With a tiny grimace, the waiter turned to me. "Miss?"

"Fish and chips." I grinned and handed him my menu.

The waiter left, and a tense, aware silence filled his wake before Luther leaned back in his chair, letting out a roaring laugh. "Well now. I guess we know who the princess is!"

Nana became a prune again. Great.

Sam leaned forward, planting two solid arms on the table. "How long you here for?"

"Two weeks," Nana told him, pulling her hand sanitizer out of her purse.

"We're doing a month," Luther said, and beside him, Sam picked up a piece of bread from the basket at the center of the table and wolfed it down in a single clean bite. I worried they'd ordered a while ago, and our appearance had really delayed the delivery of their meal. "Here for a couple weeks as well," Luther continued, "then up to the Lake District. Where are you staying in London?"

"The Marriott." My voice carried the same reverence I'd use to tell him we were staying in a castle. "Right on the river."

"Really?" Sam's eyes darted to my mouth and back up. "So are we."

Nana's voice cut in like a razor: "Yes, but we'll be moving as soon as we can."

My jaw dropped, and irritation rose in a salty tide in my throat. "Nana, we don't—"

"Moving hotels?" Luther asked. "Why on earth would you leave that place? It's beautiful, historic—it's got a view of everything you could possibly want."

"Our room doesn't. In my book, it's unacceptable to pay

what we're paying for two weeks, just to look at a row of parked cars." She immediately handed the water glass back to the waiter when he put it in front of her. "Ice, please."

She's tired, I reminded myself, and drew in a deep, calming breath. *She's stressed because this is expensive and we're far away from home and Mom is alone there.*

I watched the waiter turn and walk back toward the bar; I was mortified by her demands and her mood. A tight leaden ball pinballed around inside my gut, but Sam laughed into another sip of his own water, and when I looked at him, he grinned. He had my favorite kind of eyes: mossy green backlit by a knowing gleam.

"This is Tate's first trip to London," Nana continued, apparently ignoring the fact that it was her first trip here, too. "I've been planning this for years. She should have a view of the river."

"You're right," Sam said quietly, and didn't even hesitate when he added: "You should take our room. Twelfth floor. We have a view of the river, the London Eye, and Big Ben."

Twelfth floor. Same as us.

Nana blanched. "We couldn't possibly."

"Why not?" Luther asked. "We're barely ever there. The better views are outside, when you're out and about."

"Well of course we won't be sitting in the *room* the entire time," Nana protested defensively, "but I assumed if we're paying—"

"I insist," Luther broke in. "After dinner, we'll trade rooms. It's settled."

★ ★

"I don't like it." Nana sat by the window while I shoved all my clothes back in my suitcase. Her purse on her lap and the packed suitcase at her feet told me she'd already decided to trade rooms, she just needed to make a show of protest. "Who offers to give up a view of the river and Big Ben for a view of the street?"

"They seem nice."

"First, we don't even know them. Second, even with *nice* men you don't want to be obligated."

"Obligated? Nana, they're trading hotel rooms with us, not paying us for sex."

Nana turned her face toward the window. "Don't be crude, Tate." She fingered the organza curtain for a few quiet beats. "What if they find out who you are?"

There it was. Reason number one I'd never traveled east of Colorado before today. "I'm eighteen. Does it even matter anymore?"

She started to argue but I held up a hand, giving in. It mattered so much to Nana that I stayed hidden; it wasn't worth pushing back.

"I'm just saying," I said, zipping up my bag and rolling it toward the door. "They're being nice. We're here for two weeks, and glaring at that street will drive you crazy. Which means it will drive me crazy. Let's take the room." She didn't move, and I returned a few steps closer to her. "Nana, you know you want the view. Come on."

Finally she stood, saying, "If you'd be happier with it," before leading me out. We fell silent as our suitcases rolled dully behind us, wheels rhythmically tripping over the seams in the sections of thick carpet.

"I just want your vacation to be perfect," she said over her shoulder.

"I know, Nana. I want yours to be perfect too."

She hiked her JCPenney purse higher on her shoulder, and I felt a pang of protectiveness. "It's our first trip to London," she said, "and—"

"It's going to be amazing, don't worry." The café did well for a café in a small town, but it was all relative; we'd never been rolling in cash. I couldn't even fathom how long it must have taken her to save for all this. I mean, I'd seen her itinerary and it was packed: museums, Harrods, shows, dinners out. We were going to spend more in two weeks than Nana probably spent in a year.

"I'm already so excited to be here," I said.

Sam and Luther emerged from their room; Luther was rolling a bag behind him, and Sam had a duffel slung over his shoulder. Once again I experienced a weird physical leap inside at the sight of him. He seemed to completely fill the hallway. He'd pulled a worn blue plaid shirt over the T-shirt he wore earlier, but at some point he'd taken off his green Converse, and now padded his way down the hall only in socks. It was oddly scandalous.

Sam lifted his chin in greeting when he saw me, and smiled. I don't know if it was the smile or the socks—the hint of being undressed—but a shiver worked its way down my spine.

I'm here for museums and history.
I'm here for the adventure and experience.
I'm not here for boys.

Sam was right there, four, three, two feet away. He blocked out the ambient light coming in from a row of narrow windows—I barely came up to his shoulder. Was this what it felt like to be a moon orbiting a much larger planet?

"Thanks again," I mumbled.

"Are you kidding?" His eyes followed me as we passed. "Anything to make you smile."

★ ★

The new room was exactly the same as our old one, except for one important detail: the view. Nana unpacked, hanging her clothes in the narrow closet, lining her makeup and lotions on the wide granite counter. Against the swirling black and cream, her drugstore blush and eye shadow palettes looked dusty and faded.

Within only a few minutes she was in bed, beginning her ritual of foot cream, alarm setting, and reading. But despite the time difference and long flight, I was still buzzing. We were in London. Not just down the freeway in Santa Rosa or San Francisco—we were actually across an entire *ocean*. I was exhausted, but it was in that speedy, jittery way where I didn't want to sleep. In fact, I didn't think I ever wanted to sleep again. I knew if I got into bed now my legs would wrestle with the sheets anyway: hot, cold, hot, cold.

Anything to make you smile.

I hated to admit it, but Nana was right: the view was spectacular. It made me itch to slip out like a shadow into the night and explore. Right there, just outside the window were the Thames and Big Ben, and just below was a manicured garden. The grounds were dark, spotted with tiny lights and fluttering shadow; it looked like a maze of lawn and trees.

"Think I'll sit outside and read for a bit," I said, grabbing a book and trying to hide how on edge I felt. "Just in the garden."

Nana studied me over the top of her reading glasses, practiced hands rhythmically rubbing in hand cream. "By yourself?" I nodded, and she hesitated before adding, "Don't leave the hotel. And don't talk to anybody."

I kept my tone even. "I won't."

The real directive remained unspoken in her eyes: *Don't talk about your parents.*

My own answered in kind: *When have I ever?*

★ ★

I could legally drink in England, and part of me really wanted to sneak into the hotel bar, order a beer, and imagine the day when I'd be here on my own, untethered from Mom and Nana and the weight of their pasts and the burden of their expectations. I wondered if I might look like I belonged . . . or more like a rebellious teenager trying on adulthood for size. Looking down at my tight jeans, my baggy cardigan, my battered Vans, I suspected I already knew the answer.

So, with my book in hand, I bypassed the bar and headed out the wide set of doors on the ground floor. The garden was irresistible: it had that tidy, manicured look that makes every shrub look like it needs to be brought in at night, too precious for the elements. Yellow lights sat at even intervals, each lighting a cone of brilliant green grass. The city was

could take them back, and a brush fire of panic flared to life beneath my ribs.

"Really?"

I hummed, noncommittal, and he returned his attention to the sky.

"Yeah, I guess Roberta has everything she needs in Vermont," he said.

I attempted to steer us back to safer territory. "Then why did you and Luther come to London?"

"Luther always wanted to go."

"No wonder he's so excited."

It was Sam's turn to hum and the silence swallowed us up. Sam was right, though. The more I looked for them, the more stars I saw. In a rare twist of nostalgia, I remembered lying in bed while Dad read *Peter Pan* to me, and we picked our favorite illustrated page. Mine was Peter Pan peeking in the window, seeing the Darling family embracing. Dad's was Wendy and Peter fleeing in the night sky, sailing clear past Big Ben.

Out of the quiet, Sam's voice rumbled over me. "Want to hear something crazy?"

Interest piqued, I turned my head to see him. "Sure."

"I mean." He exhaled slowly. "*Really* crazy."

I paused. My world for the past ten years had been a bubble: the same five people orbiting around me in a tiny tourist community. For nine months out of the year—all but the summer—we were Hicksville, California. We never heard any crazy stories—unless they were about my dad, and I rarely saw or heard those anymore, Nana ensured it.

"Sure."

"I think Luther is dying."

Shock passed over me in a cold wave. *"What?"*

"He hasn't said anything. I just . . . have this sense, you know?"

I barely knew Sam, barely knew Luther, so why did this possibility feel devastating? And what must that feel like? To sense someone close to you was *dying?*

The only person I knew who had died was Safeway Bill. I didn't even know his last name, just that he was a regular at the café and when he wasn't sitting at the corner table getting free pie, he was sitting near the Safeway, panhandling and probably drunk. I think Bill lived in Guerneville even before Nana did; he looked about a hundred years old—leathered and with a tangled, messy beard. Tourists used to give him a wide berth when they passed, headed to Johnson's Beach with their inflatable rafts and white sunscreened noses. Bill was the safest thing in that town; way safer than any of the frat boy tourists coming through, getting messy drunk and harassing people just minding their own business at the Rainbow Cattle Company on Friday nights. Nothing made me madder than seeing people look at Safeway Bill like he was going to stand up and turn violent.

Nana heard from Alan Cross, who worked over at the post office, that they found Bill dead near the bus stop one morning. Nana showed her emotions in these tiny rare flashes. She stared out the window when Alan said this, and asked, "Now who's gonna love my peach pie the way he did?"

But Luther was nothing like Bill. Luther was vibrant

and alive and right upstairs. He worked and had a family
and *traveled*. I'd never known anyone who looked healthy
like Luther and just . . . died.

I was quiet too long, I think, because I heard Sam swallow in the dark. "Sorry, I guess I just needed to say it to
someone."

"No, of course," I said in a burst.

"He's not my grandfather by blood—I mean, I guess you
figured that, since I'm white and he's black. He's Roberta's
second husband. They both raised me," Sam said, and then
reached back to tuck his hands behind his head again. "Him
and Roberta."

"Could you ask him?" I said. "Whether he's sick?"

"He'll tell me when he wants to tell me."

God, this conversation was surreal. But it struck me that
Sam wasn't self-conscious about discussing this with someone he hardly knew. Maybe the fact that I was a stranger
made it easier to talk about.

More words bubbled to the surface. "Would it just be
you and Roberta, then? If . . ."

Sam took a deep breath, and I squeezed my eyes closed,
wishing I could pull the words back in my mouth and swallow them down.

"I'm sorry," I said quickly. "That's none of my business."

"Neither is Luther being sick, but that didn't stop me."
While my brain chewed on this, he shifted beside me,
scratching his ear. "It's just me, Luther, and Roberta, yeah."

I nodded in the darkness.

"As the story goes," Sam continued, "a young woman
from Ukraine named Danya Sirko came to the States and

found herself in New York." Sam paused, and when I looked over, I caught his wry smile aimed at the sky. "Danya became the nanny to Michael and Allison Brandis's three young children in Manhattan."

I could feel him turn to look at me, waiting.

"Okay . . . ?"

Sam hesitated meaningfully. "Incidentally, Danya was also very beautiful, and Michael was not a faithful man."

Realization settled in. "*Oh*. Danya is your mom, not Allison? Michael is your dad?"

"Yeah. He's Roberta's son. Luther's stepson." He laughed. "I was the dirty little secret, until my mother was deported—by Michael, sort of. I was two, and he wanted nothing to do with me, but Danya wanted me to be raised here. Luther and Roberta took me in when they should have been retiring and taking it easy."

My stomach bottomed out. There he was, spilling the soap opera version of his family's history, and I wasn't even allowed to talk about mine. It felt unfair.

"I'm sorry."

He laughed lightly at this. "Don't be."

"You know what I mean."

"I do. But I have to think it was worlds better to be with Luther and Roberta than Michael, even if that had been an option."

"So . . . you don't know your dad?"

"No." Sam blew out a breath and arced a smile over at me. He let the confidence settle between us for a few quiet beats. "What about you?"

My heart slammed against my breastbone, and Nana's stern warning expression was printed on the inside of my eyelids. This was where I always played my part: *My dad died when I was a baby. I was raised by Nana and Mom.*

But the thing was, I'd spent my whole life with the truth trapped in my throat. And with Sam's enormous backstory out there between us, I didn't *want* to lie again. "Me?"

Sam tapped his knee against mine, setting off an electrical storm along my skin. Even when he wasn't touching me, it was impossible not to feel how close he was. "You."

"I grew up mostly in Guerneville." The truth rattled a cage inside my ribs. "It's a super small town in Northern California. I'm moving to Sonoma for school—which isn't very far." I lifted my hands in a shrug and let a hint of the truth slip out: "I was raised by my mom and Nana."

"No dad, either?"

I swallowed. The easy, familiar lie was right there, on the tip of my tongue—but I was under the London sky, thousands of miles from home, and a rebellious, impulsive flash streaked through me. This had always been such a bigger deal to Nana and Mom than it had ever been to me; why was I still protecting their story? "He sort of . . . fell away."

"How does a dad fall away?"

I became aware, while I was lying beside this completely earnest stranger on a damp lawn, that it was weird that I'd never really talked about this. In part, I didn't talk about it because I knew I wasn't supposed to. And in part, because it was unnecessary: the one person in my life who learned about it—my best friend, Charlie—had watched the drama unfold in real time, in bite-sized servings that grew spaced farther and farther apart. I'd never needed to summarize it or spin it into a story. So why did I suddenly want to?

"My parents got divorced when I was eight," I told him, "and Mom moved me back to her hometown. Guerneville."

"Back from where?"

I peeked over the edge of this canyon, and I didn't know what it was about that garden or Sam but I decided: *Fuck it.* I was eighteen and it was *my* life, what's the worst that could happen?

"LA," I said.

I blinked in the direction of the hotel again as if I expected to see Nana racing toward us, shaking her fists.

Sam let out a low whistle, as if this even meant anything yet. And maybe it did; maybe to a farmer from Vermont, LA seemed as exciting as it could get.

I had only tiny, pulsing memories of living in the city: foggy mornings, hot sand on my bare feet. A pink ceiling that seemed to stretch into space above me. Over time I'd started to think maybe I remembered LA the way Mom remembers childbirth: all of the good parts, none of the obvious pain.

The quiet swallowed us again, and in it, I felt the adrenaline ebb. I grew aware of the contrast of the cold at my back and the heat at my side. I'd shared a tiny slice of my history and the sky hadn't opened up and rained fire. Nana hadn't materialized from behind a tree, intent on dragging me back to California.

"So, divorced parents, Mom moved back to Guerneville. Now you're on your way to Sonoma? I told you about adultery and a secret love child. I'm disappointed, Tate," he teased. "That wasn't very scandalous."

"That's not exactly *all* of it, but . . ."

"But . . . ?"

"I don't know you."

Sam rolled to his side, facing me. "Which makes it even better." He pointed to his chest. "I'm nobody. I'm not going back to *Vermont* of all places and telling everyone this beautiful girl's secrets."

My thoughts tripped on the word *beautiful*.

Torn, I searched out the thread on the hem of my fraying sweater, but I was distracted when Sam reached out to pluck a blade of grass from my hair. The tip of his finger grazed the curve of my ear. Heat blazed from the point of contact and down across my cheek, scalding my neck. Could he see my blush in the dark?

He waited one . . . two . . . three seconds before he rolled onto his back again.

"Anyway," he said, "I guess that's why I said that about Luther. I sure can't talk about it at home. He and Roberta are the bedrock of our community, and for as independent as she is, I don't know how Roberta would survive without him. If he's sick, I'm sure that's partly why he hasn't told anyone. Like I said, I think I needed to put it out there." Scratching his jaw, he added, "Does that make sense? Saying it out loud makes it real, means I can work on dealing with it."

What he was saying, what he was describing—it was like a deep gulp of cold water, or the bursting first bite into a perfect apple. I knew, in some ways, that my life had been entirely constructed as a safe little bubble. Dad was loaded, but I wasn't sure we even took money from him, because we'd never had a lot. We had enough. I had freedom within a small geographic range, the best friend I could have ever hoped for, and a mother and grandmother who adored me.

All I had to do was keep the secret.

The problem was that I didn't want to anymore.

"I'm not supposed to talk about this," I said, and I could feel the shift in his focus, how he was really looking at me now.

"You're not *supposed* to?" He held up a hand, and quickly added, "Okay, in that case—"

I shoved the words out: "My dad is Ian Butler."

Even if he was going to let me off the hook, I wanted to say it. I wanted to name it, like he did, so it could stop being this thing that threatened to burst out of me.

Sam was quiet before he pushed up onto an elbow, eclipsing the stars as he hovered over me. "Shut up," he said, laughing.

I laughed along with him. I'd never said that sentence out loud before; it sounded ridiculous to me, too. "Okay."

"Wait." He held a hand out, palm down. "You're serious?"

I trembled, nodding. I knew I'd just dropped a bomb— my father was arguably the biggest movie star of his generation. He'd won back-to-back Oscars twice, was constantly on magazine covers and entertainment news shows everywhere, and I sometimes wondered whether there was a human alive who hadn't at least heard his name. But all I could imagine right then was the way Sam looked above me.

The way he'd look on top of me.

"Holy shit," he whispered. "You're Tate *Butler*."

It'd been ten years since someone called me that. "I go by Tate Jones, but yeah."

Sam blew out a breath, eyes cataloging every one of my features: the oval face and high cheekbones, the beauty mark near my lip, whiskey-colored eyes, heart-shaped mouth, and dimpled smile that made Ian Butler the only man who'd been *People*'s Sexiest Man Alive a record three times. "How did I not notice it before? You look *just* like him."

I knew I did. I used to watch his movies in secret and marvel over seeing my face on the screen in front of me.

"Everyone wondered where you went." Sam reached forward, gently tugging at a wayward strand of my hair. "And here you are."

two

"WHAT DID YOU DO last night?" Nana spooned some melon onto her plate and moved down the line to the tiny, decadent pastries.

The second-to-last thing I wanted to do was have next-morning processing with Nana about Sam. The *last* thing I wanted to do was lie to her about him. My heart took off at a gallop. "Just hung out in the garden."

She looked over her shoulder at me. "Is it pretty?"

I could still see the looming shadows of the manicured trees, still feel the chill at my back and the heat of Sam on the lawn beside me. "Yeah."

My answer was intentionally lackluster. If I'd told her what it had really been like she might have wanted to see for herself, and I didn't want her anywhere near the scene of the crime.

"How late were you up?"

She asked this kind of semi-controlling question so

habitually, like my schedule was hers to manage. Would it still be like that when I'd left for college and she didn't know the parents of every person I went to school with? I knew she'd hate my answer, too: *I don't know how late we were up.* That first morning, my eyelids felt dry and wrinkly. My limbs were slow. I wanted to sleep, but more than sleep, I wanted to see Sam again.

He and I stayed up well past midnight, talking. It started heavy—with his details about Luther, about Danya and Michael—but once we touched on my parents, and my past, he pivoted. He didn't ask a single thing about my personal life in LA. Instead, we talked about movies, and pets, and favorite kind of pie, and what we wanted to do today when the sun came back up. He was right that it was easy to talk to him because who cared what he knew? I'd never see him again after this. I wanted to capture the night on film and show it to Mom and Nana later to say, *See? I can tell a stranger who I am and they don't turn into an obsessed maniac and run to the press. He didn't ask me for Dad's phone number, okay?*

I fell asleep next to him on the lawn, and when I woke up he was carrying me inside. In his arms.

"Late?" Nana prompted.

"Pretty late," I agreed. "It was nice out."

My stomach dropped at the memory of feeling Sam's arm banded beneath my knees, the other curved around my shoulders, and the steady pace of his footsteps across the marble lobby. I woke up with my face pressed to the collar of his flannel shirt and my arms around his neck.

Oh my God. You don't have to carry me.

I don't mind.

Did I fall asleep?

We both did.

I'm sorry.

Are you kidding? I came to London and slept with the prettiest girl I've ever seen. I get to say that now.

He put me down once we were inside the elevator, but it was a slow, intimate process. My front sliding along his chest until my feet landed safely on the floor. He kept his arm around my shoulders, one huge hand stretched across, cupped possessively on the other side. I wanted to ask exactly how many girls he'd carried. How many he'd made lose their minds over his thick arms and broad chest, his honesty, and the tiny comma scar under his lip. How many girls he'd slept with, on the grass or otherwise.

Thankfully, Nana moved on. "I've scheduled the British Museum for us today." She nodded so that I'd follow her to the table. In my daydreaming, I only managed to put a piece of bread and cheese on my plate. "Then have lunch at Harrods."

The sleep—not to mention the view—she scored last night seemed to have served her well: she was smiling in that modest, contented way of hers and wearing her favorite red cardigan from Penney's, which could only mean she was in a decent mood.

It was either that or the simple truth that Nana loved nothing more than a schedule. Other than Christmas and New Year's Day, she opened Jude's at six thirty every morning and closed at four every afternoon, on the dot. And in between, she prepped pie crust, put in her vendor orders,

checked and double-checked the cash registers, butch-
ered and marinated the chicken in buttermilk and paprika
for frying the next day, made all the side dishes fresh, and
slow cooked the brisket while I washed dishes, mopped
floors, and set tables. Mom made lemonade; peeled apples,
peaches, and potatoes; made lemon curd; and then took
whatever leftover food we had from the lunch crowd down
the road to Monte Rio, where the same people waited every
night for the one meal they'd get that day.

Nana waved at someone over my shoulder, pulling
me out of my sleepy thoughts. I assumed she was flagging
down the waiter for some coffee, but Luther's voice rang out
across the restaurant: "Our two favorite ladies!"

Heads turned, and the girls at the table beside ours
gaped at Sam as he made his way over. A weight dropped
from my chest to my stomach. I knew I'd see him again—
hoped I'd see him again—but I didn't think it would be over
breakfast with Nana, before I'd had a chance to remind him
not to mention what I'd said about Dad.

"Okay if we join you?" Sam asked.

He must have directed the question at me, because a
beat of silence passed before Nana jumped in: "Of course.
We just sat down."

Across from me, beside Sam, Nana pulled her napkin
onto her lap, smiling up at him, and then over to Luther,
who sat down to my left, patting my knee affectionately.

I finally worked up the nerve to drag my eyes to Sam's
face. His arms were enormous—an anatomy lesson in indi-
vidual muscles, tendons, and veins. His blue shirt stretched
across his chest—Bob Dylan's face was mildly distorted by

pectorals. There were a few lines on his left cheek, like he'd come straight from the pillow to the hotel restaurant.

Although he looked as exhausted as I felt, he met my gaze with a lazy, flirty grin and I was reminded again of the way our bodies dragged against each other when he put me down last night. I hoped the flash of heat that blew across my skin didn't show on my face, because I could feel Nana looking at me.

He blinked away and nodded when the waiter asked if he'd like coffee, and then lifted a hand to his stomach, mumbling, "Starving," before wandering away toward the buffet.

The teenagers at the table next to ours followed him with their eyes glued to his back, all the way to the spread of meats and cheeses.

Beside me, Luther seemed content to enjoy his coffee, adding four packs of sugar and a generous helping of cream. "I hope you woke up to a beautiful view?"

"We sure did." Nana shifted uncomfortably in her seat. I knew her well enough to understand that she'd already thanked him—she didn't want to have to say it over and over. "Many thanks . . . again."

Waving a hand to dismiss this, Luther lifted his cup to his lips and blew away the steam. "Women care more about those things than men do."

I felt a defensive wave rise up inside me, and saw it mirrored in Nana's expression. She forced her face into an amiable smile. "Hmm."

Luther tilted his head to me. "These two were out late last night, huh?"

Tires screeched, laying down black rubber tracks in my brain.

Nana went still, before tilting her head in question. "These . . . *two*?"

He glanced from me to where Sam was presumably tearing his way through the buffet. "Our grandchildren seem to have hit it off." I would have taken a moment to appreciate Luther's delighted laugh if he hadn't been currently destroying my life.

Nana looked at me again, eyes sharp. *"Really."*

At this, Luther's delight visibly wilted. "Oh. Oh, dear. I hope I haven't gotten Tate into any trouble," he said. "I'm a light sleeper and woke up when Sam walked in around three."

THANKS, LUTHER.

Nana's eyebrows disappeared beneath her bangs. *"Three?"*

I pressed my hands to my forehead just as Sam returned to the table with a plate piled high with eggs, sausage, potatoes, bread, and fruit. I'd never stayed out past curfew—eleven—and Nana thought *that* was too late a curfew for me.

"Three?" Nana asked him. "Is this true?"

Sam slowly lowered himself into his chair, looking around the table in confusion. "Three what?"

It was so unbelievably awkward.

Nana pinned him with her deeply intimidating brown eyes. "You were out with my granddaughter until *three in the morning*?"

"Well, yeah," he said, "but we were asleep for a lot of it." He did a double take at her deepening horror. "On the lawn. Just—sleeping."

Nana's face had slowly gone from ashen to pink to red, and Sam winced over to me, stage-whispering, "I'm not helping, am I?"

"Nope." My voice echoed from where I was trying to crawl into my cup of tea.

"Tate," Nana hissed, "you are not allowed to stay out with *strangers* in the *garden* of a hotel until *three o'clock in the morning!*"

I was having flashbacks to the time Nana walked in on me and Jesse tangled on my bed, shirtless, and chased him out of the house with a spatula.

And the time she found us making out in his car and wrote down his license plate and called Ed Schulpe down at the police station, who came and rapped his heavy police flashlight against the window, scaring the crap out of us.

Even the time she found us lying innocently on the couch watching television—barely touching—and reminded me that high school relationships end when high school does because there's a whole big world out there.

"I know, Nana."

"*Do* you?"

Luther and Sam both fixed their attention on the table-cloth.

My jaw clenched. "Yes."

★ ★

"Are you having fun, muffin?" Mom asked, and although I'd spoken to her on the phone thousands of times, knowing how far away she was made her sound *really* far away, and I got a sharp pang of homesickness.

"So far, yeah." I peeked at the closed bathroom door, lowering my voice. "Just one day in, and Nana is still calibrating."

"Meaning," Mom guessed, "that Nana is being uptight and miserable?"

I laughed and sat up straighter when I heard the toilet flush. "She's okay. We're headed to a museum today, I think. And lunch at Harrods. Then *Les Miz!*"

"I know you're dying for the theater, but oh my God: Harrods!" She paused before quietly adding, "Tater Tot, Harrods is really nice. Try to have a good attitude."

"I *do* have a good attitude!"

"Good." Mom sounded unconvinced. "And make Nana buy herself something fancy." Something clattered in the background—a pan against the stove, maybe—and even though I wasn't hungry, my mouth watered for home cooking. I did the brief math—it was midnight there. I wondered whether she was getting a snack before bed, wearing her favorite flowery turquoise silk pajama pants and *I'm a Proud Artist* T-shirt.

"*You* tell her to buy herself something fancy," I told her. "I'm not saying that. I'm already highly aware of how much this trip is costing."

She laughed. "Don't sweat the money."

"I'll try, somewhere between handling Nana's controlling questions and having a good attitude."

Mom, as ever, was unwilling to engage in bickering. "Well, before you go, tell me something good."

"I met a boy last night," I said, and amended, "Well, maybe more guy? Man?"

"*Man?*"

"Guy-man. He just turned twenty-one."

My mother, ever the romantic, became dramatically—*comically*—interested. "Is he cute?"

A twisting ache worked its way through me. I missed Mom. I missed her easy encouragement that I find adventure in safe, tiny bites. I missed the way she balanced Nana's overprotective tendencies without undermining her. I missed the way she understood crushes, and boys, and being a teenager. I didn't actually think she would be angry with me for telling Sam about her and Dad—not anymore, now that I was officially an adult—but on the phone, across an ocean, was not the time or place to open that can of worms.

I'd tell her everything when I got home.

"He's really cute. He's like eight feet tall." As expected, Mom *oooh*'d appreciatively. Just then, Nana turned the water off in the bathroom, making me rush to get through it. "Just wanted to tell you."

Mom's voice was gentle. "I'm glad you told me. I miss you, muffin. Be safe."

"I miss you too."

"Don't let Nana make you paranoid," she added just before we hung up. "No one is going to chase you down in London."

★ ★

Sam and I met on the lawn again that night.

We didn't plan it. We didn't even see each other after breakfast. But after Nana and I returned from the show, I snuck out into the garden beneath the sky full of stars, and Sam's long body was once again stretched out on the grass, feet crossed at the ankle. He was a life raft in the middle of a green ocean.

"I wondered if you'd come," he said, turning at the sound of my footsteps.

I'm not sure I could stay away, I wanted to say. Instead, I said nothing, and lowered myself down next to him.

Immediately I was warm.

We were both smarter that second night, layering up: He was wearing track pants and a Johnson State sweatshirt. I was wearing yoga pants and a 49ers hoodie. Our socks were bright white against the dark grass. My feet could have worn his feet as shoes and still have had plenty of room.

"I hope I didn't get you in trouble with Jude this morning," he said.

He did a little, but it wasn't worth dwelling on because thankfully, Jude didn't. After we left the hotel, she was swept up in the Tube, in the museum, in the glitter and pomp of lunch at Harrods. And then we walked, for hours, before ending the day with a production of *Les Misérables* at the Queen's Theatre. My feet were still vibrating with the echo of my steps on pavement. My head was full of all the information Nana had tried to cram in there: the history she'd read of royalty, and art, and music, and literature. But my heart was the fullest; I was absolutely besotted with the story of Valjean, Cosette, Javert, and Marius.

"She's fine. And she's asleep," I reassured Sam. "I think she only got one foot moisturized before she nodded off."

"Think she'll set an alarm to make sure you're back in the room by midnight?"

"She might . . ." It hadn't even occurred to me that she would do that, but it should have. That was absolutely the kind of precaution Nana would take to make sure I was safe. And midnight—*ha*. If an eleven o'clock curfew was considered late, midnight would be scandalous.

God, I was so torn. On the one hand, what else could I do to prove to her that I wasn't Mom? I wasn't going to run away to the big city, get married at eighteen and pregnant soon after, chase fame and find heartache. I also wasn't going to tip off the paparazzi and get us all swarmed on opposite sides of the world. I got why she was nervous—she lived through the chaos of my parents' marriage dissolving and remembered the specifics far better than I did—but it was getting harder and harder to live under a constant veil of paranoia.

On the other hand, would being a little like Mom really be so terrible? Sometimes Nana acted like Mom couldn't possibly take care of herself, but that hasn't ever been true. It was like Nana saw Mom's pure spirit as a weakness, but Mom found joy in every tiny moment and had the enormous heart of a romantic. Nana might not have relished the decade Mom spent with Dad, but without him, there'd be no me.

"I probably won't stay out quite as late," I admitted, pulling myself out of my mental spiral.

Sam sounded both teasing and disappointed when he whispered, "But I liked being out late with you."

"I'll sleep in my *bed*," I said, grinning at him. Why had I bothered with lip gloss and blush before coming outside? My face was bright red even without it.

"Now *that's* a shame."

I stared up at the sky, unsure what to say and wondering if he could sense the way my blood seemed to simmer just beneath my skin. I didn't remember him falling asleep last night, so I must have first. Did I curl into him, throw a leg over, press my face to his neck? Maybe he gripped my hip and pulled me closer. How long did he lie there before dozing off, too?

"Nana would murder us both if it happened again."

"You're eighteen, Tate. I know she worries, but you're an adult."

How was it that being told I was an adult made me feel even more like a child?

"I know," I said, "but—and I realize how this sounds—my circumstances are a little different."

In my peripheral vision, I could see him nodding. "I know."

"I don't think anyone cares where Mom and I are anymore, but . . ."

I trailed off and we both fell silent, leaving me begging wordlessly for the ease of last night to return, for the effortless unrolling of conversation. Last night was like falling into a pool of warm water, of knowing you have the entire day to swim in the sun, and nothing to do at the end of it but sleep.

"What'd you do today?" I asked.

"Luther wanted to re-create the *Abbey Road* cover, so we found a couple of random dudes to round out the

Beatles with us." He smiled over at me. "Had lunch from some curry place, and then went shopping for some things for Roberta."

"I feel like my day was a lot fancier, but you're rounding the day out pretty well: those track pants are way nicer than my pajamas."

He laughed, glancing down as if he hadn't really noticed what he pulled on after dinner. The realization made me glow inside. For the first time all day, it didn't occur to me to be self-conscious about what I was wearing; the only downside to our first day had been my constant awareness that the department stores at the Coddingtown Mall in Santa Rosa clearly couldn't compete with the fashion scene in London. In Guerneville, the things Mom bought for me felt edgy and modern; in London, I just felt frumpy.

Sam's smile turned contemplative. "Can I ask you something?"

His cautious tone made me uneasy. "Sure."

"Has your life been happy?"

God, what a loaded question. Of course I was happy, right? Mom and Nana were amazing. Charlie was the best friend I could imagine. I had everything I could possibly need.

Though maybe not everything I'd always wanted.

The thought made me feel supremely selfish.

When I didn't immediately answer, he clarified, "I've been thinking about this all day. What you told me. I remember seeing your face plastered all over the cover of magazines down at the grocery store—*People* and whatever. Most of it wasn't even about you, it was about your dad, and the affairs, and how your mom just . . . disappeared with you. But then I looked up Guerneville, and it seems like a really nice place, and I thought, 'Maybe they had a better life there.' Like I did with Luther and Roberta." He rolled to the side, propping his head on a hand, just like he did last night.

"Guerneville is nice but it's not, like, *nice*," I told him. "It's funky and weird. There are maybe four thousand people who live there, and we all know each other."

"That sounds enormous compared to the one thousand who live in Eden."

I stared at him. Maybe his life had been just like mine, only on the complete other end of the country.

"So, *have* you been happy?" he asked again.

"Do you mean have I been happy in general or happy with my parents?"

His attention was unwavering. "Either, both."

I chewed on my lip while I thought through it. Questions like this were such weird little provocations. I rarely thought about my life before, and I certainly tried not to feel sad about Dad. The entire world seemed to know him so much better than I did, anyway; I figured maybe when I was older, Nana wouldn't mind so much letting me know him, too.

I'd been stupid in a lot of things—my crush on Charlie's cousin from Hayward our freshman year, and the scores of letters I wrote him; loving Jesse but never having sex with him even though we both wanted to, simply because I never had any privacy; the early days of being so enamored with Jesse that I drifted from Charlie when she was dealing with her own family drama—but one thing I'd never done is

disobeyed Nana and Mom when they asked me to be careful, to keep our seclusion a secret to protect me and Mom.

"It's okay," Sam said after a couple of minutes, "if you
don't want to talk about this."

"I do." I sat up, crossing my legs. "I just never have."

While he waited for my words to come, Sam sat up too.
He pulled up a blade of grass and drove it in and out of the
lawn, like a tiny car winding around a complicated neigh-
borhood.

I studied his downturned face, trying to memorize it.
"Mom and Nana are great, but I won't lie and say that it's
not hard to know that there's this whole other world and life
out there that I don't get to know anything about."

Sam nodded. "That makes sense."

"I like Guerneville, but who's to say I wouldn't like LA
better?" I peeked over at him, and my heart climbed a little
higher in my chest. "Don't laugh at this, okay?"

He glanced up at me, shaking his head. "I won't."

"Part of me really wants to be an actress." I felt the sensation rise in my throat like it always did, like I was choking
on the dream of it. "I think about acting all the time. I love
reading scripts and books about the industry. If someone
asked me what I want to do, and I was being honest, telling
them that I want to act would explode out of me. But, God,
if I said that to Nana she would flip."

"How do you know?" he asked. "Have you talked to her
about it?"

"I tried out for a few school plays," I said. "I even got the
lead in one—*Chicago*—but she always found a reason why
it didn't work. To be fair, our schedule at the café is really

crazy, but I think mostly Nana just didn't want me to fall in love with it."

Sam chewed his lip and dropped his blade of grass, wiping his hands on his thighs. "I know what you mean there." He went quiet for a few beats. "I always wanted to be a writer."

I looked over at him, surprised. "Yeah?"

"I love to write," he admitted, sounding almost reverent. "I have all these stories in notebooks under my bed. But it's not an obvious choice for someone raised on a farm who's expected to take it over someday."

"Do Roberta and Luther know you do it?"

"I think so, but I don't know if they realize how seriously I take it. I sent this short story I wrote to a bunch of literary magazines. I got rejected immediately from all of them, but it just made me want to try again."

"You should." I tried to keep the fondness from my voice, but it was hard because I felt like he was showing me a side of himself that not everyone got to see. "What would they say if you told them you wanted to write?"

"Luther would tell me writing is a hobby," he said. "Something to enjoy but not something I can expect to pay the bills. And Roberta might not even be that enthusiastic."

"If I told her that I wanted to take up acting once I get to college—and working in the café isn't an issue anymore—I think Nana would flat-out tell me I'm not allowed to."

He laughed, and it crinkled the corners of his eyes. "Yeah. I love Roberta to death, but she's practical almost to a fault sometimes. She doesn't have a lot of time for dreamers."

"What kinds of stories do you write?"

"Maybe that's part of it," he said, shrugging. "Why I don't tell them much about my writing. Most of my stories are about people in our town, or made-up people who might live in our town. I like to think about how they became the way they are."

I pulled up my own blade of grass. "I remember we had this whole discussion in history class a couple years ago, how history is subjective. Like, who is telling the story? Is it the person who won the war or lost the war? Is it the person who made the law or was jailed because of it? I kept thinking about that so hard afterward, like—and I totally get that I'm just one person, and not, like, important—but I wonder what's the actual story between my parents?"

Sam nodded, riveted.

"Mom told me once that Dad fought for me, but in the end it was better for us to be up in Guerneville, away from the media." I wrapped the long blade of grass around my fingertip. "But how do I know whether the stories they've told me are true, or whether it's what they wanted me to hear so that I'm not sad about it? Like, I know LA wasn't a good environment for her, and I know the circumstances about why they split up, but I don't actually ever talk to my dad anymore. I wonder how much Dad fought her leaving. Did he miss us? Why doesn't he call me?"

He hesitated at this, and I wondered if he knew things I didn't. It was entirely possible.

"I've seen some headlines," I told him, "and it's impossible to miss his face on the magazines at Lark's—sorry, our drugstore—but even though I know Mom's version of things, is it weird that I haven't ever gone online and read the articles written about my parents?"

He glanced up. "Not really, I guess."

"I mean, I'm so obsessed with Hollywood but can't even be bothered to read about my own family." I paused, tearing up my blade of grass. "How accurate are the stories out there? I wouldn't even know. I can't know how he looked at her or what things were like between them when it was still good. I won't ever know what kinds of things he did that made her laugh, but I don't even know what people say about the whole thing." I gave him a winning smile, but inside, I was a yarn ball of nerves. "I sort of want you to tell me."

Sam's mossy-green eyes went wide. "Wait, really?"

When I nodded, he leaned in, intense now. "I mean, I'm not going to lie and say I didn't read up on this on Yahoo for hours last night."

A giggle burst free. "I'm sure you did."

"Seems the story goes," Sam started, clearing his throat and coming back with a deeper voice, like an announcer, "Ian Butler and Emmeline Houriet met when they were young. Emmeline was insanely hot—which I'm sure you've heard from all your dude friends—Ian was Mister Charisma, and they fell in love and moved to LA, where his career took off. Hers . . . not so much. He *was* crazy about her. According to a profile in *Vanity Fair* back in the day," he said with a self-deprecating little wink, making me laugh, "anyone who saw them together could tell."

Sobering, I looked down, trying to not seem too affected by this—the suggestion that it hadn't always been misery for my parents.

"He started on a soap, but then he got a supporting role beside Val Kilmer, and his next one was a leading role. He wins an Emmy, a Golden Globe shortly after, and around that time your mom had you."

I nodded. "1987."

"Then your dad had the first affair—or the first one the press knew about."

"Biyu Chen."

"Biyu Chen," he agreed. "You were . . . two?" he asks, seeking confirmation.

"Yeah," I said, knowing this part, too.

"Your mom stayed with him. More big roles. More awards. Apparently everyone thought Ian was sleeping around pretty much constantly after Biyu. But the affair that caused all the problems was Lena Still."

Without realizing it, my fingers had curled into fists. I remembered when a Lena Still movie was playing at the Rio Theater. She was cast as a warrior in a dystopian future, the sort of Chosen One trope. I never saw it, of course, but it felt like I did because of how much everyone at school talked about it. I couldn't say to anyone except Charlie that year how much I hated going to Halloween parties with my peers dressed as ten different homemade versions of Lena Still.

"So, in 1994, Lena was only twenty, and she slept with your dad." I bit back the reflex to remind Sam that Dad was only in his early thirties—he was being gross but not *that* gross—but I didn't understand where the defensiveness came from and certainly didn't want to give it room to breathe.

"She got pregnant," Sam said, "and the press found out about it." He paused, pressing a hand to his chest, and giving me a playfully earnest aside: "Many believe that *she* tipped off the press."

Many, meaning almost everyone.

"But then they got in that car accident," he said, "after the wrap party for their movie, and she lost the baby, and everyone felt so bad for Lena, not Emmeline."

Those headlines I'd seen. It was impossible to miss them, even when I was eight. I wondered how many times a day those supermarket tabloid headlines flashed through Mom's thoughts, unwelcome and obtrusive. Bright yellow words:

LENA STILL'S LOVE CHILD LOST. DEVASTATED, IAN BUTLER BACKS OUT OF BOND ROLE.

Little mention of a wife or a child at home—and Mom said the ones that did mention it made her sound like an unreasonable clinger, a crazy woman.

"And so much speculation about your mom."

"You really did spend some time on Yahoo today, didn't you?"

He gave a sheepish little smile before lying back in the grass again. "Even I remember seeing it. I was eleven. Your face was everywhere for a few months—those enormous eyes. Where did you go? Did she kidnap you? Were you being kept from Ian? Had you gone into witness protection? All that stuff."

Really, the truth as Mom laid it out was much more banal: cheating husband, toxic culture, mother takes the child and leaves LA to go live in a nowhere, Podunk town.

It just happened that my father was one of the most beloved actors in the world, and it's hard for the public to realize that the actor and the man aren't always the same person. People couldn't believe that he'd done something terrible to her, and the noxious Hollywood environment nearly broke my mother.

But again, what was the real story? In a weird way, it felt like we were talking about someone else's life.

"I mean, I was a kid during all of this, right?" I said. "In a tiny private school with other actors' kids, and we're all insulated from this stuff. Basically, Mom came to get me during school one day. She had the car packed full of suitcases, and the dog. We drove for hours—it felt like forever, but seriously, it was like six hours."

Beside me, Sam laughed.

"We got to Nana's house on the river, and I think that was the first time I asked whether we were going to go home. Mom said no." Pausing, I pulled up another blade of grass. "I didn't even get to say goodbye to him."

"Does anyone in Guerneville know who you guys are?"

"Probably some of the locals, yeah. I mean Nana has lived there forever, but everyone just knows her as Jude. I bet the only one who knows her last name is Houriet is Alan, the mailman. Mom grew up there, but she cut her hair, dyed it brown, goes by Emma now, not Emmeline, and we both use the last name Jones. Almost everything is in Nana's name and it's not like *Emma Jones* would mean anything to anyone." I shrugged. "It seems like anyone left in town who knows who Mom is and why she came back also didn't need to get into her business, if she felt like hiding."

"But you have friends who know?"

"My best friend, Charlie, knows. That's it."

Guilt started to creep in, spreading from the center of my chest outward until I felt cold all over. It was both good and terrifying to talk about all of it. I was spilling *everything*. I knew Mom and Nana built this secluded bubble to protect us, but talking about it was a little like unleashing a creature we'd kept in a basement for years. Nice to be rid of it, but now the world could see the ugliness for themselves.

"There were some pictures of you from LAX, weren't there?" he asked.

"Oh, right." I settled back beside him, and he surprised me by taking my hand. My neck and face burned with nerves, but I didn't let go. "It was the first approved visit I had with Dad after the divorce—when I was nine. Mom bought a ticket for me to fly down. She walked me to the gate, hugged me about a thousand times before she'd let me leave with the flight attendant. She was more freaked out about me flying alone than I was, and even more freaked out that I would be hounded by the press when I was out with Dad. I landed in LA, got off the plane with the escort, and waited."

I told Sam about the rest of it then: about feeling like I was waiting a long time—long enough for some people to figure out who I was, and for a couple of them to take pictures of me. After a while I realized the airline people were figuring out which parent to let me go home with, because Mom flew down and got me.

"I guess she was too worried about me being in LA, and in the papers. She said Dad was waiting, but he would understand, and I guess he did, because she took me home."

Sam went still next to me when he heard this, and his lingering silence made me uneasy.

"What?" I asked, after his silence started to feel like a thick fog.

"You really haven't read the articles about this, have you?"

I turned my head, looking over at him. He wore the expression of someone who was about to break terrible news. "What do you mean?"

"I mean," he started, looking back up at the sky, "the story that's out there is a little different."

I waited for him to tell me, but it was clear that I was going to have to confirm that I really wanted to hear it. "Is it that bad?"

"I . . . it's pretty bad?"

"Just tell me."

"I think your mom had to fly down because your dad didn't show up," Sam said quietly. "At least, that's what I read."

A chill spread down my arms. "What?"

"I mean, there's not a ton. But I remember it because there aren't any pictures of you after you left LA—except for these. I saw pictures of you waiting in LAX, and witnesses who said that the gate attendants were trying to get ahold of Ian Butler, but couldn't."

My history crumbled the tiniest bit. Did I *really* want the truth? Or did I want the story that let me feel better about my silent father? I supposed it was too late now.

"He put out a statement," Sam said, and turned back to look at me, eyes searching. "You never heard this?"

I shook my head. The only time Charlie and I had

worked up the nerve to look up Ian Butler online, the first hit was a strategically posed naked photo shoot for *GQ*, and that was enough to kill the urge to do it again.

"He basically threw his assistant under the bus, saying she had written the time down wrong, and explained how heartbroken he was."

Shrugging, I said, "I mean, it could be . . ."

"Yeah, that's true." Another long pause, and my hopeful grip on this possibility loosened. "Did he fly up to see you after that?"

I closed my eyes. "Not that I know of."

Sam cleared his throat, and the uncomfortable fallout silence felt like a weight on my chest. "I mean," he said, clearly scrambling for something to say, "maybe it's for the best. Charlie sounds pretty nice, but if you lived in LA, maybe your best friend would be Britney. And we all know she's a ticking time bomb."

I laughed, but it sounded hollow. "Totally."

I riffled through my thoughts, digging for something more to say, a different subject to discuss, but just when I thought my heart was going to roll over in my chest from the tension, Sam rescued us both: "You know, I have this theory about cats."

I blinked over to him, confused. "Cats?"

"Yeah, I don't like them."

"That's your theory?"

He laughed. "No. Listen. I don't like cats, but whenever I go to a house with cats, they always come over and sit on me."

"Because they take one look at you and think you're furniture."

This made him laugh harder. "Sure, that's another theory. But here's mine: those anti-cat vibes would be weird for a human—like when we sense someone doesn't like us, and it's just really uncomfortable—but maybe for a cat, those weird vibes are *comforting*."

"Bad vibes are good for cats?" I asked.

"Exactly. There's something about the tension they like."

I stewed on this one a little, thinking. "If that's true, cats are sort of evil."

"Without a doubt they're evil. I'm just finding the root of it."

I looked over at him. "I think cats are cute. They're not needy, they're smart. They're awesome."

"You're wrong."

This made me burst out laughing, and I let it roll through me, pushing out the residual tension over Dad, and what I'd learned from Sam. But just thinking about it again brought some of the tightness back to my chest.

Maybe he sensed it, because Sam squeezed my hand. And then I knew he sensed it, because he said, "I'm sorry your dad sucks."

This pulled a surprised laugh out of me. "I'm sorry your dad sucks, too."

"I'm never seeing another Ian Butler movie ever again." He paused. "Except *Encryption*, because that movie is the fucking bomb."

"Hey!"

"Sorry, Tate, it's just science."

three

MOM MUST HAVE SAID something to Nana—telling her to go easy on me, let me have some fun, *something*—because without any complaint or even a whiff of displeasure from my grandmother, Luther and Sam became our regular companions in London. Each morning I bolted from bed and raced through the process of getting ready, eager to sit across from Sam, to wander the city together, to *see* him. We talked for hours in the garden every night. He said he'd lived in a small town for all but the first two years of his life, but he had more stories and random theories than anyone I'd ever met.

At breakfast each morning, they were across the table from us: Sam with his flirty smile and plate piled high, and Luther with his highly sugared cup of coffee. On the street, they were usually a few steps behind us, wrestling with the giant map Luther insisted on using and arguing over alternative Tube stations when we found Paddington closed.

On a particularly gloomy day, we avoided the rain by visiting the Natural History Museum. Luther made up funny—and very loud—fictional stories about each of the dinosaurs in the Blue Zone, and even managed to coax Nana into dropping her plans for lunch at an old hotel she found in a guidebook. Instead, we ate burgers at a dark pub and laughed hysterically as Sam told us about things going disastrously wrong with the milking equipment on his first morning shift alone at the farm.

Not only did Nana not seem to mind our new traveling sidekicks, she genuinely seemed to enjoy Luther's company. After lunch, they walked on ahead, and Sam came up alongside me while we strolled, bellies full, to the Baker Street station.

"What's the craziest thing you've ever done?" he asked.

I took a few quiet seconds to think while Sam and I wove in and out of pedestrian traffic. Together, apart, together. His arm brushed against mine, and in a heated breath I registered that it didn't feel accidental.

"Nana's house is on the water," I told him. "It's raised on stilts, overlooking the Russian River and—"

"Wow—stilts?"

"Yeah, I mean, the river floods a lot, so most houses near the water are on stilts." When his eyes went wider, I said, "Don't get a mental image of some sort of elaborate castle. It's really just a three-bedroom, plain house on stilts. Anyway, we're not supposed to jump from the deck because it's so high up. The river is pretty deep there, but our toes always brush bottom, and the depth changes year to year. Someday we'll jump and it'll just be riverbed."

Sam's hand brushed mine when we sidestepped a man on the sidewalk, and this time it was accidental: he apologized under his breath. I wanted to reach out and make the contact permanent.

"Charlie and I would jump off the deck when we were home alone. I'm not even sure why."

"Of course you know why."

"To be scared?"

"To feel a rush, yeah." He grinned over at me. "What would you think about when you jumped?"

"Just . . ." I shook my head, trying to remember the feeling. "Just that there was nothing else in that moment, you know? No school, no boys, no drama, no chores. Just jumping into the cold water and feeling crazy and happy afterward."

"You're pretty cute if that's the *craziest* thing."

I wasn't sure whether I was more thrilled that he called me cute, or embarrassed to be exposed for being so tame. I held in a shaky breath and laughed. "You know me." And in a weird way, I felt like he did. "What about you?"

Sam hummed. "Tipping cows. Drinking beer in the middle of nowhere. Weird races and games in cornfields. Trying to build an airplane." He shrugged. "I don't know. It's easy to be crazy on a farm."

"Is it?"

"Yeah, I mean," he said, ducking around a man walking aimlessly with his eyes on his BlackBerry, "everyone in Eden's always saying when you live in the middle of nowhere it's impossible to get into trouble, and I think it gives parents a sense of ease, like even if they can't see us, what's the worst thing that could happen? Drinking some beer in a field? But knowing they think that, I don't know . . . it feels sort of like a challenge sometimes."

"Did you ever get hurt?"

Sam shook his head. "Hangovers? Sprained my ankle once. But it's mostly just a group of us being idiots. Most of the girls around are way smarter than we are and could kick our asses. It kept us from going too far."

Nana turned around, waiting for us to catch up. "What are you talking about?"

I grinned over at Sam. "He's talking about drinking beer in fields, tipping cows, and building an airplane."

I expected Luther to say something about the cows or the beer, but he just nodded proudly. "That plane nearly flew, didn't it?"

Sam looked down at me, grinning. He knew exactly what I was trying to do—get him busted—and when Nana and Luther turned back around, he dug a long finger into my ribs, tickling. "Looks like that backfired, missy."

Mom called me that night, right as I was slipping out the door to meet Sam. I took my flip phone out of the room with me, not wanting to wake up an already-snoring Nana.

I'd been wondering whether Mom was lonely with us away in London, though I knew how much work it took to keep the café open, and even with a couple women from town helping her while we were gone, I was sure Mom didn't have a lot of time to think about anything but work. Still, if it was nine o'clock at night in London, it was one in the afternoon at home; Mom should have been running around like mad handling the lunch rush. Unless . . .

"What's wrong?" I asked immediately.

She laughed. "Can't I miss my kid?"

"You can," I said, "but not when you're supposed to be at the café. Nana will lose it."

"It's Tuesday," she reminded me. "We're closed. I'm actually still in my jammies."

I pressed the down button on the elevator, relieved. "I have no sense of what day it is."

"That's the best thing about vacation."

This triggered a small, guilty realization. "When was the last time you took one?"

The only one I could think of was when she took me to Seattle for a weekend a little over a year ago. Other than that, it felt like Mom had become a happy, settled fixture of Guerneville. Just like Nana.

"Seattle," she confirmed, and I felt a weird wiggle of guilt that we didn't just close up the café and bring her along. "But don't worry about me. You know I love summers here."

I always had, too. The heat came rolling in across the river and down the dried creek beds bursting with fat blackberries. The air grew so sweet and the sun heated the beaches and sidewalks so hot, we couldn't go barefoot for even a few seconds. If we needed a reprieve, we drove just a few miles west, where the ocean met the Russian River. On the coastal beach just past Jenner, we would be blasted with air so cold we needed jackets in the middle of July. The town filled with tourists and their money and there was always a line outside Nana's café, all day long.

"Maybe once I start school, over a break we can go on a trip, me and you," I said.

"That sounds nice, muffin." She paused. "Are you walking? What time is it there?"

Guiltily, I admitted, "I'm sneaking out to hang out with Sam."

"Do you think you two could make it work?" she asked. "Cross-country?"

"*Mom.*" A bright flash of genuine irritation jetted through me at how quickly she went from me hanging out with Sam to imagining a long-distance relationship. I loved her romantic streak, but sometimes it was more pushy than anything. "I'm eighteen, and we aren't a *thing*."

"I'm not setting you up to be a child bride, Tate. But to just . . . have fun. *Be eighteen.*"

"Isn't it your job to discourage this kind of behavior?"

I could almost see her waving this concern away. "You get plenty of that from Nana. I'm just dreaming, you know me, having the fun conversation and what-ifs."

"I like him but—I don't want to get my hopes up and start talking about what-ifs."

"Why not?" she asked. "It's not like you won't be disappointed regardless if nothing happens. I don't know why people think permanent denial is better than temporary disappointment."

I knew she was right, allowing myself a few moments of fantasy as I made my way from the elevator to the back doors that led to the garden. My only boyfriend to date lived a half mile down the road from me. What would it be like to date someone in another state, clear across the country?

"I mean," I said, giving in, "he's so cute, Mom. But he's more than that, he's really easy to talk to. I feel like I could tell him anything."

Mom paused again, and in that silence I heard how quickly the unspoken question formed. Finally: "Did you?"

What was I hearing in her voice? Fear or excitement? Sometimes they sound the same—thin and tight, words clipped.

Would she be angry if she knew I'd told him? Or would she understand my desire to lay claim to this glimmering history of ours? Sometimes I got the weird sense that I was disappointing her by not rebelling and shouting from a megaphone who I was, who she was, where we came from. In London, I wanted there to be a reason for my small-town clothes, bland ponytail, outdated style. I told myself it could be fun, playing the role of the country mouse in a big city. But in the privacy of my own thoughts and as selfish as it sounded, I wanted the world to know that it was just an act, that I wasn't meant to be a fish out of water in this land of cosmopolitan women.

Daughter of world's most famous actor has been living a simple life in a tiny town and never learned fashion. She's so down-to-earth!

But I told Mom a lie instead of the truth. "No way, Mom. I would never."

She exhaled, humming quietly. "Okay, muffin. Let's talk tomorrow?"

I blew her a kiss before hanging up, feeling the sour weight of the lie settling in my gut.

The guilt melted away as soon as I stepped out into

the dark, glimmering night. Sam didn't look up as I settled beside him on the chilly grass, but I could feel the way he shifted, sliding just a little bit closer.

"'Bout time," he said. It was dark but I could hear the smile in his voice. "I was getting sleepy."

The urge to reach out and hold his hand spread through me like an electric wave. "Sorry. My mom called to see how things are going."

He turned to me in the dark. "Is she jealous, with you and Jude all the way out here in London?"

"I wondered the same thing." I sat up and crossed my legs, looking down at him. Inside, I felt keyed up, sort of jittery.

"You okay?" he asked.

"She asked me whether I told you about Dad."

Sam smiled up at me. "You mentioned me to your mom?"

"Yeah."

"And?" He waggled his eyebrows. "What'd you say?"

"That I met a guy named Sam."

Playful disbelief took over his expression. "That's it?"

I hoped he couldn't see my flushed neck and cheeks in the darkness. "What am I supposed to say?"

"That I'm handsome, and both talented with words and know my way around a farm."

This made me laugh. "I'm not sure you're talented with words or farms; I haven't seen proof."

"I notice you didn't argue with me about being handsome."

"Are you trying to impress my mother?"

He pushed up onto his elbows, giving me flirty eyes. "What did you tell her?"

"I told her you're nice and—"

"No," he said, waving me off. "I mean when she asked whether you told me about your dad."

"Oh." I bit my lip. "I lied. I said I hadn't."

This seemed to surprise him. "Would she be mad?"

"I don't know." I tucked my hair behind my ear and noticed that his gaze was following the path of my fingers. "I don't think she would?" I looked up at him and then winced. "But I was thinking about it the other day, and I realize this sounds totally spoiled, okay? But part of me wants to get to enjoy the perks of being Ian Butler's daughter a little."

"Why on earth do you think that makes you sound spoiled? Everyone in your position would want to be able to see how the other half lives."

"I think because that life ruined my mom, and here I am, wanting a reason to go back there."

"*Did* it ruin her?" he challenged me. "Or did she just have a shitty marriage?" He ran his fingers through the grass. "Roberta had a crappy first husband. Got her pregnant so young, cheated on her. She was different after that, I bet, but then she moved to the farm and fell in love with Luther and they've sort of become these bedrock citizens. Everyone relies on them for advice and help and just wants to soak up their wisdom. She'd've never met Luther if she hadn't had a bad one the first time around, and I know she'd never tell me not to get married just because it didn't work for her once. I don't imagine your mom would want you to avoid something just because it didn't work for her."

I could see the storyteller in him, the biographer. He didn't even know my mom, and still he drilled down to something so quintessentially true about her: she would never tell me to stay away from LA if that's what I really wanted.

The idea of chasing that dream—of really stepping out into the sun and owning that legacy—set something afire inside me, and when Sam caught my eye and held my gaze, I could tell he saw it too.

four

ON OUR SIXTH DAY in London we watched the changing of the guard at Buckingham Palace. The crowd was heavy and our bodies were pressed close as we all jockeyed for the best vantage point through the gilded iron fence. Sam's proximity made me drunk. I would never have anticipated how longing could be so dizzying, how it could feel like he belonged to me without any proof or history at all.

In the jostling, Sam looped his pinky around mine. I was a tiny fish; he had me hooked. It felt almost criminal the way the physical reaction snaked up my arm, down my torso, between my legs.

He looked down at me and smiled, winking.

"Don't forget to tell your mom I'm an all-around talented guy," he said quietly.

I think he knew exactly what he was doing. Was it a good sign or a scary one that he seemed to enjoy how flustered he made me?

On a particularly crowded train on day eight, we let Nana and Luther have the only empty seats. Sam insisted I take the bar near the bench in the back, while he stood behind me, easily able to reach the handle directly overhead. It took a few minutes of a rocky ride for me to realize that he'd chosen that spot to protect me from the group of rowdy guys just behind him. And, with him standing so close, I felt the heat of him along the full length of my body, his front pressed to my back, rocking against me as the train slipped around curves and bends in the track. I was flustered and flushed by the time we reached Westminster station, tense with an unfamiliar ache.

Sam just grinned knowingly as we parted ways off the elevator, telling me under his breath that he'd see me later.

At nine, I found him sitting on the grass, facing the door when I emerged. As usual, the garden was empty. I felt grateful for this location in a new way; yes, it was a beautiful view, but the surrounding monuments were also a pretty capable distraction from the jewel of the garden; no one else was ever out here with us.

Sam smiled as I approached, watching me walk the entire distance from the back door of the hotel to where he was sitting with his legs stretched out in front of him, leaning back on his hands. In the past two days, it seemed like everything had shifted; we'd stepped across the unspoken line from acquaintances into this new intimate *awareness*. I still felt clumsy in it. I wasn't nearly as casually flirtatious as Sam, which made me feel young and inexperienced and constantly hyperaware of everything I said. It was growing simultaneously exhilarating and exhausting.

I was barely seated before he told me, "You are so fucking gorgeous. Do you know that?"

He didn't look away or soften the moment at all, and my first instinct was to duck my head or pretend I needed to tie my shoe, or do something else dismissive and bashful. I'd never had a guy say something like that to me, let alone practically growl it.

I looked up at him and smiled, and the expression on his face made my heart race. "Thanks."

He ran a finger beneath his lip, contemplating something. "I liked being with you on the train today."

"That was you behind me?" I deadpanned.

Sam burst out laughing. "Okay, okay," he said with a wild grin and snapped his fingers. "Lie down. Tonight is the clearest night we've had so far."

I settled on the grass, his instructions to *lie down* playing on a loop in my brain. Sam surprised me by putting his head next to mine, and stretching his body out in the opposite direction. We were a set of propellers, ready to take flight.

He pointed out Jupiter, so bright above us, and told me, "I used to want to be an astronaut."

"So did Charlie," I said. "She made a rocket out of a cardboard refrigerator box and still had it when I moved to town in fourth grade."

"Tell me more about her."

It was weird to feel so far away from that world, and so deeply rooted in this new routine with Sam. "She's my best friend back home."

"Right." He hummed. "Charlie is a rebel name for a girl."

"It is?" I turned my head before remembering that he was *right there*, and our eyes were almost aligned. He was blurry, but even so I could see that he was smiling. We both turned our faces back to the sky.

"It totally fits, then," I said. "Charlie is the best. Her mom is a former model. She's so insanely beautiful, but basically her entire life is focused on maintaining her looks, which is hard to do where we are because there aren't, like, gyms or plastic surgeons. They live up on the hill, in this McMansion. Nothing else around us looks like this house. It reminds me of a ski lodge in pictures of the Alps, with those sloped roofs and big windows."

"Yeah," Sam said, a rumble from somewhere deep inside him.

"A few years ago, her dad just didn't come back from a business trip in China, where he's from. Turns out her parents never really got married, so it's just Charlie and her mom now."

In my peripheral vision, Sam lifted his hands, wiping his face. "Wow."

"Charlie went through a pretty rebellious phase that year, but she's chilled out a little. As much as she ever will, I guess. Charlie's pretty awesome. You'd love her."

Was this a sufficient description of Charlie? With her crazy style that stood out nearly as much as a half-Asian girl would anyway on River Road? With her love for stray dogs and the lemonade stands she'd organize to give money to homeless kids? I was growing to despise this CliffsNotes version of my life. I'd never done this before—let someone completely in from start to finish. I wanted to plug my brain into Sam's and simply download everything in one go.

Sam adjusted his position; I imagined him crossing one long leg over the other. "So, you have Charlie, and there was a boyfriend named Jesse. Who else?"

Frankly, it was embarrassing to have the tiny scale of my life measured like this, but those two were and had always been the bulk of my social world. I couldn't even think about Charlie going to UCLA, and Jesse going to Wesleyan, because it would remind me that I'd need to make all new friends at Sonoma State.

"That's pretty much it," I said. "I mean, El Molino is a super-small school and I'm friendly with almost everyone, but I guess I was never one of those social butterflies who spent time with big groups of people. We had the popular clique, and they're fine, but I'm not really part of it." I pulled away a little so I could look at him. "I bet you were."

"Yeah, I guess." He shrugged and scratched his eyebrow. "But my school was really small, too. Like four hundred kids total. I had my group of guys I'd hang with. Most of them go to State with me, so I see them all the time. Eric. Ben. Jackson. A few went farther away—probably won't come back. It'll be interesting to see who's still there with me in twenty years."

"So for sure you're going to go home and run the farm?" I asked.

My stomach did the familiar clenching-drop combination it did whenever I imagined staying in Guerneville and taking over Jude's Café. Every time I tried to imagine that future, everything turned blank.

"That's the plan." He took a deep breath. "I love it there. I know it as well as Luther does now. It's so peaceful at night; the sky gets so dark you can see everything. But they're getting older, and if Luther really is sick . . . I don't know." He paused, wiping a hand over his mouth. "I might be taking it on earlier than I thought. Which is fine, because let's say someday I want to write a book? I can easily do it there. I keep telling them they can live there and let me take care of them for once. Roberta probably won't hear of it until I'm married, though."

A tiny shiver worked its way down my arms. "Do you have someone back home?"

Sam laughed at this, and the sound was so low he seemed much more man than boy. "No, Tate. There's no one right now." He looked at me, both amused and incredulous. "Wouldn't they be pissed to find me lying on the lawn with the beautiful daughter of the most famous actor alive?"

"It's not like we're doing anything," I reminded him, but the words came out all wobbly, like I knew they weren't entirely true.

In response, he gave the moment a heavy, lingering beat of silence before he grinned over at me. "We sure aren't."

I grew hot all over, and a nervous laugh escaped when neither of us spoke for five . . . ten . . . fifteen seconds.

"What are you thinking about?" I asked him.

"You."

I was positive he heard the way my voice shook when I asked, "What about me?"

"That I like you," he said with gentle urgency. "That it's weird to already like you so much. That I want to spend time with you—alone—during the day, and get to know you better, but don't know how we could make that happen."

"What would you want to do?" I asked.

Sam sat up, reaching to brush the damp chill of the lawn off his back. "I dunno. Just walk around. Talk more like this, but in the daylight so I can see you properly." He turned and looked down at me, a smile slowly lifting the corners of his mouth. "Lie down together on a different lawn somewhere."

★ ★

"You want to spend the day *alone*?"

I didn't miss the edge of hurt in Nana's voice.

"Not because I don't want to be with *you*," I insisted. "I'm leaving soon, to school in Sonoma, and I like the idea that I can walk around a big city alone and navigate it by myself. I just . . . want to try for a few hours."

I held my breath while she lifted her arms, clasping pearls at the back of her neck. "I suppose I could visit Libby tomorrow without you."

Libby, from deep in Nana's past, owned a tiny London hotel. Even the way my grandmother said *Libby* with a particularly lilting emphasis on the first syllable made me see that she thought her old high school friend must be impressively cultured.

"Exactly," I said, exhaling at the appearance of this convenient excuse: an old friend. "You wouldn't want me there, either. I'm sure I'd keep you from gossiping your faces off."

Nana laughed, swatting at me with her sock before sitting to put it on. "You know I don't gossip."

"Sure, and I don't like pie."

She laughed again, and then looked up at me from where she sat at the edge of the bed. Her expression straightened from her brow to her mouth, and, at rest, her lips pulled down in a natural pose of displeasure. "Where will you go?"

I tried to look undecided, but the plan flashed in my head like a marquee. Gambling that she wouldn't follow to check up on me—I didn't think even Nana was that paranoid or controlling—I said, "Not sure. Maybe Hyde Park?"

"But hon, we've planned that for next Tuesday."

"Maybe I could go out on a paddleboat?" I tried to make it sound more like it had only just occurred to me, and not like Sam and I had already discussed the idea. "It looks fun, but I don't think you'd want to do that with me."

Nana wouldn't step foot on a paddleboat, but wouldn't want to stop me from doing it, either. She nodded slowly, bending to pull on her other sock. I could see I'd won.

"I guess you'd be fine." She looked up. This was such an enormous leap of faith for her. She would never let me even go to San Francisco or Berkeley alone.

And here I was, asking to walk around *London* alone— as far as she knew, that is. "You're sure you'll be fine?"

I nodded quickly, working to speak past the sun rising in my chest. "Totally fine."

five

"YOU ARE A MASTER manipulator." Sam handed a few pounds to the man at the Bluebird Boats rental kiosk and looked over his shoulder at me. "I thought for sure she'd say no. How did you get Jude to go for it?"

"I told her I wanted to be independent and ride a boat. I knew she didn't want to go on the lake, so . . ."

He reached out for a high five, and we followed the man along the dock to where our blue paddleboat was tethered to a wide metal hook. The mechanics of powering the boat with our feet seemed pretty straightforward, but the man explained it anyway: how the pedals worked, how to steer, what to do if we got stuck far out and the wind picked up across the lake. Had he not looked up and seen the freight engine that was Sam standing right in front of him?

"If we get stuck," I said, hooking my thumb toward the mountain of a man beside me, "I'll just make him climb out and tow me back to the dock."

The man sized him up with a raised brow. "Well, off then. Stay on this side of the bridge, all right?"

Sam steadied me with his hand on my arm as I climbed into my seat, before following me in. The boat dipped noticeably under his weight. "We're going to be paddling in circles," I joked. "Maybe you should only use one foot."

He looked at me, eyes glimmering. "You're in an especially good mood."

I liked that he saw it. He was right, too. I was nearly light-headed I was so giddy to be out on my own, especially with Sam. We had only a handful of days left together, and I was already dreading having to say goodbye.

We backed up and play-fought over who got to steer, finally agreeing that I'd go first, then he'd get a turn.

"Girls usually like to be driven around," he said when he ceded control of the simple lever.

"Careful," I growled darkly, but playfully, over at him. "You wouldn't want to sound sexist."

With a sweet smile, he held a hand to his heart. "I sure wouldn't."

It was windier on the lake than it was on the paved trail, and steering proved harder than I'd expected. Paddling was comical. I was pushing with every bit of strength I had and still barely managed to keep us moving in a straight line.

"Canoeing is way easier," I whined. "Mental note to request they stock canoes when we return."

"Or kayaks."

"We have these huge lines of canoes at the beach in town," I told him, already breathless. "They used to be metal and would get hot as hell in the sun. Now they're these thick inflatable ones. Yellow rubber. You'll see tourists all over the river, tipping over where it gets gnarled just before Jenner."

"You get a lot of tourists?"

"In the summer, yeah." I stopped, working to catch my breath. "Wine country. The river. I get it—it's a nice place to stay . . . for a few days."

He laughed at this and again, we veered left because he was pedaling so much more forcefully than I could.

"Lend me one of your legs," I said.

He reached over, tickling my side, and then shifted his hand behind me, letting it rest around my shoulders. "This okay?"

I had to swallow past a thick swell of *YES* in my throat, and managed a garbled "Of course."

"Sorry we cut out of breakfast so early."

For once this morning, Sam and Luther were downstairs before we arrived, and they left only a few minutes after we'd returned with our plates of food. "Is Luther okay?"

"Not sure. He hasn't been eating much."

Now that he mentioned it, I'd noticed it, too.

His hand curled around the back of my neck, warm and firm. Changing the subject, he asked, "Is it weird to be on your own in a big city?"

"A little. Mom and Nana don't really let me go anywhere alone."

"Were they worried about something happening related to your dad?" He squeezed my neck gently. "Or are they just overprotective?"

"I don't think they were worried about Dad. More the

media, I guess. Or . . . it just became habit to worry. Every day, up until I graduated, one of them would drop me off and pick me up from school."

He looked floored. "Seriously?"

I nodded. "I have a driver's license, but I've driven alone only a handful of times, and only ever around town. I've been to movies with friends without Nana or Mom, but am required to check in immediately after the show ends."

"But now they're letting you move to Sonoma? How far is that?"

"Fifty miles. It's about as close as I could be." Regret pulsed like a twin heartbeat inside me. "I also got in to Santa Cruz, University of Oregon, and UC Santa Barbara—but they just felt too far."

He hummed and slid his fingers into the hair at the nape of my neck, sending an electric pulse from my scalp to the base of my spine. I could feel his fingertips, the way his hand flexed. He made tiny circles with the tip of his index finger, and the sensation traveled down my body; an anticipatory thrum settled low in my navel.

"By the time I was twelve," he said, "I was out in the barns at dawn, and then earning money mowing lawns, pitching hay, you name it. Luther and Roberta rarely had any idea where I was when I wasn't at school or the dinner table with them. I think that kind of supervision would've driven me crazy."

"Probably. It drives me crazy, and I'm used to it."

"Could I come see you in Sonoma?"

My legs stiffened so suddenly that we tilted left. Sam's hand came over mine on the steering lever, gently guiding

us away from an oncoming boat. Once we'd paddled ourselves clear, he let go and looked over at me, amused. "Did
I freak you out?"

I shook my head, but couldn't manage to spit out a
simple no. I mean, obviously I'd been wondering the same
thing—hoping that I could see him again after we left
London—but some fantasies are easier to play with when
they seem impossible. Now, not only was I imagining a
dorm, a roommate, classes, and fifty miles separating me
from Mom and Nana, I was imagining Sam there, too. It
seemed like an infinite abyss of unknowns.

"I just had a moment where it really hit me that I'm
leaving home," I admitted, "and I'm going to be on my own.
I can't even fathom living in a new place, let alone having
you come see me outside of this London bubble."

"You're so brave, Tate." He took a few quiet moments
before speaking again. "But am I wrong to think there's
something happening here?"

I looked at him and waited for the right words to come.
I'd had exactly one boyfriend. Jesse kissed me sophomore
year at homecoming, and that was that. No discussion of *do
you want this* or *should we try that*. In fact, we were never
great when it came to discussing anything—we'd known
each other since fourth grade, so romantic arbitration still
eluded me. But I did know what Sam *meant*. It was why,
even though I was on a trip with my grandmother, I'd been
more careful with my makeup. It's why I agonized a little
every morning about what I was going to wear. It's why my
favorite part of the day was when I saw him.

"Tate?" he prompted when I remained silent.

"No, you're not wrong," I said.

"You feel it too?"

I wondered if he could hear my heartbeat. "Yeah. Sorry. I'm not very good at . . ."

He slowed his pedaling. "Is it too early to be talking about this?"

"I mean, I don't know how college students–slash-writers-slash-farmers do things in Vermont, but it's not too soon for me. Just new."

But Sam didn't laugh. He leaned over and pressed the slightest kiss to my neck, just beneath my jaw.

From my chest to between my legs, everything went tight. I could smell strawberries on his breath.

"You smell like strawberries."

A rumbling laugh escaped, and he leaned back a little. "I had a crepe while I was waiting for you. Want to get off this lake and go get one?"

★ ★

My legs were weak from the effort it took to paddle the boat against the wind back to the dock, but I was well aware Sam did most of the work. As he collected his deposit at the kiosk, he wasn't even winded—he probably could have taken off and run twenty miles if I asked him to.

We bought two more crepes and found a spot on the grass, in dappled shade beneath a maple tree. I had the strange sense of being precariously suspended above a canyon, almost like the way I feel in a dream when I'm floating and look down and realize that I'm actually falling. This felt like the start of something new, something scary but glorious. It felt like I was deciding not just whether I would kiss this man, but whether I would chase every other dirty thought I had, too.

He let out a satisfied moan when he finished the last bite of his food and fell back on the lawn with a grin aimed at the sky. "Damn, I could fall asleep right here."

Out of instinct, I pulled my phone from my bag and sent Nana a quick text to let her know I was okay. She had brought Mom's BlackBerry; she despised all manner of mobile phone, but Mom insisted.

Nana replied shortly with *I'm at Libby's for the next few hours. Meet me in the lobby at five, please.*

I stared at my phone and felt something weightless inside me expand. It was only eleven in the morning, and I had an entire day of freedom.

I turned to find Sam already watching me. "What?"

He smiled and rolled onto his side, propping his head on his elbow. "We seem to spend most of our time together on lawns."

The words burst free: "And horizontal."

"And horizontal," he agreed through a grin.

"At least it's daylight." And looking at him in the light— in a way I hadn't been able to when we were out together during the day with Luther and Nana—was like chugging down a glass of cold water. His skin was smooth and clear, eyes like glass surrounded by generous lashes. He couldn't have inherited anything from Luther genetically, but he sure did have the same wide smile.

He seemed to be taking me in just as carefully. His eyes swept over the long waves of my hair, across my cheeks, to my mouth—where they lingered. And then he met my gaze and grinned, pulling a small dimple into his left cheek. "You have amazing eyes."

With a tremble in my stomach, I rolled to my side too, stacking our empty paper plates and moving them out of the way. "What do you feel like doing today?"

His pupils swelled, turning his eyes nearly black, and in the brief reaction I read the forbidden thoughts there. I wondered whether they mirrored my own: Sam's mouth on mine, the heat of his palm beneath my shirt, the way he would block out the sun if he hovered over me.

He shrugged. "What do *you* feel like doing?"

"Things I'm not sure we could do in a park."

His brows shot up, and a laugh burst out of his mouth. "Tate, holy shit."

"Don't tell me you weren't thinking it too. I could see it all over your face."

He looked at my mouth again, and a lazy grin settled on his. "You always this honest?"

I was already shaking my head. "Absolutely not."

Sam's brows pulled closer together. "Why with me?"

"I don't know." He just seemed to pull everything out of me: my truth magnet. Maybe it was because he already knew my secret; there was nothing else about me that I'd ever have to hide. "I just feel safe with you."

"I could ask you anything, and you'd tell me?" he asked.

He was so close, maybe only six inches away, and my heart was a jackhammer. I could lean forward and press my lips to his. I was 99.8 percent sure he'd let me.

"You can try," I said.

I watched his tongue dart out, wet his lips. "Hmm."

"I could ask you anything too," I ventured.

"Sure."

But all my thoughts were more . . . physical. I was wiped clean of any questions. Maybe he could see it too, because he smiled a little wider and reached out to pull a strand of hair from where it was stuck to my lip. "So you've had one boyfriend?"

"Yeah. But we didn't have sex."

His hand fell away leisurely, his breathing slowed, and he let my words settle between us. I felt everything come to a stop inside me, immediately wanting to swallow back what I'd said, wanting to stand up and walk away and dive under the covers back at the hotel room.

"I don't know why I just said that," I admitted.

"Because you're thinking about it."

If my heart was racing before, it was torpedoing now, a wild metronome inside me that couldn't keep pace with this song.

"Don't be embarrassed," he said quietly. "I am too."

"You've done it before?" I wanted to shove my fist in my mouth over how naive I sounded.

He let out a sweet laugh, a gentle "Yeah."

At first, I thought I was only imagining that he moved closer, but then his mouth was on mine, just once: a pressing, lingering strawberry kiss.

"That okay?" he asked, his words whispered against my lips. He pulled back, taking me in. His breath was warm on my skin.

"I've been *kissed* before."

With another quiet laugh, he leaned in again, and this time he brought one hand up, cupping the side of my face, before sliding it into my hair. His mouth opened, warm and careful, and he tasted me, pulling back again with a smile. "Now *you* taste like strawberries."

I may have tasted sweet, but I'd become a monster, a shark given a whiff of blood. With a hand on his neck, I pulled him back, urging him partway over me so his chest covered mine. He came readily, groaning, and was careful not to crush me, putting his weight on an elbow, propping his other hand beside my ribs.

I couldn't get enough, couldn't kiss him deep enough or press my mouth hard enough against his. I wanted him so intensely; it had been building only for days but it felt like months, and it made me ache in this agonizing, impatient way.

He pulled away a little, breathless as he kissed my chin, my neck, and then pressed his forehead to my shoulder. "Easy, Tate. I still have to walk out of here."

His ear was so close to my heart, I was sure he could hear the way it flipped around inside me. "Nana's gone for the next few hours," I said.

Slowly, Sam lifted his head and studied me. "You wanna go back to the hotel?"

When I spoke, I sounded like I'd been running all morning: "Yeah. Hotel."

six

MY HAND SHOOK AS I slid the key card into the slot in the door. I was distracted and rushed by the sensation of Sam's fingers bracketing my hips, his mouth moving up the side of my neck to my ear. I didn't know what I was doing—*this was crazy*—but the hunger was greater than the trepidation that loomed like an anxious shadow in the back of my thoughts. Housekeeping had already been through, and the beds were immaculate, surfaces shining.

We closed the door, hooked the safety lock in place, and then stood, staring at each other.

"We don't have to do this," he said.

Before nerves could get the best of me, I turned and walked over to my bed, scooting toward the headboard. Sam climbed after me onto the mattress, kicking off his shoes.

It was so quiet I could hear a taxi driver on the street yelling to someone on the sidewalk. I could hear the even ticking of the alarm clock on the bedside table. I could hear the uneven pulls of Sam's breath.

"This is crazy," he said, finally moving closer and punctuating every sentence with a kiss to my jaw, my cheek, my ear: "Change your mind anytime. I mean. We just met. Your grandmother could come back. Tell me to stop."

I couldn't seem to pull enough breath into my lungs, and my words came out as a gasp. "She won't. And I don't want to stop."

I imagined we had at least a couple hours, but still, it felt like we threw our clothes onto the floor in a frenzy, teeth and chins knocking in sloppy, undressing kisses. He asked me again, and again—while we kissed, and touched, and explored—whether I was sure.

I'd never been naked with someone before, and I'd also never been more sure about anything.

He kissed down my body, loving my breasts, kissing between my legs until I was crying out into a pillow and holding him there by a fist in his hair. And then he was over me, massive and bare, asking me one more time.

"You trust me?"

It was strange, but this question drew the moment to a quiet standstill. I could tell by his expression that I could take my time to answer, that I could say no and we would put ourselves back together and go out to the garden, or down the street for lunch. He wasn't just asking if I trusted him to be careful with my body, but whether I trusted him to be careful with me.

With a nod, I pulled him back down over me, closing my legs around his hips. I felt him press against me, warm and inflexible, but he moved away before I could react, jogging toward the bathroom. I was unable to look away from the architecture of him, the sheer bulk of muscle and height. When he reappeared, my eyes dropped below his navel . . . and then over to the towel in his hand.

"Just in case," he said.

He tucked the towel beneath me, kissing my chest, my neck, my mouth so sweetly, and he returned over me, climbing between my legs and kissing up my neck.

The sheets beneath me were so soft, so perfectly white. Sun slanted into the room, trapezoiding across our naked skin.

"You okay?" he asked one last time.

"Yeah." I ran a hand up from his stomach to his collarbone. "Are you?"

"I'm nervous," he admitted. "But yeah. I'm good."

"You've done this before, though."

"I've never done it with you."

I was shaking. I could feel it, and I knew he could, too. But he just kissed me over and over, like he did at the park, until I was hot, and squirming, until I'd forgotten the pleasure he'd already gifted me and was demanding more, for the press of him, that instinctive desire to feel him inside.

He had a condom—thank God, because where was my head?—and I watched him roll it on, suddenly questioning my sanity, the logic that he'd somehow fit inside me. He put a gentle hand on my hip, guided himself with the other. With his eyes on my face, Sam went slow, so slow, careful to stop when I made a squeak of pain, slow again, and then deep, and then he was moving and it was okay, I was okay.

I was better than okay. I was lost in him, in the feel of

his back growing slick under my hands, and his mouth on my neck, and his waist against my thighs. Lost in the feel of the sun on my skin, the way it poured in from the window to spill across the bed. I was lost in the sense of pleasure flirting under the pain, and his breath growing hot and hungry on my neck.

He was telling me it was good,

it was so good,

did I think I could come again?

Did I want him to finish?

I did but I didn't, because I knew we wouldn't ever be back in that exact moment, my first—our first—and I knew, too, that as soon as it was over I'd have to face myself and this wild decision. So I told him to wait, please, I didn't want it to end.

He did wait, or at least he tried to, with gritted teeth and fingers that pressed almost too hard and still not hard enough. But when I hooked my ankles at his back and moved with him from below, he groaned out an apology and swore, shaking under my hands.

We fell still, and the ache in me turned sharp, more discomfort than pleasure. Sam carefully pulled back. There was blood on his fingers when he took off the condom, but he didn't look worried. He just cleaned me up, bent to kiss my forehead, and walked to the bathroom.

I was shaking so bad I pulled the covers over me, all the way up to my chin.

I barely heard the toilet flush above the ringing in my ears. I didn't even feel like the same person. Tate Jones wouldn't have sex with a guy she knew for a matter of days.

Tate Jones wouldn't fall for someone so fast, so immediately. But apparently Tate Butler would.

Sam walked into the bedroom, pulled on his boxers, and climbed back onto the bed, bracing over me on all fours, sweetly trapping me under the blankets.

"Are you cold or hiding?"

"Cold."

With a little growl, Sam climbed under the covers with me and curled on his side, bracing on an elbow to look down at me. He was smiling like an idiot, but—to my horror—I felt the burn of tears across my eyes. I was so scared of the moment he left this room, and hesitation pushed out the certainty that this had been the right thing to do.

"Tate," he said, eyes flickering across my face, worried now.

I pressed a hand to his bare stomach. "Yeah?"

He closed his eyes and then bent so his head rested between my breasts. "You're crying," he whispered.

"I'm just overwhelmed," I admitted. "With good feelings, I swear."

"I don't want you to feel weird about doing this."

Struggling to put myself back together, I promised him, "I won't."

He shook his head, and then kissed my breast, gently biting. "This is a big deal," he said once he released me. "Having sex. I know why I did it—I'm crazy about you—but why did you?"

"Can't my reason be the same?"

He laughed against my skin. "It can."

★ ★

We didn't see each other after he kissed me before leaving my room at three thirty. I remade the bed and turned on the shower with a numb hand, climbing in and staring at the tiles for twenty minutes, alternating between thrill and panic.

Will he think less of me now?

Has he slept with a hundred other girls?

We used a condom but how would I know if it broke?

Will Nana be able to tell what we did? Will she see it on my face?

In the end, Nana seemed pretty oblivious. She happily caught me up on all of Libby's gossip during dinner at Da Mario, and then we saw *Hairspray* at the Shaftesbury Theatre. At eleven, we fell like rocks into bed. I would have texted Sam to tell him that I couldn't come to the garden, that Nana insisted I get to bed early . . . but he didn't have a cell phone.

I barely slept that night. Every time I rolled over, my aching body remembered, and then I opened my eyes, stared up at the dark ceiling, and wondered whether Sam was awake down the hall, whether he was happy or regretting this, or feeling something else—some other emotion that usually follows sex and which I didn't even have a name for.

At breakfast, my stomach felt like it was full of squawking birds, but when I came back from the buffet with just a piece of toast, Nana sent me away for protein, fruit, *something substantial, Tate, we have a big day today.*

I immediately felt Sam step up behind me when I was deciding which of the cold cut selections I could stomach, and my skin broke out in a warm shiver.

"Hey you," he said quietly, reaching forward to run two fingers down my arm.

I chanced a look at him over my shoulder, and my pulse became a stampede. He was sleep rumpled, hair mussed and eyes still tired. "Hey."

"Are you okay?"

I frowned, turning back to the trays of meat. Was my mental clutter visible all over my face? "Yeah, I'm great. Why?"

"You didn't come to the garden."

Oh. I nodded, stepping down the line. Sam grabbed a plate and followed me. "We got back late from the play," I explained, "and Nana wouldn't let me head out." I smiled up at him, face heated. *We had sex.* Was he remembering it too? "You'd know this if you had a phone."

Sam laughed. "What do I need a phone for?"

"So you're not sitting out in the garden waiting for me."

He scooped two fried eggs onto his plate. "It was worth it."

"Why?" I asked, laughing. "Did someone else show up?"

He bumped my shoulder gently. "Seriously, you're okay?"

"I'm good."

"Not . . . hurt?"

Oh. If I thought my face felt hot before, when his meaning hit me, I grew feverish. "A little, but . . ." I looked over at him. His mossy eyes were studying me so intently, his lips parted. Truth magnet. I mirrored his words: "It was worth it."

His gaze dropped to my mouth. "That's a pretty good answer."

"I think I'd worried you'd be weird today."

Putting down the bacon tongs, he looked at me, confused. "Weird how?"

"Just—"

"This is what I meant," he interrupted with quiet urgency, looking over my shoulder to make sure we weren't being watched, "how it happened fast, and I didn't want you to regret it afterward."

"I don't."

"*I'm* not being weird," he insisted, holding a very solemn hand to his chest.

I bit back a laugh at the earnest gesture. "Well I'm not being weird either."

With a flirty grin, Sam reached up, tugging on a long strand of my hair. "Good."

I reached up too, pressing my thumb to his comma scar. "Good."

seven

NANA AND LUTHER ATE like sloths. At every meal, each bite was carefully cut, poked, chewed, swallowed. Pauses were taken for sips of water or wine, and there was far too much conversation. In contrast, Sam and I shoveled our food in our faces, and then sat, waiting—staring while Luther and Nana nattered on, oblivious to our brain-melting boredom. Meals—particularly lunch—were becoming a drag, and neither Sam nor I had any patience for sitting for two hours in the middle of the day.

Plus, afterward, Nana always ordered coffee, but then had to sit and wait for it to cool to room temperature before she could drink it. At lunch, just twenty-four hours after we had sex—it was all I could think about—I looked at Sam, who, as soon as Nana lifted her hand to get the waiter's attention to order coffee, was already looking at me with *Get me the hell out of here* written all over his face.

Finally, I broke: "Nana, can we go outside and walk around?"

She gave her order, and then looked over at me, concerned. "'Walk around'?"

"I mean," I amended, "just sit outside and people-watch?" I winced apologetically. "It's hot in here, and I am super bored."

This was enough teenage attitude to earn a lecture later, but if she let us out into the fresh air, it would have been worth it. With a tiny flick of her wrist, we were dismissed.

We didn't wait for confirmation: both Sam and I were up and bolting from the dark, subdued restaurant before either she or Luther could change their mind.

There was a bocce court in the back garden of the restaurant, and a few small tables with chessboards. The bocce court was occupied, but Sam pointed to a chess table and I followed him over, hoping my rusty skills would return quickly.

I sat in front of the white pieces; he sat in front of the black, looming over the table. With a tiny tilt of his chin, Sam smiled over at me. "You start."

I moved my king's pawn two spaces and opened my mouth to speak, but stopped when I heard Luther's voice just on the other side of the window. All of that internal flailing over our boredom, and we'd only managed to move three feet away.

Sam laughed quietly, shoulders pulled up to his ears, and he was so adorable I wanted to stretch across the table and put my mouth on his. The day before was still a fresh, singing echo in my thoughts and all over my skin.

I think he could see the memory in my eyes, too, because his attention dropped to my lips and he rumbled a quiet "We could go make out in the bushes."

My reply that making out would be way more fun than chess but also way more punishable by grandmother-inflicted death was cut off when Nana's voice filtered out to us: "No, actually. My husband died when I was thirty-five."

Across from me, Sam's flirty smile seemed to dissolve.

"On the one hand," Nana said, "I had a six-year-old daughter to raise alone. But on the other hand, I was no longer being yelled at for not keeping the house clean enough." I heard her pause and imagined her lifting her cup, inhaling the coffee before deciding it was still too warm and putting it down again. "I have the restaurant, and it makes enough to support us. So, no, I never wanted to marry again."

My chest pinched in, and every thought seemed to slow in my head. Nana never liked to talk about anything longer ago than the previous weekend. Said it did us no good to live in the past. I always knew Mom was raised without her father, same as me, but it didn't seem to sink in until that moment that Nana wasn't bothered by it in the slightest.

"That's how my Roberta was," Luther told her. "Didn't want to marry again. Even with a young son, she was stubborn as all get out to do it all on her own. I put on the hard sell. Told her nobody was telling her she needed a man, but if she wanted one, I was throwing my hat in the ring."

I looked across the table at Sam and could tell he was listening just as intently as I was, and it made me wonder how much he could know about their past. I imagined

Luther was in his late sixties; if he and Roberta met years before Sam was born, it couldn't have been easy for a black man and a white woman to be together in a small town.

Nana grew quiet, and I wondered if the same question was said too quietly for us to hear, or maybe just communicated in her eyes, because Luther added, "We went through a lot in those early days. Lot of folks didn't appreciate me walking around town with her."

"I'd imagine."

"She didn't care one iota." Luther laughed again. "Even when they set the barn on fire."

They what now? Sam didn't seem at all surprised to hear this; he just lifted his brows and nodded at me like *I know, right?*

"You raised Tate's mom all on your own?" Luther asked, turning the conversation back to us.

Sam studied me, and it was a little like being stuck in quicksand. I wanted to escape, but couldn't. I'd never heard Nana talk about this before.

"We did fine, the two of us. Emma was a good girl," Nana told him, using Mom's new name. Emma now, not Emmeline. "She married too young, though. Met a boy when she was only eighteen, and it just moved too fast."

Sam's eyes snapped from the window back to mine, and I knew we were both wondering what Nana would actually divulge to Luther.

On the other side of the window, the old man hummed sympathetically. "I worry when it happens, Sam will fall too hard, too fast," he said quietly. "He wears every feeling on his sleeve. Always has."

Sam turned a bright tomato red and reached for his piece on the table, mirroring my opening move, king's pawn. "You know, we could turn this into strip chess," he said awkwardly, too loudly.

I leaned forward. "If we can hear them, they can hear *us*."

He paled, whispering, "Do you think they heard me ask you to go make out?"

"Or plot how to get me naked?" I asked, stifling a laugh.

Nana's voice returned, and our questions were answered in the obliviousness of her tone. "He's a sweet boy, but strong. He'll be fine."

"I hope." A pause, and then, "If you don't mind me asking, is Tate's father still in the picture?"

"Oh, Emma's ex-husband? He was awful," Nana said. "Cheating all the time. Could barely be bothered to spend time at home with his girls."

A knife slowly worked its way into my chest, and Sam abruptly stood with a look of urgent sympathy, gesturing for me to follow him away from the table. But I couldn't. My entire life Nana had been a stony vault when it came to Dad. Whenever I asked about him, she usually answered with a simple "You're better off here." I felt like there was some information I could glean in eavesdropping, something that would explain why Dad never came for me, or why Mom never let him.

"Emma is a passive one," Nana continued. "Sweet— maybe too sweet. But the husband? My goodness. I suppose it's hard to see someone's true colors when you're in love like that, but I've never met a more selfish man. Everything was about appearance."

Luther hummed low in his throat, a quiet *mm-hmm* of understanding. "He have any contact with Tate?"

"No." She paused, maybe finally drinking her coffee. "He gave little indication that he wanted any."

This stabbed fully into me; a sharp splinter into my thoughts. I had memories of sweetness with my father: in his arms on the sidewalk, lying head-to-head in bed, reading books, splashing in the waves on the beach. I wanted to believe that he gave me up for my own protection, that he did it out of love. He may not have fought for me, he may have forgotten to pick me up at the airport . . . but what Nana said meshed too well with the unwelcome sense I got from Sam that night he told me what he knew: that Mom might have given me a better impression of Dad than he deserved.

Finally I did stand, realizing that there was nothing in this conversation I wanted to hear. I didn't want my memories to be washed in hindsight with Mom painted as a weakling and Dad as a deserting father who didn't want me at all.

Sam jogged after me. "Tate."

I marched past the bocce court and into the thin patch of trees just behind the restaurant.

"Tate." He caught up with me, falling into step to my right. "Hey."

Stopping at a low bench, I sat, leaning my elbows on my knees.

"You okay?"

I let out a short, dry laugh. "The thing is, she won't talk about Dad with me. But she's talking about it with Luther?"

"Maybe because she doesn't think anything will come of talking to him about it?" he asked carefully.

"You heard her. She's so set against him. I get her being mad over what he did to Mom, but I'm his kid. You know?" I looked over at him. "And I never even got a choice. If you could have a relationship with your dad, wouldn't you try?"

Sam shook his head. "No. But the situation is different, and even if it weren't, you and I wouldn't have to react exactly the same way." He took my hand, turning it over to draw on my palm. "My dad sent me away. Your mom took you away. Those might seem like small differences, but they aren't. They're enormous."

"I know." I turned to look up at him and the sight of him, close enough to kiss, made desire mix strangely with sadness. He bent, sliding his mouth over mine. We weren't that far from the restaurant, but the feel of him was such an immediate comfort that I didn't care who saw us. I leaned in for more, to put my hands in his hair, to hold him to me.

Finally, he pulled away and his eyes had that same heaviness they had yesterday when he was braced over me, asking if I was sure.

"I want to take you back to Vermont with me," he said quietly.

"I'd go."

He leaned in for another kiss. "I'll make you a deal," he said. "When I come out to California to visit you soon, if you want to go to LA to meet up with your dad, I'll take you."

★ ★

I hadn't imagined there was any way that Sam and I could be together again, but that night, after the loop of Nana's words had formed a dull, persistent rhythm in my thoughts,

I met him in the garden at midnight, kissing him frantically until our mouths were raw. Whether or not he knew I needed distraction as much as I needed him, he didn't make me talk about it again. Instead, he slid his hand into my pants and stared at my face while he touched me, almost delirious with want—and let out a relieved moan when I reached for him, too.

I didn't even know what was really happening between us, how it seemed to balloon so quickly or how it could be sustained. It felt both inevitable and foolish to give my heart away like this, to let myself fall so hard for someone I might never see again. I immediately pushed the thought out of my head as soon as it entered.

When I spoke to Mom every morning, I dropped little bits of information about how things had progressed with Sam. But no matter how much she seemed to delight in my romantic vacation, I still wouldn't dare tell her that I lost my virginity to him or that every time I saw him, my head started singing a tiny, beautiful, terrifying four-letter word.

The following night in the garden, his hands were on my face, but I wanted them on my skin. His hands were on my chest, but I wanted him over me. His body was on top of mine in the shadows, but I wanted him moving into me. I wanted to possess him and be possessed by him in a way that made me feel nearly wild.

When I reached for his track pants, he went still, his voice unsure in my ear: "We should stop."

"I don't want to stop."

"I don't want to either, but I also don't want to get *arrested*."

"Just . . . let's be fast."

In the end, we came together, frantically, behind a row of trees. And afterward, while I was staring up at our stars, he turned to look at me, saying, "It's so crazy to think that things that I thought only lived in my imagination can be real." He reached out, tracing my mouth with his fingertip. "But then I touch you, and it's like every fantasy I ever had coming true."

I closed my eyes, feeling, for the first time all day, a sense of reality closing down on us. "You can't say things like that."

Sam pushed up on an elbow. His hair was messy from my hands, his mouth swollen. "Why not?"

"Because it will make it that much harder when we go home."

He didn't say anything to this, he just stared down at me, half-amused, half something unreadable.

"When you look back at this," I started, already hearing the unreasonable in my voice, "do you think you'll remember it as just sex with a girl in London?"

Sam laughed, giving me a simple "No." He kissed me again. "I could have *just sex with a girl in London* if that's what I wanted. I already told you I'm going to come see you. I like being with you just as much when we have our clothes on. That's part of what I mean about the fantasy."

Pulling back, I looked over at him, not entirely sure why this made me feel even sadder. No matter what my infatuated heart said, could there really be hope for us long term? Other women would eventually get this careful, attentive person, and I hated every single one of them. No matter how much bigger Sonoma was than Guerneville, there wouldn't be anyone like Sam there.

When we stood, my legs felt rubbery. I was so physically and emotionally exhausted, I could have fallen asleep standing up, if required. Inside the elevator, Sam pulled me in against his chest. "Does your dad know you're going to college?"

"No, I don't think so," I said. "I mean, I don't really know how much Mom talks to him, but I don't get the feeling that she tells him anything."

"So you really haven't heard from him?" Sam asked.

I reached up and pressed a fingertip to his comma scar. "He sends me things at Christmas. Usually something techy. He must not write anything, or Nana must take whatever note he's written, because there'll be a tag on it in her handwriting that says, 'To Tate, from Ian.'"

"But not money? He's a bajillionaire and—" He paused, and the corners of his mouth lifted in a small, apologetic smile. One didn't have to be the most observant person to notice the way Nana calculated everything down to the last dime. Ian Butler might be a bajillionaire, but we were not.

"Not money. I mean, maybe, but it doesn't seem like it. But we're doing okay."

"Michael—a ridiculously rich Wall Street guy— wouldn't send Luther and Roberta money to help raise me," Sam said. "Forget presents. Sometimes I wonder whether he remembers that he has another kid."

I thought this last part was hyperbole, but it was hard to tell. "Is Roberta still in touch with him?"

"She sends him cards on holidays." Sam squinted, thinking. "I think they talk a couple times a year, maybe. But I know he never calls. If they talk, it's because she's calling him."

"He sounds like trash. Is it weird that I'm imagining Christian Bale as Patrick Bateman?"

"Actually, that's disturbingly accurate."

"And it doesn't bug you that he's so . . . lame?" I asked.

"Honestly? Not really. Luther and Roberta are the best parents I could have had."

God, he was so levelheaded. And what different lives we'd lived. Me, cherished, but held beneath two sets of very neurotic thumbs. Sam, given all the freedom he could handle—and then some—with just as much love.

The elevator doors opened, and we stepped apart. Usually, Sam went to his end of the hall and I went to mine, and we would wave at the door before ducking silently inside. But that night, he walked me down the hall to my room.

"I don't like what you said," he whispered outside the door, stilling my hand before I could use the key card. "Earlier. About it just being sex for me. You think I'm like that?"

"No. I don't." I looked up at him, taking in his tight, controlled expression. "It's just this awesome-terrible situation. I feel more for you in the past week and a half than I did for Jesse in three years. And it's going to end. It just . . . sucks."

He pulled back, alarmed. "Why's it going to *end*?"

"Because—"

He bent, cutting off my words with his mouth, the sweetest kiss, stopping me in my mental tracks. Pulling away, he cupped his hands to my face and looked me square in the eye. "Because *nothing*," he said, "okay?"

I nodded, a little breathless. "Okay."

Sam kissed me one more time and then hesitated. His cheeks flushed just before he admitted, "I think I'm falling in love with you. Is that crazy?"

Biting my lips was the only way to hold in my elated scream. Finally, I managed, "No. It isn't crazy. Because, me too."

eight

I COULDN'T EVEN LOOK at him at breakfast when he arrived at our usual table, because I knew I would burst into a giant, stupid grin and Nana would realize not only that I was infatuated with this guy, but probably that we'd had sex and were pretty much thinking about only that whenever we were together.

I think I'm falling in love with you.

"Where's Luther?" Nana asked.

But at this, I looked up. Usually Sam grabbed his plate after a quick hello and made a beeline for the buffet. But that morning, he looked haggard, pulling out a chair and sitting heavily down. "He's still in bed."

Sam caught my gaze, and his normally smiling eyes were oddly flat. He winced, opening his mouth to speak before seeming to think better of it, and broke his gaze away, looking out the window into the garden. I watched him lift a hand, chew his thumbnail, and we all fell silent for a good ten seconds, unsure what to say.

My lungs, heart, and stomach seemed to fall away. Nana and I exchanged anxious looks.

Worry etched another crease into her forehead. "Are you okay, hon?"

Blinking back over, he inhaled sharply, as if he'd forgotten where he was. "Yeah. I'm good. Hungry."

Without another word, he stood, walking away toward the buffet.

Nana watched him go, but I focused on my mostly empty plate. His mood very well might have had something to do with Luther, but he'd been worried about Luther this entire trip and hadn't ever been cold to me because of it.

The only thing that had changed from yesterday was that he'd told me he loved me.

"Well, he doesn't seem like himself." She picked up her fork. "But then again, Luther's been looking pretty gray lately. Wonder if that has Sam in a mood."

Sam returned with his usual loaded plate and proceeded to shovel food into his mouth.

"Sam," I said quietly, as soon as Nana stood to get some fruit.

He looked up at me, chewing, unspeaking, with his brows raised.

"You sure you're okay?"

We held eye contact for ten bewildering seconds before he swallowed and looked down to spear another forkful of eggs. "Not really."

He didn't look back at me, so we finished breakfast together in silence broken only by the scrape of silverware on porcelain.

★ ★

I couldn't talk to him on the elevator ride back up to our rooms because Nana was there. And when I knocked at his door while Nana was using the restroom, no one answered.

He and Luther were nowhere to be seen when we were ready to head out for the day.

Sam wasn't in the garden after dinner.

He didn't come to breakfast the next day.

"I wonder if they left for the Lake District early," Nana mused, staring distractedly out the window. It must have been weird for her, too, to have them so abruptly disappear.

"Sam told me that he thinks Luther is sick," I told her.

She nodded. "I think so too."

And with that, I didn't feel like eating. Everything tasted the same: bland and gluey.

"Honey," she said gently, "I know you were fond of him. I'm sorry."

Fond.

I was fond of chocolate. I was fond of my red Doc Martens. I was fond of sunny days out on the water. I was not *fond* of Sam.

But still, I nodded, trying to work a piece of grapefruit down my throat.

On the phone with Mom after breakfast, I knew I sounded flat. She was used to me talking more, and when confronted with my monosyllabic answers, she grew concerned—asking about Nana, about Sam, about me. I gave her the barest of facts: that Sam and Luther had left, and no, I didn't think we'd keep in touch. That Nana and I were heading to St. Paul's Cathedral that day.

A wave of nausea rocked me when I remembered what he'd said about coming to California, traveling with me to LA and supporting me when I reunited with my dad. It wasn't that it couldn't happen without Sam, but he was the first person in my life to encourage me to try. He gave me a bravery and sense of strength I hadn't felt before. I had no way of finding him. He didn't even have my number, either.

I hung up and slid the phone into my purse.

Numb, I followed Nana down the hall, into the elevator. I let the flatness take over. It was like folding a piece of paper, tucking it under a stack of books, letting the weight of some other story take over whatever interesting thing had been written there.

"Ready to explore?" Nana said too brightly. I could tell she was trying to put on a happy face, to show me how one soldiers on from a disappointment.

I grinned back at her, feeling the shape spread across my mouth, knowing it was more of a grimace.

"Okay, hon," she said with a gentle laugh. "Let's go."

She marched ahead, shoulders squared, chin up, pushing through the doors to the sidewalk. And because I was looking at the ground, I didn't notice when she pulled up abruptly. I walked into her back, causing her to stumble forward.

An explosion of cameras caught the awkward collision on film. I'd see the photos everywhere for weeks to come. A chorus of voices shouted my name—*they knew my name*. Nana turned, grabbing my hand and jerking me back into the hotel. It took me a long time—far longer than it took her—to figure out what was going on.

nine

LOST NO LONGER:
Tate Butler Steps Out in London

The famed daughter of Ian Butler and
Emmeline Houriet surfaces, and tells her story
of a life of hiding, secrecy, and fear.

Screen legend Ian Butler's only daughter vanished completely from the public eye when she was only eight, spurring wild conspiracy theories that would plague him and enthrall fans for years. But this week in London, Tate Butler has resurfaced and spilled the details about her life in seclusion.

Once a doting husband and father who was often photographed on the red carpet with his wide-eyed and smiling daughter in his arms, Ian became tangled in scandal following an affair with co-star Lena Still. His wife and daughter fled Los Angeles, leaving the public without a clue to their whereabouts. Indeed, for nearly a decade the world has wondered what happened to the girl with her father's million-dollar smile, and—moreover—what happened to her mother, rising starlet Emmeline Houriet.

The truth about what happened next comes from the daughter herself, Tate Butler, now eighteen. A close friend of Tate's tells the *Guardian* that she has graduated from high school; is attending college in Sonoma, California, this fall; is obsessed with the idea of following in her father's footsteps; and "is ready to move beyond her secretive past."

As it turns out, Tate was taken by Emmeline to a small town north of San Francisco, where she assumed the name Tate Jones. Emmeline—who managed to stay under the radar as Emma Jones—has lived a quiet life in the small resort town of Guerneville, California. Although custody battles raged behind the scenes, eventually Emmeline won full custody of Tate, and worked to keep her away from Ian, and the spotlight.

Tate's first trip out of the country was to London, and it was here that she told a trusted confidant everything.

"I don't get the impression that he was a very good father," the source says. "Despite his side of the story, Ian didn't make many attempts to connect with Tate. She has been incredibly sheltered. No one—except maybe three or four people—knows who she is. It was a priority for her mother and [her grandmother] Jude to keep Tate out of the spotlight, and they've done that. But she's an adult now. It's time for her to start living her life freely."

ten

I WAS HYSTERICAL ON the phone—a bubbling cauldron of panic. After Mom admitted that there were photographers outside the house back in Guerneville, she could barely get a word in edgewise.

"I'm sorry, Mom, I'm so sorry."

"Baby girl, listen," she said, "this was going to happen at some—"

"But I told him *everything*. I told him about you," I choked, "and Dad. What is Dad going to say? Is he going to sue us?"

At this Mom laughed. "Don't be silly."

Don't be silly.

She sounded so sure. So unworried.

Meanwhile, Nana paced the room behind me, on the phone with the airline, trying to rearrange our flights. Once that was sorted, she called Mom's old agent, coordinating to have someone meet us at Heathrow, to get us home without incident.

I was just holding the phone to my ear, listening without hearing the words Mom was sending across the line. Soft sounds of reassurance, telling me she loved me, it would all be okay.

But it wasn't okay. I knew I'd made an enormous mess.

And a small voice in the very back of my head kept whispering, *He's going to remember he has a daughter now.*

★ ★

A man met us at the airport. He opened the door as our car pulled up to the curb. Before I could catch a glimpse of his face, the door closed again and he shuttled Nana past a throng of photographers, into a tight circle of airport security guards. And then he came back, holding his hand out for me.

He smiled. "Hey, Tate. I'm Marco."

He was in his late twenties: fine, carved features, jet-black hair, penetrating blue eyes—and yet somehow he managed to exude calm rather than panic, like he'd navigated this sort of thing a thousand times before. I took his hand; it was warm. His skin was soft, but I could feel the strength of the tendons and bone beneath when he tugged me forward, out of the backseat.

To my surprise, Marco didn't pass me off to a crew of security guards. He ushered me in under the blinding hail of flashes, hiding me beneath his own coat. The airport wanted even less to do with this madness than we did, so they let us through a private security line and into a secure room while we waited to board our flight.

Nana stepped out, telling me she needed to call Mom, needed to get water. To me, it felt like she needed to get away from me and my terrible decisions for a few minutes. My eyes were puffy; so puffy I felt like I could see my own eyelids. My nose was sore from being wiped on tissue after tissue, my lips were chapped. I hadn't brushed my hair.

I looked up at this polished, composed stranger, and his expression was exactly the same as it was when there were a hundred photographers on our trail: mouth a faint upward curve, eyes steady.

"You okay?" he asked.

"Are you kidding?" I ran a shaking hand over my hair. "I'm great. You?"

He burst out laughing, but I couldn't keep up the surreal joke. I felt the tears swell in the back of my throat.

"I didn't mean for any of this to happen," I told him, voice thick.

"Of course not." He waved like my intention was the least of his concerns, and a smile lit up his entire face. He was too pretty to be very masculine. Elfin. I remember seeing *Lord of the Rings* with Charlie and laughing for hours when she quipped that Legolas was the prettiest woman in the movie. Marco was like that.

"Ian has been on four major magazine covers this month," he said. "So finding you is the biggest story anyone has on either side of the ocean. There's no way around this circus."

Whether we were past it or not, I needed to know. "Not to be rude . . . but who are you?"

He pressed an apologetic hand to his chest. "I'm sorry.

Of course. My name is Marco Offredi. I'm a PR manager. I was hired by your trust to handle all of your publicity-related concerns for as long as you should need."

"My . . . trust? Hired you?"

He laughed. "Technically. The trust pays my salary, but your father called me."

I squeezed one eye closed, squinting the other at him. My thoughts were windmilling around my head. "I'm so confused. I haven't spoken to my dad in ten years. I didn't know I *had* a trust."

If this surprised Marco, he hid it. "From my very basic understanding, all the money your father owed in child support was set aside." He spread his hands, and the gesture opened my entire world. "The trust covers anything you might need after you leave home."

Slowly, my head started to spin. I was a carousel, gathering speed. "Who's in charge of the trust?"

"You are, as of your eighteenth birthday."

"But," I spluttered, forcing the right questions to form in my mouth, "who was in charge of it before me?"

"Your parents."

Blackness threatened at the edges of my vision, and Marco became blurrily framed. "Both of them?"

"Ian and Emmeline." He leaned in, his light eyes steadying me. "When the news broke, Emmeline called Ian, and Ian called me."

"I didn't even know they were speaking."

"They hadn't been," he said. "Not outside of the occasional legal correspondence, anyway."

But they were now.

"There is nothing sinister happening," Marco assured me, maybe sensing my panic. "Your parents don't get along, but the priority here is you. I am not here for Ian, or for Emmeline. I am here for Tate Jones, Tate Butler—whichever Tate you want to be. I work for you."

This entire situation was a chaotic mix of titillating and alarming. Beneath the guilt and devastation I felt, there was a curiosity lurking, an odd sense of power.

Marco seemed to see this reaction pass over me. He reached into a leather laptop case near his feet and produced a bag of trail mix, handing it to me. "Want to tell me everything?"

Managing my first smile in what felt like days, I admitted, "Not really."

"I'm not here to judge," he said. "I know the story of your mom and dad, but I don't know anything about you after you left LA. Why don't you tell me a little bit about who I'm working for?"

I glanced anxiously at the door. No sign of Nana yet.

When I looked back to Marco, he didn't look away. He blinked slowly, giving me that same gentle smile. There was something in his posture—he exuded a sense of tenacity and loyalty that made me want to go sit next to him and cry for an hour. I wanted to trust him, but I trusted Sam and look where that landed me. What if my internal compass was broken?

"I confided everything to the wrong person," I told him. "That's how we ended up here."

"I'm sure that makes it hard to say it all over again. Can you tell me about him?" When I remained quiet, he added, "It will help me know how to best manage this for you."

"I thought he felt the same way I did," I said quietly. "We . . . yeah."

My face crumpled, and his expression morphed from gentle calm to genuine empathy. "He broke your heart."

So I spilled it all. Every last detail. I told him about the garden, about meeting Sam every night. I told him about all the things I confided and about our day of freedom in the paddleboat. I admitted that I slept with him that day and nearly every day after. I told him that Sam seemed like the first person who knew me as me—the Tate I felt like I'd never been allowed to be.

"What do you want to do?" he asked once I finished.

"Whatever Mom has planned." I shrugged, feeling sick. It was both the truth and a lie. I wanted to do whatever made this easier for her and Nana, but there was something else glittering there, winking at me from a distance. "I'm not sure what she and my dad will want me to do once we're home."

"I'm not here for them. I'm asking *you*, Tate," he said. Marco leaned his chin in a cupped palm. "What do *you* want to do now?"

Shaking my head, I asked him, "What do you mean?"

"Do you want to live in the sun?" he asked quietly. "Or do you want to go back in the shadows?"

eleven

SEPTEMBER
Now

IT'S NOT UNTIL I'M facing the entrance to Twitter headquarters that I realize I've personally only tweeted from my account twice in ten years. Even so, I have over four million followers and I'm supposed to do a live chat in ten minutes. I can already see an enormous crowd of bodies just inside the doors and have no idea how I'm going to do this without screwing up.

"So, if I start the tweet with someone's Twitter name," I say, looking up from my phone, "everyone who follows me can see it?"

Marco is leaning back in through the passenger window, telling the driver where to meet us, and when. He straightens, glances at my phone, and waves me away. "Don't worry about any of that. I have all the answers typed out for you. Just use the hashtag, and you'll be fine."

I take the folder he hands me, scan the questions and

answers inside, and gaze up at him with melting gratitude. "How would I function without you?"

"You'd be curled in the corner of your messy house, eating Lucky Charms out of the box by the handful." He checks the time. "Five questions, and then we're out. Don't get chatty. We need to get on the road by noon."

I salute him obediently and follow him up the steps.

"Here we go," he says under his breath. And then, he turns to me, asking more seriously: "Are you ready for this?"

He's implied this question every time I've had to sign my name on a contract, every time a piece of this collaboration moves forward. But there's a duality there now: he's asking whether I'm *really* ready for what we're about to dive into promoting headlong—my seventh feature film, but the first I'm making with my father. Awareness pulls me up short in a bright square of concrete.

"I hope I am." I gape at him, heart pounding as if maybe I've made a huge mistake. It happens a little bit each time I start something new: the sense that I'm really a fraud, that I don't actually know what I'm doing, that I somehow got into acting on a technicality and not because I earned it.

Usually the feeling evaporates pretty quickly. This time, though, it's hung around since I officially agreed to take on the role of Ellen Meyer: farmer, local civil rights activist, and badass extraordinaire. Some of that has to be due to the pressure of leading a film with my extremely famous father in only a supporting role. And some of it has to come from knowing that we'll be on a rural location together for a month and a half, and I have no idea whether it will bring us closer at all.

And on top of that—the pressure of acting with Dad aside—I've never done anything like this. *Milkweed* is a subtle script: the story about a tenacious woman who comes back from heartbreak to find the love of her life and help shape her small Iowa community, while going through the pain of losing a parent to dementia. It's brilliant but entirely character driven, and will require acting chops I'm not even sure I have, under the guidance of one of the best directors in the world.

"What if I'm *not* ready?" I ask, chewing my lip.

"The correct answer was yes," Marco says, tapping my chin so I'll stop biting down on my abused bottom lip. "You are."

His confidence in my ability has always been solid, but I know this right here is part bravado, too: the pressure for Dad and me to do a film together has been slowly building to a hysterical frenzy. It's no longer a *When Will They?* headline, it's become a *Why Haven't They?* Admittedly, as Dad's career has slowed down and mine has picked up, it feels like the perfect time for our Jane-and-Henry-Fonda moment. The script is incredible, the timing works, and I wouldn't even be relying on Dad's celebrity to get me in the door: if I back out now, it would be a PR nightmare for Marco.

"You *are*, Tater Tot." A sweet smile and a wink take the edge out of Marco's next words: "Don't make my life a living hell."

He pulls open the glass door, gesturing for me to go ahead of him. Cameras flash, applause rises in welcome, and although my brain is still stalled out, my body makes the subtle shift from Me to Tate Butler: My eyes widen, and an easy smile spreads across my face. I stand a little straighter, walk a little looser.

A tight semicircle of people waits just inside the gleaming lobby, and a stocky, bald man with a salt-and-pepper beard steps forward, hand extended. "Hi, Tate; hi, Marco. I'm Lou." Lou Jackman, according to the notes I crammed in the car. Twitter's VP and head of community engagement. "It's fantastic to meet you."

I grip his hand. "Thank you for having us today."

He laughs. "Are you kidding? Anytime. We're grateful you made room in your schedule."

"Let's hold off on the gratitude until you see me tweet," I tease. Flashes pop in a constellation behind him.

"I think you underestimate how many people are looking forward to this." Lifting his chin, Lou pulls my attention across the room to where a table has been set up with two laptops side by side, two elaborate black desk chairs, and a small vase of flowers. A bowl of Skittles tells me someone did their homework on the famous Ian Butler sweet tooth. An array of cameras on tripods are set up in front of the table, waiting to catch every one of my fumbling typos. Awesome.

Dad is already here, his charm having been quarantined in a green room until I arrived and they pulled him out from a hallway to greet me. He waves with the trademark crinkly-eyed Ian Butler smile as we approach each other.

My stomach tilts; I saw him only four days ago at the agency offices in LA, but when he stands to give me a hug, a thousand flashes burst as though we're being reunited after a decade apart all over again—capturing my smile over his shoulder.

The narrative is that we're as close as any father and daughter could be. The narrative is that we're together at holidays, birthdays, vacations. The truth is he drops in for a quick glass of wine on Christmas; his assistant Althea recruits Mom's help to choose something lavish and semi-personalized for me on my birthday, and we've never taken even a day of vacation together. Clearly, the narrative is bullshit.

Dad turns to face the room of press and Twitter employees, throws up his arms like this is the greatest welcome he's ever received, and hurls a smile at them so supremely trademark Ian Butler that a few people actually cry out "Oh my God." Even with the more stoic men in the room, I sense the collective, vibrating thrill of being so close to a celebrity of his magnitude.

And I get it—he's an icon. I *still* have that momentary buzz of adrenaline when I see him. It doesn't seem to matter that he's no longer the Ian Butler of fifteen years ago—he's fifty-six now, at the top of the extended hot years (for men) in Hollywood—he is still charisma personified.

From across the room, Marco is watching me carefully and I know our thoughts are aligned: This is it. I'm about to launch into Ian Butler's orbit for a solid fifty days in a row. I know we're both gauging how well I'm going to handle it. I can be surrounded by functional relationships—with my mom, my best friends, even Nana—but five minutes with my father and I'm an insecure, awkward mess.

Looking at Dad's face still feels like a trick of the imagination. Other than the shape of my ears, which I got from Mom, I take after him completely: the brown hair, the honey-brown Butler eyes, the full mouth. We even share a beauty mark, though his is just at the top of his right cheek-bone, and mine is lower. His is a face that should feel so familiar—I see it in the mirror every morning—but it's still so disorienting to get a good, long look at him. Even four-teen years after our chaotic reunion, I'm pretty sure I've still seen his face more frequently on magazine covers than in person.

We sit at the table with an enormous screen mounted on the wall at our backs. With a laptop stationed in front of each of us, we look up expectantly at Lou. Behind him, Marco regards Dad and me with a faint smile. Publicist Marco wants to remind me to keep my smile natural for the cameras. Friend Marco wants to give me a hug and tell me, *You don't have to be so nervous. You don't have to prove anything to him.*

Dad's elbow knocks into mine and he reaches over, cupping it gently, paternally, saying a quiet, "Sorry, baby."

Another staccato of flashes captures the moment.

"The questions you'll need to answer are from the main Twitter account," Lou explains. "So they'll be from 'at Twitter.' These are the questions we sent over last week."

Behind him, Marco motions for me to pull my answers from the folder.

"You'll probably also get some questions from other users," Lou says, "in the hashtag—which is just 'hashtag AskButlers'—and although it's by no means required, you're welcome to answer any of those that you like. We just ask that you try to remember to include the hashtag in your re-plies." He gives me a teasing wink. "Sound good?"

We nod, relatively unconcerned because this is a fairly

simple ask. It's not like the tearful reunification interview
Dad and I did with Barbara Walters only a week after I returned from London. It's not like the *Vanity Fair* shoot we
did six years ago where we were required to be in near constant physical contact for over seven hours. And it certainly
doesn't compare to the exhaustion of the one and only time
I walked the red carpet with Mom on one side and Dad on
the other. The only reason Mom agreed to come was because it was my first Emmy nomination and the speculation
about whether my parents were bitter enemies was reaching an exhausting fever pitch. Even tourists in Guerneville
were stopping her in the café to ask her about it. As Mom
said to me that night while we got ready, "To be bitter enemies, I'd have to give a shit."

Marco and Mom: my two calm, stoic constants.

Nana, on the other hand, doesn't ask about any of it.
When I come home to Guerneville, I may as well be visiting
from a space station or coal mine.

I settle in front of the computer, waiting for the first
tweet to appear. Beside me, Dad shifts. "How was your
flight from LA, kiddo?"

Flash. Flash. *Over here, Tate!* Flash.

"It was fine," I say. Ever the performer, Dad nods and
casually goes back to scrolling through Twitter, but the silence that follows is heavy and loaded. Marco reaches up,
pulling on his ear—his sign that I need to relax. I look at
Dad and give him a goofy smile. "It was only an hour but I
fell asleep and am pretty sure I drooled the entire flight."

Dad roars with laughter at this, and the press gobbles it
up. My heart is a tiny, anxious bird in my chest.

You don't have to prove anything to him.

"Here we go," Lou says, and a tweet appears in the column.

@Twitter: This is your first project as co-stars. What aspect of the process are you most looking forward to? #AskButlers

Ducking, Dad immediately begins typing. He's so good at this; he's been doing all kinds of press tours for so long that he doesn't even question anymore whether he'll come off as natural. Everything he says is adored. Without referring to notes, he hunts and pecks enthusiastically at the keyboard. Surreptitiously, hoping that the press doesn't realize I'm not writing this from the gut, I peek at the answer Marco has crafted, typing the words and double-checking for typos before hitting send. My tweet pops up only a second before Dad's does.

@TateButler: Milkweed is the project we were always meant to do together. It may sound silly, but I just can't wait to be on set with my dad.

@IanButler: Working with my daughter is the biggest item remaining on my bucket list. It's all going to be a joy! Tate is the best actress of her generation, and a true gift to me as a father. #AskButlers

My heart is a beast with claws that extend, wrapping around the compliment. I gobble it down.

"Tate," Lou says gently, "if you could use the hashtag . . ."

Oh, shit. "Sorry, sorry."

Beside me, Dad beams in my direction. "I thought I was supposed to be the technologically impaired one."

I toss my head back and laugh. Ha, ha, ha. Inside, I am mortified.

When it's just me—Tate Butler, actress—I'm not intimidated by flashing cameras, by probing interviews, by the heated press of fans. I'm not the wide-eyed, wobbly-chinned girl anymore, sitting on the couch between Dad and Mom, giving my well-rehearsed answers in front of a camera crew. But when I'm near Dad, the entirety of who he is seems to dwarf me. I feel a little like a computer with a glitch.

The second question comes in, and I find myself holding my breath, even though I know it won't be personal. It's asking for a short summary of the movie. And the one after that asks what films or shows we've seen lately and loved. Two more softball questions, and we'll be done.

I type Marco's answers, add the hashtag, and try to keep my heart rate as even and slow as possible. It isn't the official Twitter questions that bother me—those are all standard—it's the others I notice, the ones I know see right through me.

Why would you do a movie with that piece of shit womanizer? #AskButlers

I want to have Ian's babies and don't even care that he could be my grandpa. #AskButlers

Wait, I thought they hated each other? #AskButlers

If Tate hates him so much, she can get the fuck out of the way. #AskButlers

This is such an act. They look like strangers. #AskButlers

IAN BUTLER I WANT TO HAVE YOUR BABIES! #AskButlers

The feed scrolls continuously on the enormous screen above our heads, and I can see the press reacting to every single tweet—pointing at some, laughing and nodding at others. Dad remains oblivious, seeing only what he wants to see and happily typing out his perfect, off-the-cuff answers. He's used to living inside the heat of the sun, the pressure of the public opinion. Fourteen years later, I'm still figuring out how to navigate the good and let go of the bad.

When the chat finishes, Marco is up front, apologizing immediately and explaining that we need to get rolling. But Dad stalls us, managing to give me a tiny look that communicates, *This is your job, give them what they want.* What they want is us embracing, his lips pressed to my cheek, and—just before Marco hauls me out of there—Dad picking me up around the waist in a hug, swinging me around as I laugh in delight.

Finally, we push through the doors and into the suffocating September heat. It's so warm the concrete weaves in front of us.

"Okay, let's hustle," Marco mutters, and waves as our car pulls around the front of the building. We're leaving straight from here to go to the farm in Northern California where we'll start shooting tomorrow. I can tell Marco doesn't want the press to catch on that we're not sharing a car up there with Dad.

But Dad stops us just as I reach for the car door. "Cupcake," he calls out, and his smile is captured by a photographer only a few feet away. But then his voice goes soft enough that only I can hear it. "Everything okay, kiddo?"

"Yeah," I say, and motion for Marco to climb in ahead of me. "Just excited and anxious, I think."

"Okay, good. I wanted to check in." He smiles warmly at me, but there's an edge there I can't miss. "You weren't your usual perky self in there."

My stomach tilts. "I wasn't?"

"A little off, I guess?" He presses a hand to my face, eyes wide and so full of concern that even I could believe it's real. "Be sure to rest up next time we have to do some press together. We always want to finish strong."

The rebuke lands like a small shove, and I nod quickly. "Absolutely."

"Just remember," he says, and his hand slides up from my cheek so he can tug on my earlobe, "people want to see us having *fun* together."

With a little wink, he strides off to the other car at the curb, where Althea waits by the open door.

A few photographers linger nearby, snapping pictures of Dad's departure. I struggle to look nonchalant and tack on a breezy smile as I climb into the car.

As soon as I sit down, Marco says without even blinking, "You were not *off*."

"I don't know, maybe I was."

"No." He turns to face me as the car surges forward and we pull away from the curb. "If you were off, I would tell you to get your shit together. I'm not telling you that, because I don't need to." He lifts a hand, holding up one finger. "Pay attention, Tate, because what I'm about to tell you is something you're going to have to repeat to yourself a thousand times in the next month and a half. Are you listening?"

I smile at his ready-to-battle tone. "Yes."

"Your dad is insecure," Marco says. "He's not the name he used to be."

This pings a strangely tender, protective bone in my chest. "I know."

"You are on your way to becoming a huge star," he continues, "up-and-coming. *You* are the lead of this film. He is in a *supporting* role."

"I know."

"But he's still Ian Butler, and he's going to make sure you know your place."

I swallow, hating that he's right. It's another point of contrast between my two parents: Mom lifts me up. Dad lifts me up so that he has a higher perch to stand on.

"Some people rise to the top on their own merit, and some people get there by stepping on heads." Marco reads my mind. He takes both of my hands in his. "Do not let him step on you."

I take a deep breath and let it out slowly. "Okay. I won't."

★ ★

It's a three-hour drive to set, and both Marco and I pass out for the first hour of the drive. But when I wake up, he's thumbing through a stack of photos.

"What's that?"

"These are the *Vogue* covers. We have approval in the contract."

I peek over at them. In the first, my hair is a wild halo of shimmering auburn. Crystal earrings dangle from my ears to my shoulders, and my makeup is an aggressive streak of black across my lids. The coolest part of the photo (and thank God because it took nearly four hours): my shoulders, arms, and face are dotted with thousands of tiny crystals.

"Wow," I mumble, pointing. "I like this one."

"Me too. You're like a glammed-up Imperator Furiosa."

I high-five him, and he slips it to the back of the pile. In the second photo, my hair and makeup are done in the style of my breakout role—the crafty and complicated vampire Violet Bisset from *Evil Darlings*, the sexy, campy, and totally addictive CW show that ran first in its time slot for six consecutive seasons. I suppose it's meant to show the *grown-up* side of Violet/Tate: I'm kneeling on the sofa with my back to the camera, looking over my shoulder at the photographer. And, I'm naked. My breasts are pressed against the back cushion, but my ass is almost completely exposed. It's a great ass—I work hard for it—but . . .

"I mean, I like this one," I admit, "but I'm not sure I want it on the *cover* of *Vogue*."

"Agreed. I think it would be great to include in the profile inside." Marco slides it to the back.

The final one makes something itch along my skin, and I'm not entirely sure why. I remember the styling and liked it at the time, but here . . .

I'm a modern-day Audrey Hepburn: smooth hair, artfully jagged bangs, pearls, wide eyes. The beauty mark near my lip, admittedly my trademark feature, is a dramatic and perfect circle; a bold, bombshell flirtation in stark contrast to my soft pink mouth. Discomfort works through me at the round innocence of my gaze, the surprised circle of my lips.

Marco takes it from me, studying it. "I absolutely adore this one. You look innocent, young." He glances at me, reading my expression. "It reminds me of when I first met you."

The twist in my gut intensifies. Is that what I don't like about it?

I rarely let myself think of what brought us together, but the sense of calm I felt that first day in London when he pulled me out of the black car into the chaos and ushered me into the quiet room—the reassurance that everything was under control, and that Marco was there for me and me alone—has never wavered. He was in his late twenties then, with the same dark hair and chiseled features, but he's wiser and seasoned now. We've grown up together, sort of.

I like my face, my body, my mind so much more than I did back then. This picture sends me tumbling back in time. Makes me realize that I've grown into myself, that I've had to work to do it.

He blinks up at me, gauging my reaction. "You okay with me sending this one? I can see it makes you uneasy, but Tate, it's so fucking beautiful, I'm genuinely speechless."

Objectively, it *is* a beautiful photo. I hand it back to him, choosing to let it go. Marco's instincts are razor-sharp. He'd never steer me wrong. "Either this or the first. No naked Tate on the cover."

"Done." Marco lifts my hand, kissing my knuckles. "Now let's get up on set and crush this." He smiles over at me. "I smell life-changing. I smell critical darling. I smell awards season."

I laugh. "I smell pressure."

twelve

THE TIRES CRUNCH OVER gravel, and I stir awake at the sound: we've reached Ruby Farm. I'm nervous and excited and feel the proverbial weight of a thousand pounds on my chest, but still—something tight inside me unwinds instinctively at the unfolding green serenity directly ahead of us.

We pass through the gates, waving to a guard there who notes the license plate and, I assume, checks the box to indicate Tate Butler has arrived.

I am officially on set.

Marco and I came up to Ruby Farm a few weeks ago for the hair and makeup test, and to choose my on-site cabin for the duration of the shoot. Even having grown up on the Russian River, I can say there's nothing quite like the peace here. It's 240 acres of serenity. The moment I stood in the Magnolia cabin, in front of a mirror and wearing a beautiful wig and the housedress the wardrobe stylist, Naomi, picked out for me? I *felt* like Ellen Meyer. I'd never felt so powerful, so excited to start a shoot, like being shot through with adrenaline at the possibilities.

On paper, Ellen is formidable. In my everyday life, I want to have a tenth of her strength and composure. But in that costume, in the cabin on the farm, I saw her fire in my own eyes. It made me itch to get back here and get working.

Our car slows in front of the Community House, which is a long wooden structure immediately neighboring the enormous barn. For the time being, the Community House appears to have become the social center and craft services hub where we'll take most of our meals, and the barn seems to be where the props master has brought in all of the props and set pieces. I grab my folders and reach for the door handle, but the door swings open seemingly on its own to reveal the irresistible, smiling face of Devon Malek, the 2nd assistant director.

"Tate!" He reaches a hand out, helping me from the car and giving me a warm embrace. His sparkling brown eyes, dimples, and flirty mouth make my stomach do a fluttery nosedive. "How was the drive?"

"Easy for me." I inhale as deep as my lungs will let me. "I slept." The air isn't like this in LA; not on the coast, not even in the mountains.

Marco steps out, shakes Devon's hand, and then stretches his long, lanky frame while we all look around at the work the art department has done so far.

"Looks like things are getting close," Marco says.

"We're ready to roll for the first week," Devon tells us, "everything after that is at least partly under construction, so we're in really good shape."

As he speaks, my pulse is machine-gun fire inside

my chest. The Community House is directly across from an enormous green field, where a replica of Ellen's wide-porched yellow Iowa farmhouse has been meticulously constructed, down to the weathering of the clapboards. It looks breathtaking—better than it did even in my imagination.

In the distance, I can see they're beginning construction on the replica barn—in a few weeks they'll be done . . . and we'll watch it burn to the ground.

All around us, activity is buzzing. It seems like hundreds of cameras are being assembled; at least five people are moving various cranes into place. Lighting structures, scaffolds, and temporary sets are being built by a dozen crew members. This is an enormous production—on a scale I've never experienced before. I want to bend over and put my head between my knees to catch my breath. The pressure is almost debilitating, but it is also delicious.

Marco puts a steadying hand on my back, and we follow Devon and his clipboard down a soft dirt path toward the cabins. He chats over his shoulder to us, about the weather being unreal, the crew getting settled in the tent cabins on the other side of the hill, the transformation of the Bright Star cabin into the interior of Ellen and Richard's farmhouse.

"You sure you're okay staying on-site?" Devon asks, and grins at me because he knows it's an absurd question; Ruby Farm is spectacular. Most of the time on location, I'm put up in a hotel, sometimes an apartment. I never get to live in a communal bubble like this, and I love that we'll all be together in this setting: rustic, quiet, away from everything. It's like summer camp out here. A glance at my phone tells me I don't even have cell service. Bliss.

I see Marco pull out his own phone and frown down at the screen. The 1st AD and line producer always have good Wi-Fi, so I know what he's going to ask before the question even emerges: "Where are Liz and Todd's trailers?"

Devon tilts his head to his left, indicating up the hill from us. "Just over there, with Gwen and Deb."

Marco catches my eye, gauging my reaction to the name. I have been dying to work with Gwen Tippett ever since I first stepped into the industry as a wide-eyed eighteen-year-old. Gwen is in the Spielberg and Scorsese stratosphere—a director actors can spend an entire career hoping to work with. But, as is the way of Hollywood, it took Gwen seven nominations for Best Director before she won last year for her film *Blackbird*, about a son who takes his dying mother on a road trip across the States. Everyone I've spoken to about *Milkweed* has asked whether this will be the one to get Gwen back-to-back Oscars.

"Nick is there," Devon tells us, pointing to my co-star's cabin, just north of mine. "I'm past that batch of trees. Our screenwriter is that cabin, there . . ." He points. "Your dad is down the hill to the right, in Clover." Devon looks at me and winces as if in apology. "I meant to ask: Do you want us to refer to him as your dad? Or would you just prefer Ian?"

"Dad is fine." I smile through the unease his question triggers. How successful have the gossip rags been? Does the crew know there is tension there? If so, we'll have to fix that, pronto. The last thing I need when I'm trying to play the role of my lifetime is micro-aggressions from Dad about how I need to appear to love him better.

Devon stops in front of my cabin and gestures for me to head inside. "Obviously most of your stuff is in wardrobe, but they brought a few pieces down they still need to check." He glances at his watch. "You have about fifteen minutes till final hair and makeup consult." Devon points to a row of trailers back up the way we came and then smiles over at Marco. "Are you staying tonight?"

Marco shakes his head. "I'm headed back to LA after the read, but I can come back up at any point if you need me for anything."

"We should be fine." Giving me his bright, dimpled smile, Devon says, "We'll start at six in the Community House. Sound good?"

The tightness in my stomach returns. I've done dozens of table reads in my lifetime, but none will have been anything like this: with the studio heads in town for the first day of shooting, and everyone dying to get a look at Ian and Tate Butler doing their first read together. Some of it will be filmed for marketing and bonus DVD material, which means the room is likely to be packed. Yep, no pressure.

With a wobbly smile, I nod. Marco kisses my cheek and then follows Devon back up the path to gather whatever remaining information he needs before heading back home to LA.

I've been dreaming about the smell of Ruby Farm—the fresh tang of grass, the sweetness of the apple trees, the bright wide-open sky framed on one side by redwoods and on the other by the snaking Garcia River—so the last thing I want to do is go sit in a trailer, but fortunately there is also no more joyous place on a set than hair and makeup.

Dropping my purse on the bed just inside the cabin door, I turn around and head back up the hill, toward hair and makeup and the one and only Charlie.

★ ★

The music is already blasting; I can hear it from thirty feet away. Today it sounds like Beyoncé. Tomorrow it might be some French singer Charlie discovered and wants everyone to hear. Or maybe Malaysian hip-hop. Whatever it is, Charlie will be right in her assessment: it will be fantastic. Hair and makeup is always an actor's first stop, and Charlie learned early on that her space sets the tone for the entire day. I'm grateful that my career has landed me in a place where, contractually, I can request my own hair and makeup people on a shoot; as Head Makeup Charlie has glam and happiness down to a science.

I pull open the door, and she turns, hurling herself into my arms with an eardrum-piercing scream. My closest girl-friend, my oldest friend: when I find my people, I try to keep them. When she pulls back to inspect me, I feel comparably dull: She's wearing skintight leather leggings, stilettos, and a tank top with a series of strategically placed rips. Her thick black hair is pulled into a high ponytail, and her wild makeup is so intricate, I don't think I could re-create it even if she gave me all her tools and an entire day.

"Wow, hi." I pinch her hip. "You look *good*."

"You will too. Sit." She motions me to the chair in front of the wide mirror, and Trey—1st Assistant Makeup—comes over to peck my cheek and give me some water. A few weeks ago, we decided on a soft palette for my makeup: lots of pinks and soft browns. A series of Polaroids are taped to the mirror—photos of me from all angles and in a variety of early-1960s outfits with the corresponding wigs and makeup. They'll be Charlie's reference throughout the shoot.

Beside them is a series of photos of my co-star Nick Tyler in costume. Trey is handling Nick's makeup, and I can see the excitement in his posture, the way he fidgets with the tools on the counter beside Charlie's, arranging them, rearranging them.

"I heard you get Nick." I lean into the name and wink at him.

"I will never survive this shoot," he says. *"Never."*

"He seems really nice." And it's true. Not only is Nick Tyler hot to the point of distraction, he was lovely during our screen tests together and has a good reputation on set.

"Really?" Trey asks.

"Yeah. We've met a few times but I mean, we don't hang out." My films to date have mostly been glossy Chosen One paranormal flicks, girlfriend comedies, and rom-coms. Nick has done sports films and a couple bigger action movies. Gwen and the studio heads at Paramount are really taking a big risk on both of us in this nuanced, cinematic feature.

Anxious fire reignites in my chest.

"Maybe you'll start hanging out now." Trey leans back against the counter, facing me while Charlie cleans off my face with a wipe.

"Romance on set," she sings. "God. Just think about this place. All the sneaking around and making out against trees." As much as cast and crew hookups are technically frowned upon, they still happen. Just more quietly than they did in my dad's day.

"Ruby does feel a little summer camp," I admit. "I'm sure there will be cabin visits aplenty. Time to place our bets."

"Tate and Devon Malek," Charlie says automatically.

I gape at her. "Can you see *directly* into my brain?"

"I know you have a thing for those obscenely deep dimples, and those flirty eyes? Forget it. I know your weakness."

I tilt my chin up for her to clean my jawline. "I feel exposed."

"You need to get some action going," Charlie says. "I'm tired of knowing the tabloids are lying about all these men you supposedly have on the hook."

Trey samples a few shades of lipstick on his arm. "My vote was going to be Charlie and the writer guy."

"The screenwriter?" I ask.

Charlie nods and begins blending foundation into my skin.

"Oh yeah?" I ask. She nods again. "A pretty, creative type?"

She looks at Trey over the top of my head, squinting. "I wouldn't say *pretty*, exactly. I'd say gorgeous, bearded, looks like he could throw someone around a bed pretty well." She looks at me, takes in my skeptical expression. "I'm not joking, Tates, he did immediate things to my blood. Think Tom Hardy but taller, and I bet he's even more capable with his hands." Pausing for effect, she says, "I mean, he wrote a screenplay about a lovesick farmer."

"Is this why you're wearing leather pants your first day on set?"

"I will neither confirm nor deny."

I frown. "I guess I assumed the writer would be the usual: nerdy and bald, or willowy and sensitive. I'll have to mentally realign."

Trey pulls out the chair beside me. "Can we talk about me now?"

I laugh. "Yes, Trey baby."

"Are we *sure* sure Nick Tyler is straight?"

"I'm pretty sure he's hard-core into the ladies," Charlie says. "And a bit of a player. Related: he's my second bet for Tate getting laid on location."

"You seem awfully sure I'm going to be getting laid when you know pretty well it's been dry as the Sahara around here."

Charlie grins. "I'm getting back-to-nature, wild-farm vibes. It can't be helped. There's something in the air out here." She looks at me, and the exact angle of her face, of her expression reels me back to when we were kids, running down the creek bed together, our hair in tangles behind us, fingertips blackberry-stained.

"Remember that summer?" she says, and I don't need her to say more. It was 2004, a sweltering summer in Guerneville, with the heat warping the pavement, the river a clear, glittering green, and the lingering scent of charcoal barbecue lasting all day and night. My childhood sweetheart Jesse and I couldn't keep our hands off each other, and Charlie could barely keep her hands off all the tourists.

"The Sexy Summer," I say, nodding. God, that feels like a different lifetime.

She snaps her fingers. "It's gonna be another one."

"But it's already September," Trey offers helpfully.

"Fine," she says, waving him off. "The Sexy September."

Frowning, Trey says, "That feels a little more pumpkin spice latte and a little less sweaty roll in the hay, but it works. Putting my money on Tate and Devon, Tate and Nick, or Charlie and Hemingway."

"Or Trey and the shy adorable camera guy who surprises you one night with a kiss up at the Community House," I suggest, and his eyes light up.

He laughs. "Oooh, or maybe a sassy, sarcastic grip pulls me behind the trailer for a grope?"

"Why not both?"

The door to the trailer swings open, and Nick Tyler ducks as he steps in, already smiling that panty-dropping smile. In his reflection in the mirror, I see Trey waver where he stands.

"Were your ears ringing?" Charlie asks him. "We were just talking about you."

"Oh yeah?" His voice is a deep, Southern vibration. "What were you saying?"

"Wondering who you're gonna hook up with on set," she says.

Nick's head falls back and he lets out the laugh I've heard in theaters, the delighted, low belly rumble that makes women all over the world turn into giggling fangirls. "I thought we don't do that sort of thing these days."

"I'll never tell," Trey says.

Nick looks around at us, nodding knowingly. "So this is the trouble trailer, then?"

Charlie bends to perfect my concealer. "Always." Standing, she reaches out a free hand. "I'm Charlie. That's Trey."

He takes it. "Pleasure to meet you, Charlie. Trey."

Nick's laugh fades away, but the echo of it unknots the anxiety in my stomach.

"Hey, Nick."

"Hey, Tate."

I turn my face up to him, and he does a double take. Charlie has effectively camouflaged my flaws, but added no color. I look like one of the Precogs from *Minority Report*.

"Damn, girl." But he grins, leaning in to kiss my cheek. "It's weird seeing you all plain."

"I'm creating my canvas," Charlie says.

Nick stares at me for a lingering beat and then smiles again, as if he likes what he sees.

Maybe Charlie was onto something after all.

"Devon told me to come over," Nick says, and then looks up at Trey.

Valiantly combating his nerves, Trey motions for Nick to follow him to the other station and sits him down, drifting a drape over his shoulders to protect his shirt.

"Saw your dad," Nick says to me, and then immediately adds, "Wait. Should I call him your dad or Ian?"

Charlie laughs, but I turn, wearing a bewildered grin. "Seriously? Why is everyone asking me that?"

"Maybe because you've been acting forever and never did a movie together?" he says.

"Maybe it just wasn't ever the right time?"

Nick *mm-hmm*s and grins at me. I haven't seen him since we did a chemistry test with Gwen and the studio heads, and we had to read one of the moments leading up to a love scene, and kiss at the end. They made us do it about seven times, and—let me be clear—I was not complaining.

Nick is a star on the rise, winning Best Actor at the BET Awards last year and Best Hero at MTV. Not just handsome, he has that special something that makes it hard to look away. His eyes are wide set and hypnotic, dark and glimmering with a constant hint of mischief. His skin is a warm chestnut brown, luminous under Charlie's bright makeup lights. His hair, once cut close to his scalp, has grown out a little for the role. But he's still built like the DC action movie star he is: his Mon El feature just wrapped a couple weeks ago—it has *summer blockbuster* written all over it.

There's something about Nick's eye-crinkling smile that reminds me a little of my ex-boyfriend and former co-star on *Evil Darlings*, Chris—but Nick has a calmness about him that Chris never quite managed. Chris and I were only actually together for about seven months, but we agreed to continue the ruse of our relationship for another three years because the more enthusiastic viewers were so fanatical about Violet and Lucas being together "in real life" that our off-screen reality became an intense focus of promotion.

Unlike Chris, though, Nick has that acute kind of focus, the tendency to maintain prolonged eye contact, the slow-growing smile. Whenever he catches my gaze and holds it, I feel like he's carefully translating my thoughts directly from my brain.

"You two have *such* great chemistry," Charlie says,

glancing between us as she works. "Going to look great on-screen." I feel heat push to the surface of my cheeks.

"That's what Gwen said," Nick tells her, finally breaking eye contact. "Though I feel like now is the time to tell you: I've never done a love scene before."

"Not even in Mon El?" I ask.

"Nah, that was just some kissing."

I bite my lip and grin at him. As he knows, there are two love scenes in *Milkweed*, and both of them are pretty intense. "You'll be fine."

"You ever do one like this?" he asks. "I should've asked you this that day they made us read it."

"A few. Nothing like this, though. They're awkward, but they don't have to be too bad."

"Maybe they could even be good," Charlie says, low enough that only I can hear.

"Okay," Nick says, "so if this is the trouble trailer, who's going to give me the dirt on the crew? I've only worked with Deb Cohen before—everyone else is new to me."

I've never worked with most of them, either, but have heard enough stories from Dad over the years to have a general sense of their eccentricities. "Liz is the 1st AD, and she's amazing. Cool and organized. I've been warned not to hit snooze because Devon will come in and wake us up himself. The production secretary has decided this shoot is the best time to quit smoking so, seriously, avoid him at all costs. And from what I've heard, Gwen can be intense and a bit of a perfectionist."

"Yeah," Nick says, nodding, "I've heard that too."

"But whatever, it's Gwen Tippett."

"Right?"

"Honestly," I tell him, "I think this is a pretty solid crew."

"So, it's just us young up-and-comers trying to prove ourselves to Ian Butler," he says with a knowing gleam in his eye. "Do I have that about right?"

I laugh, melting a little. I have an ally here. "Something like that."

An alarm goes off on Charlie's phone, and I peek at it—we need to head down to the Community House for the table read. The loose-limbed ease I've found in the trailer immediately hardens back into a tense anticipation.

"Wait." Charlie halts me, finishing some work on my contour. We meet eyes and she smiles a soft smile that she doesn't give just anyone. "Don't be nervous," she says quietly, and helps me stand. "You're going to be amazing."

★ ★

Nick and I leave the trailer with the sounds of music—and Charlie and Trey laughing hysterically about something said after we left—filtering along after us. We are immediately swallowed by the serenity of the farm; in contrast to the makeup trailer, the space outside is so quiet it's a little like stepping onto an empty soundstage, with that hollow, echoing silence.

"You've known Charlie since you were kids?" he asks.

"Eight years old."

He grins back over his shoulder at the trailer. "She's a trip."

I laugh at this, nodding. But Charlie is more than a trip.

She's a sparkler, a firecracker, a fistful of gunpowder. Marco is my calm, Mom is my home, Nana is my conscience, but Charlie is my wide-open sky, my free-dancing, stargazing wild rumpus.

"There's your dad," Nick says, voice low. He clearly took my word for it that it's okay to call him "your dad," but had some reservation about whether or not I need careful warning.

I follow his attention up the path toward the Community House. Even at a distance, it's easy to recognize my father—it's his posture, the cocky lean. He's in jeans, a worn leather jacket, and sunglasses, and wearing the ubiquitous brilliant grin. Facing another man, Dad is listening in the intent way that makes a person feel like the only important thing on the planet. I have a pulse of envy that this is the only sign of intimacy I ever get from Dad—his attention, his complete focus—and it's really just something he's mastered to appear sincere. He gives it away to anyone.

Dad spots me over the man's shoulder and perks up, waving. "There's my girl!"

The other man turns. I don't know him, so my smile is that instinctive kind of bright that I've learned makes me seem friendly, chases away any potential diva concerns. He's enormous. *Oh, the writer*, my brain sings back to Charlie in the trailer. Bearded, frowning, eyes like moss, with a scar through his—

Shock is a cold hand on my shoulder, a complete standstill in my brain and chest and veins. Nick collides with my back, and reaches forward, gripping my arms from behind.

If he hadn't caught me, I would have fallen forward onto the dirty path, face-first, straight as a board.

"Tate." Nick's deep voice is surprised, and seems to come in and out. "Whoa. You okay?"

Dad's words float to me, also muted and fuzzy. "Tate! Up here!" He waves wildly, and his grin is something from a carnival; his head is too big, his mouth too wide.

I blink down to my feet; my heart is a hammer, my ribs are nails. I'm trying to put all of this together, to figure out if I knew, if someone told me and I forgot. Did I lose this important piece of information somewhere along the line? How could he just be here? The trail weaves in front of me but I stare at it, willing it to come into focus, unable to look at the man beside Dad.

His face registered immediately who I was, but his expression revealed no shock. He stared grimly down the path at me and then bowed his head, exhaling a long, resigned breath.

He knew. Of course he knew. The question is, did I?

Unable to get a word out, I turn, and start moving stiffly in the opposite direction.

I remember being drunk one night with Charlie, so drunk I could barely walk. At least, that's what she told me happened. At the time I'd felt like I made my way down the hallway in a seductive saunter. But the next morning while I nursed a lurching, debilitating hangover, Charlie told me I'd ricocheted my way down to her bedroom, stopping twice to catch my balance against the wall, before falling into her room and passing out just inside the door.

This memory rises in me like bile. I wonder how I'm

walking now; it feels like walking, but it could be crawling, tripping, ricocheting down the path. The stones leading to my cabin come into view and some internal fail-safe tells me to turn. Like a joystick has been jerked to the left, I pivot, tripping over a cobblestone and catching myself on the first step.

I hear a voice, voices.

"What's going on? What did you say to her?" It's Dad, accusing Nick of something. Nick's voice pleading innocence, his own confusion.

And then I hear the quiet words, "Let me get this."

It's the voice of Sam Brandis, jogging down the path, showing up out of the blue fourteen years too late.

thirteen

I THINK I CLOSE the door but there's no slam, only footsteps carefully making their way up the three small stairs behind me.

"Tate?" He's at the threshold now but doesn't step inside, and in this weird fugue I've entered, I find his hesitance hysterical.

Did he watch me on *Evil Darlings*? In the mirror, seeing myself in costume for the first time, I didn't look like nineteen-year-old Tate. I looked like timeless, feral Violet: ruthless, manipulative, like I could murder someone with a flash of my teeth against their neck. In every attack scene, I imagined I was attacking Sam.

But that was so long ago. Thirteen years? My life scrolls past me: lovers, sets, the swimming faces of cast and crew. At some point it stopped feeling like London actually happened. It was just a terrible dream I had once.

"Tate, can I come in?"

"No." My voice sounds far away, even to my own ears.

He doesn't leave, he just moves back from the door. Heat seems to fill the cabin, like he's standing in there, enormous, warm, alive right in front of me.

"Tate," I hear him say quietly. "We're going to have to deal with this."

I sit heavily on the couch, and the springs squeak. Leaning back, I count the number of exposed beams overhead. Seven. This cabin is old, so old and rustic and loved. I idly wonder how many knock-down-drag-out fights it's seen before.

"What is going on?" I ask the ceiling. Suddenly my head is pounding. "Seriously, what is going *on*?"

Sam seems to take this as permission to join the conversation and very slowly steps into the cabin, keeping a safe distance once the door has closed behind him.

Pressing my hand to my mouth, I struggle to not laugh. Laughing isn't the right reaction here. Dad is somewhere out there, waiting for me to come do my job and wondering what the hell just happened. Nick, too. Sam Brandis is here, of all places, for some reason? I'm grappling for logic, but it's completely evading me.

Sam steps closer, kneeling a few feet away, staring at me. I'm unprepared for how it feels to meet his mossy-green eyes; a sharp pain spears me somewhere vital, making it hard to breathe. I look back up at the ceiling.

Where do we even start in a situation like this?

"What are you doing here? And how?" I frown. "Wait. Are you here with my dad?"

He laughs out this single, incredulous breath and then

blinks to the side, like he isn't sure he heard me right. "Tate, *Milkweed* is mine. I wrote the film."

I squeeze my eyes closed. But—"The writer is S. B. Hill."

"Sam Brandis," he says quietly. "Hill was Luther's last name. I legally took it before he died."

Luther. I knew him. Can still remember his bursting laugh, his teasing, glimmering brown eyes. A tiny, conscientious part of me feels a pang at the idea of him dying. But a louder, brittle voice carries above the fray: *They used you, Tate. They probably made it to the Lake District with a shitload of money in their pockets.*

"Should I have known this?" I ask him. "That you would be here? I feel like this shouldn't have been a surprise to me today."

"It's understandable," he says quietly. "You're so busy. You have so much—"

"Don't do that," I cut in. "Don't patronize me."

"I'm not," he says quickly. Immediately. His eyes are so wide, like he can't quite believe this is happening either. "Tate. I'm so ama—"

"Who even *are* you?" I ask. "I thought you were a farmer."

"I am." He opens his mouth and then bites his lip, shaking his head as if in wonder. "But you knew I wrote, too. I write, still."

"Okay, let's be honest, Sam. If we're going to do this, at least be honest: apparently, I didn't know *anything* about you."

He looks like he wants to argue this but blinks away, seeming to search for words. "Well, I write. I've always written, but *Milkweed* is different. It's—"

"No. Stop." I lean forward, pulling my arms in, curling

into a ball. Suddenly I feel devastated: not just that he's here, but that he's a mallet and my love for this project is a precious sheet of glass, and I worry just having him near me is going to shatter it. I love *Milkweed* so much I don't want him to say a single thing that ruins it for me. "I don't care. I don't. This was the film that was going to really test me; maybe even get me short-listed for awards. This is my shot at something better. Don't try to tell me about you, or this, or why."

I feel like I'm going to cry. I take an enormous breath, pushing back the emotion until I feel nothing. I fill myself with nothing but air. It's been a while since I did this—since I felt this much and needed to tamp it down—but the instinct comes back so easily.

Sam shifts in his crouch, resting a forearm on his knee. He's wearing a soft cream Henley, open at the throat. Olive jeans. Boots. I chance a peek at his face again. The comma scar is hidden beneath the beard. He has barely looked away from my face.

"I tried to tell you," he says. "And I knew it would be hard. So I told the studio heads we might want to go a different direction for casting."

"Are you serious?" I ask, grateful for the anger rising out of the blankness, stabilizing me. "You told them you didn't want me as Ellen?"

He exhales and looks at the floor for a beat. "I said we knew each other when we were younger and I wasn't sure you'd want to take the role. Contractually, I had casting approval. They held firm, though, and I'm glad. I think you'll be great in it, Tate. I really do. It wasn't about my preference, it was about yours."

"How can I have a preference if I didn't even know there was a choice?"

He frowns. "I emailed you four times."

Liar. "I never saw anything."

"I promise: I tried to contact you."

This is impossible. And it's impossibly frustrating. I'm caught so off guard, but I don't have the luxury of working through this with some quiet and a glass of wine. The minute I step out of this cabin I have to be *on*, I have to be poised. I have to get to work.

I look up at him again, and he attempts a sad smile. His eyes search my expression. In them I see regret, but also so many other things I can't bother to decipher. It's so much—too much. He's still . . . Sam, with the dark green eyes I wanted to fall into, the mouth I kissed until it was red and bruised, the body that felt like a fortress.

"Tate," he begins, heavily, and I shake my head. Too fast; the room tilts. "God. We have so much to say to each other."

"We don't, actually." *You're a liar and a thief. You stole my shiny innocence, my belief that my first love would be pure and real and good.*

And yet he managed to write a masterpiece like *Milkweed*, with a heroine so strong and brilliant I cried the first two times I read the script, hoping alone, in the privacy of my house, that I could be even a tiny bit like Ellen someday. He wrote tenderhearted, unbreakable Richard, and the flawed, loyal William. Sam may be a monster, but every part of this gorgeous script came from his brain. I don't know how to reconcile the two.

He stands now, sliding his hands into his pockets and

bowing his head again. He stares at his feet, shoulders hunched. I'd forgotten how tall he is, how much space he takes up. Physically, yes, but in my memory, in my past—and now, in this room, on this set, in my present day, he's just so *present*.

He glances at his watch. "Tate."

"*God*, stop saying my name."

"It's six thirty."

I close my eyes—hating the weird goose bumps that rise on my skin when he speaks—but as soon as my lids close, I know I could immediately succumb to the blackness of sleep.

"Should I tell Gwen we need some more time before the table read?"

Eyes flying open, I stand, irate. "Absolutely not."

He sighs. "This is big, though. I thought you knew. I mean—really? You're going to go to do the read right now? You look like you're about to fall over."

And with the insinuation that I might be delicate or need any help from him, I feel my spine come back together, the muscles reconnecting, my brain zapping awake. I've been doing this for nearly a decade and a half. It has also been that long since he used me and ran. I am not the amateur here, and I will not let Sam see me fall apart.

"It's a shock," I admit. "And not a good one. But I'm okay. I've dealt with bigger problems than having a scumbag ex come onto the set." It's a lie, but he winces, so at least I got what I wanted. "Give me five minutes. Tell Gwen I'm on my way and you held me up." I lift my chin to the door. "And we're not friends, Sam. Keep away from me."

fourteen

WHEN THE DOOR CLOSES my bravery seems to desert me.

"You're okay. You're okay. You're okay." I repeat the words through gulps of air, willing them to be true. There's a whooshing in my ears, a pinprick that registers in a dusty, hidden spot in my rib cage.

It was only two weeks of my life, a long time ago, but I loved him. I remember the feeling; it's still the only time I've ever felt it. Maybe this is why I can call it back whenever I need to—though it's been a long time since I tortured myself that way. And it was easier in some ways not having any photos to pore over. But seeing him here—completely without warning—after not seeing his face for over a decade has me light-headed.

With shaking hands I cross the room and dig for my phone in my bag. Email won't load, but the solitary bar of signal might be enough for a phone call.

Marco's assistant, Terri, picks up on the second ring.

"Tate! I thought we lost you to the wilderness!" she says. The connection is terrible and fades in and out, but I'll take it.

"Me too," I tell her, working to keep my voice calm. "Terri, can you do something really quick? Can you search my email for me? Anything from a Sam Brandis."

I haven't said his name aloud in years.

"Sure! Just give me a second." The faint tapping of keys, and I'm barely breathing. I'm not even sure what I want her to find. "There are four." I close my eyes. Is this relief? Anger? "The subject line on all of them is *Milkweed*."

"Okay," I say quietly, voice carefully even.

"I'm so sorry, Tate. Business correspondence comes directly to Marco, or me, but I'm guessing because this person isn't in your contacts they were filtered to junk. God, I hope they weren't important."

"No. They weren't." I press my fingers to my temple and the ache that's beginning to build there. No doubt it will be a full-blown migraine by the end of the day. "And don't apologize. That's what's supposed to happen. Terri . . . could you forward them to me? I'll read them when I get service."

"Absolutely." More tapping of keys and then, "Okay, done. Anything else?"

"I think that's it. Thanks."

I end the call just as a knock comes at the other end of the cabin.

"Tate?"

Devon. Of course.

Another deep breath and I stand, tucking my phone into my back pocket. This is not how I wanted to start off.

It's well after six thirty; the table read should have started over a half hour ago.

"I'm here," I say, perfected smile in place as I open the door. "I'm sorry. This won't happen again."

★ ★

I follow Devon down a long set of wooden steps set into the hillside. Magnolia cabin sits higher than the others, with a deck built onto the front that offers a gorgeous view of the valley and the entrance to the farm.

At the bottom of the stairs a driver waits in a bright green golf cart, the knobby all-terrain tires caked with mud. Devon motions for me to take the front seat, and he climbs onto the row in the back. The driver sets off up the trail toward the Community House.

"We're good on time," he says, glancing at his watch and jotting something on his ever-present clipboard. He hands me a bound copy of the script. "You'll have a copy waiting for you, but in case you want a minute to look it over. Obviously you've done this before, but everyone should be there—probably eating—and the read-through should take about two hours. Depending on how chatty everyone gets."

"Sounds good. Thanks for getting me."

He grins at me, and as frazzled as I am, I mentally reshuffle Charlie's predictions for the shoot. If he smiles at *her* like that, she won't stand a chance.

"You say that now," he says, dimple popping in each cheek. "Let's see if you still feel that way when I'm knocking on your door at four a.m."

More golf carts line the front of the Community House,

and the main room inside is packed. Thankfully Devon was right: most people are eating or talking amongst themselves, so my late arrival doesn't garner much attention. But of course Dad notices. And Marco. I keep walking. I can't avoid Dad's disappointed glare forever, but I can at least avoid it for another five minutes. Marco knows me better than anyone. He knows that, for me, on time is as good as five minutes late and is already on his way over before I have the chance to stop him.

Reaching for my arm, he gently pulls me to the side. "What happened?" He looks closer, clearly sensing something monumental, even knowing I can't tell him about it now. His eyes narrow. "Are you okay?"

"I'm fine." Neither one of us is buying it. I give his hand a reassuring squeeze. "I'll explain later."

With a glance around us, Marco reluctantly lets me go. I take the seat waiting for me next to Nick, mirroring his tentative smile. Three long tables have been pulled together, all facing each other to form a U in the center of the room. The primary cast is at the center table, the secondary at another, and the principal crew is at the third. More people are here than I've ever seen at a table read: chairs line the walls and every inch of space is filled with someone anxious to hear the first read-through with Ian and Tate Butler.

Gwen stands and the room quiets around us. She takes a moment to thank the crew and staff that have worked so hard to get us to this point. She takes a deep breath and talks about the screenplay, how she's never read anything quite like it. I clap along with everyone else when she's finished, but the sound is like static in my ears; voices like they're coming from underwater.

I can feel the gentle weight of Marco's eyes on me, worried and constantly wanting to check in. And even though I don't know where Sam is in the room, I can feel him, too, just like I could all those years ago.

I was so angry in the months following London. Thanks to reporters and the interview I did with Dad, I was the shiny new toy and the offers came rolling in. The public was fascinated. We told a story: that Dad and Mom had agreed to take me away from LA. That Dad had always known where I was and been constantly involved. And, most important, Marco made sure to whisper to just the right people that the *Guardian* exposé was planned all along—no one *actually* betrayed us.

I did interviews with *People* and *Cosmo*, a five-page spread in *Elle*. Two days after the shoot, I got a call from Dawn Ostroff at the WB. Within three weeks, I'd signed with my manager Alec and been cast as the lead in *Evil Darlings*.

It may have begun as a campy TV show, but *Darlings* spun off an entire toy line, board games, a clothing line, and tie-in novels. It opened the door to more TV and eventually movies, helping me land the role of my dreams.

At first, acting was an escape, enabling me to be someone else and pretend that everything was okay. But it was also an active form of revenge—I wanted to haunt Sam. I loved the idea of him seeing me on his television and knowing that I wasn't his, that I would never be his again. I fantasized that he saw me and saw that he hadn't broken me; I was stronger without him. I'd imagine his regret, his guilt, his heartbreak.

For a few seconds, the fantasy would be as good as a high. But then the director would call cut and reality would crash down.

But it didn't take long to realize I *loved* acting. I loved photo shoots. I loved the travel and the promo. I loved becoming someone else. And Sam was the only one who knew how much I'd wanted acting to be my life.

Ironically, my escape into various roles helped me get over him, but the distance from Sam also gave me time to truly appreciate what Nana gave me by taking me to London. She pulled me out of my small life; she made my world expand. Without London, I would never have become an actress. This is the life I wanted, but not at all on my terms.

I scan my script and revert to old habits, surreptitiously wrapping a loose string from my sweater around my finger and pulling it so tight it sends a shock of pain through my system. It's enough to have me straightening in my seat, some of the static clearing from my ears so I can focus as the reading begins.

Because the movie opens when Ellen is a teenager, the younger cast starts the read. I look great for thirty-two, but not even Charlie's makeup can get me to pass for sixteen.

We follow along for about twenty pages as a young Ellen Meyer and her first husband, Daniel Reed, begin a secret affair and move to Minneapolis, where Daniel begins school and Ellen works odd jobs to keep them afloat. The two young actors recite their lines with only a few stumbles, and we see Daniel's infidelity, and Ellen moving to the family farm when she is only twenty-six.

We shuffle pages, everyone takes a few minutes to get some water, and when we reconvene, the silence in the room feels like it vibrates along my bones.

EXT. MEYER FAMILY FARM, FRONT PORCH — DAY

1956 Iowa. Rolling green hills and farmland surround a two-story farmhouse. A handsome but down-on-his-luck salesman, RICHARD DONNELLY (28, a physically imposing black man with wide eyes and a nervous smile) knocks on the front door. His shoes are worn but his suit is clean and pressed, his hair is short and neat beneath the brim of his hat.

When no one answers, he looks back over the scenery — there isn't another house for miles. It's hot. He's tired and hungry. He hears a woman's scream followed by loud swearing from around the back of the house. He jumps off the porch and races toward it.

EXT. MEYER FAMILY FARM, BACK PORCH — DAY

ELLEN MEYER (26), beautiful but wearing a wet dress and apron, stands with her arms submerged in the tub of a broken washing machine. She is surrounded by baskets of laundry and an empty clothesline. An open toolbox lies at her feet.

                    ELLEN
        God dammit! Piece of—

Richard races around the corner and stops when he
sees her.

                    RICHARD
        Ma'am . . . Are you okay?

Ellen turns. She places a dripping hand on her
hip, curious, but not intimidated.

                    ELLEN
        Who are you and what are you doing on my
        farm?

                    RICHARD
        Richard Donnelly. I'm here to see about
        selling you some feed for those cows.

He motions toward the front of the house.

                RICHARD (cont'd)
        Nobody answered the door and I heard
        someone shouting.

She turns back to the washing machine.

                    ELLEN
        Well as you can see, Richard Donnelly,
        I'm busy wrestling this stupid machine.
        And I don't need more feed.

                    RICHARD
        Yes, ma'am. Can I help you? I mean, you're—

She turns back to glare at him.

                    ELLEN
What? A woman?

He tries to hide a smile.

                    RICHARD
Actually, I was going to say "soaking
wet."

She looks down and tries not to smile, too.

                    ELLEN
I'm fine. I've fixed this thing a dozen
times before. I can do it again.

"Okay, so far this is . . . good," Gwen says hesitantly, and we look up at her. "Nick, I like the vulnerability, and you're really getting Richard's charm."

She turns to me, my stomach drops, and it feels like the entire room holds its breath. We all know what's coming. I know when I'm nailing it, and right now I'm about as unnatural and tense as I've ever been.

"Tate, I want you to try to capture how *disarmed* Ellen is right here. In the past years, she's become a city girl. Now she finds herself back on the farm, having to take care of everything, including her father. She's ferociously independent. She's a *feminist* before her time. She's learned the hard way that she doesn't need anyone's help, she doesn't trust men, she certainly doesn't want to be charmed by Richard, but she reacts before she can stop herself. Let's really feel that."

My face heats under the attention of the room. Dad is seated just to my left; his presence is like a pulsing light beside me. Sam's too, just down at the other end of the table. It's taking every bit of restraint I have to not lift my head and look at him.

I nod and read the scene again. It doesn't really feel any better the second time. My dialogue is forced, rushed in some places and wooden in others. But it's just a table read . . . so Gwen lets it continue.

Ellen turns away and begins tightening a bolt.

                    RICHARD
        My father owned a repair shop in
        Charlotte. I used to work there during
        the summers. These machines have really
        come a long way since then, but they can
        be temperamental.

        I really wouldn't mind . . .

Ellen ignores him. She sets down the wrench and presses the power button. She waits as the machine rumbles to life, pleased UNTIL it begins spraying water everywhere, soaking them both. A beat of silence.

                    ELLEN
        What about this scenario doesn't look
        under control to you?

"Tate, let's try that line again." Gwen nudges her glasses down her nose so she can peer over the rims at me. The action makes me feel twelve years old again, getting a lecture from Nana on how to set the café tables right. "She's freshly divorced, standing in the backyard of her childhood home, her father has budding dementia, and her washing machine essentially exploded all over her. To her, the situation is ridiculous."

Someone shifts at the far end of Gwen's table, and I blink over before I can stop myself. Sam is sitting there with his eyes down, arms folded across his chest.

My mouth is dry, but I worry my hands will shake if I reach for my water. Stalling for time—hoping to get my breathing under control—I say, "We want her to be able to laugh at herself a little."

Gwen nods, encouraging. "Exactly. This really is an *if I don't laugh, I'll cry* moment."

She has no way of knowing this, but Gwen has just crystallized the emotion down to exactly what I needed to hear. *If I don't laugh, I'll cry.*

I can certainly relate to that.

                              ELLEN
          What about this scenario doesn't look
          under control to you?

They laugh at the absurdity. With a resigned sigh, Ellen realizes she could probably use another hand.

                 ELLEN (cont'd)
Could you hand me those pliers over there?
And hold this?

Richard takes off his hat and rolls up his sleeves,
then eagerly does what she asks.

                 ELLEN (cont'd)
I don't know why we even keep this thing.
Probably faster to wash it all by hand
anyway.

They work together in silence for a moment.

                 ELLEN (cont'd)
I don't recall seeing you around.

                  RICHARD
No, ma'am. I just got into town yesterday.
I work for Whitmore Feed and was just
making my rounds.

That's why I was at your door.

Thought I'd be okay on foot, but your
farm is a bit farther from town than I
thought.

                   ELLEN
You walked all the way from town?

                  RICHARD
Yes, ma'am. I don't mind.

ELLEN

You don't have to call me ma'am.

I'm Ellen Meyer.

They shake wet hands over the washing tub.

RICHARD

Pleased to meet you, Ellen.

ELLEN

Likewise, Richard.

Richard motions to the fields behind them.

RICHARD

Beautiful place you have.

ELLEN

Thank you. Grew up here. My dad still thinks he runs the place but . . . he doesn't.

The rest of it goes unsaid. Richard moves to adjust a hose and then takes a step back.

RICHARD

Try it now.

Warily, she turns it on. It works and water begins filling the tub.

ELLEN

You did it.

                              RICHARD
             Actually, you did. I just tightened a hose.
             You'd've found it if I hadn't interrupted
             you. I can see the other repairs you've
             done in there. Mighty impressive.

She blushes, not accustomed to the recognition.

                              ELLEN
             Thank you. (beat)

             I can't send you home drenched through to
             your skin. Why don't you grab a towel over
             there and I'll bring you some lunch?

"Good job, everyone." Gwen pushes back from the
table, standing. "Let's take twenty."

I stand, stretching and working to put on a brave face.
I can blush on command, and have put on a good show of
Ellen flushing at the idea of a handsome Richard soaking
wet in her yard, but the heat on my cheeks lingers in earnest
as the reality sets in that I've just bungled my first—albeit
unofficial—performance on *Milkweed*.

I wasn't good, and everyone knows it. The lines I fell in
love with seem to drag with my delivery. The chemistry that
crackled during my screen test with Nick is nowhere to be
found. This is my movie—my dream role—and I'm letting
my head get in the way.

When I step outside, the crisp air feels immediately easier to pull in deeply. Inside the room, at the table, I couldn't

quite catch my breath, and my delivery suffered, my words coming out tight and clipped. Neon-yellow leaves crunch beneath my boots as I round the corner to the empty side of the porch. I can see the pond from here, the rows of corn that sway in the breeze, and a field of pumpkins warming in the fading sun. Footsteps sound on the boards behind me, and I turn to see Marco standing there.

"What the fuck is going on?"

I don't bother to ease him into it. "Sam is here."

"Sam? Sam who?"

"The writer, S. B. Hill? It's Sam Brandis."

It takes a moment for everything to click, and Marco's eyes widen. "From London? How did we—?"

"He wrote the script, and when I was suggested for the role he tried to email and warn me. Obviously, the emails never got through. He's here. It's completely fucking with my head."

Marco bends, meeting my eyes. "I was going to head home to LA tonight. Do you want me to stay on set?"

"No, no, but if you could kick him really hard in the balls before you go, that would be fantastic."

Marco laughs.

"And get this," I say, looking around to make sure no one can hear us. "On top of everything else, all the millions of questions I have and all the shit this brings up? He wasn't sure he even wanted me for the role."

"He *what*?"

I nod. "Yeah, so he's still a monster. Good to know."

God, what a potent reminder that there's no room in

this industry for self-sabotage. Other people will be more than happy to do it for you.

"Keep your head down and just get the job done," Marco says. "You were born for this role."

"Maybe, but I was awful in there." I press my hands to my face and feel Marco reach for them.

"You were surprised. Of course you're off your game." He turns and leans against the railings. "Jesus. What are the odds?"

"What am I supposed to do now? Do I try to get out of it or—?"

"This is *your* movie, Tate. You're not going anywhere. He's the writer, not your co-star. If you have questions about the script you talk to Gwen or Todd. There's no reason you and Sam need to interact, and he can stay the hell away. I assume you told him as much?"

"Yeah."

"Good. Just give yourself some time. You're not the teenager he remembers. You haven't been Tate Jones in years. You're *Tate Butler* now, and he'd better watch himself or he's going to answer to me, too. Though I'm nothing compared to what he's got coming."

I look up at him, confused. "What do you mean?"

"Charlie is going to fucking murder him."

fifteen

SOMEHOW WE MAKE IT through the read. By the time we're standing, shaking hands with studio execs, telling each other how excited we are to get rolling tomorrow, it's a wonder that there's anyone left in the room who has any confidence in me. Gwen's enthusiasm is too big, too bright for her normally understated personality. I hear Marco with our producer Deb and one of the studio heads, Jonathan Marino—who looks like a Ken doll wearing a brown swim cap—talking about how "Table reads aren't really Tate's favorite. She likes to be in there, on set. Tomorrow will be amazing."

Everything inside me feels droopy: my spirit, my pulse, my energy. I expect Dad to come find me immediately afterward but—even worse—he just shoots me a tight smile before finding a woman seated at the periphery. He helps her up and then kisses her.

Blinking, I take a closer look. No way is she a day over

twenty-five. My father is late-fifties now, dating a woman younger than his daughter. It's such a tired story, and now I'll have to see it every day on set.

Drained, I smile, hug, and handshake my way over to Marco, who maneuvers me out of the room. We don't say anything as we leave the Community House and tromp down the dusty trail toward my cabin. Finally, the silence feels like a two-ton weight on my chest.

"That was terrible."

"It wasn't that bad, sweetie."

I groan. "You 'sweetie'd' me. That means it was awful."

Marco laughs and then rakes his hands through his hair, turning his face skyward. "Who would have guessed this?" He laughs again and his genuine disbelief, his bursting amusement, is almost enough to make me smile too. "I was watching Sam on and off after the break. It's so weird to see him in person."

I feel like a jerk: of course this would be weird for Marco, too. There would be no Tate-and-Marco if there hadn't been a Sam Brandis first.

"Is he what you expected?"

"He's . . ." Marco trails off, and I watch him struggle for words, assuming—based off his sly smile—that he's trying to find a way to say how sexy Sam is without actually saying it. Sam's size, his composure, his eyes, the rugged look of him—he's objectively captivating. "It helps me understand, let's put it that way."

This makes me burst out laughing, finally.

"Look," Marco says, bringing his hands to my shoulders, "this whole situation is so weird. Frankly, it's beyond comprehension. But you—*we*—have to get it together. You are the same person who stepped out of that London hotel directly into the spotlight and never let her smile waver. You are the world's favorite broken, manipulative, good-hearted vampire. You are the woman who made millions of people laugh as Tessa in *Rodeo Girls*, as Veronica in *Pearl Grey*. You are beloved." He crouches so we're the same height. "Sam or no Sam, I truly believe you'll crush this. In fact, I have no doubt. He's a complication—an annoyance. You're so far above that."

I nod in his hands. "Keep talking."

He kisses my cheek and releases me. "Sadly, I need to hit the road if I'm going to catch my flight. Your call time is at five tomorrow morning. First up it's you and Nick, almost exclusively. Which is good," he reminds me. "You don't have baggage with Nick. It'll give you time to settle in. You *have* to nail this."

I may not have baggage with Nick, but *nailing it* still means I have to push everything else aside. Nothing else can matter but fully becoming Ellen, and what would Ellen do in a situation like this? She'd give herself an hour to be mad, to be sad, to be whatever she needed to be, and then she'd buckle down. No excuses.

I hold Marco tightly, wondering if I made a mistake and should have asked him to stay. But no—I don't need babysitting.

Become Ellen.

I know who can help me get my head on straight. Releasing Marco, I say, "Have a safe trip back." I pause. "Do you know where I can find a landline?"

With a smile, he points back to the Community House. "The office, upstairs."

He doesn't even have to ask who I'm calling.

★ ★

Mom answers on the fourth ring, harried, dropping the phone before she can even get a *hello* in. I imagine her in the kitchen, still using the landline with the enormous cord she winds around her hand as she chats, pacing the wide, bright room.

"Hello?"

"Mom?"

She lets out a happy little gasp. "Tatey!" A chair screeches on the tile. She's going to sit, but I know it won't last long.

"Hey, Mama."

"Tell me everything."

Before I can even get started, I hear her push back to stand. While she paces, puts away dishes, seems to start cooking something—but then heads outside into the garden, pulling the long cord behind her—I tell her about the farm, about my cabin, about the makeup trailer with Charlie, Nick, and Trey.

And then I tell her everything about running into Sam. About how Ruby Farm initially felt like an endless expanse of green, but now feels like a tiny green bubble.

It's weird that Mom never met Sam, has no idea what he looks like. Weird, because the sensation of seeing him again still pulses through me like an extra heartbeat, and it makes it hard to explain why it threw me to see him with a beard—because somehow I always knew he'd grow one.

Weird, because it's hard to explain how his eyes look exactly the same but entirely different, too. There's wisdom there now that I have no part of. I've had meaningless flings that lasted longer than my entire relationship with Sam, so why am I jealous of fourteen years? Why am I jealous at all?

"Because he was your first," Mom says, like I'm a sweet idiot. "Not just the first guy you had sex with—"

"*Mom.*"

"—but the first person you ever shared who you *are* with. He's the first person you ever consciously confided in about your dad. He's the first person who ever knew that you wanted to be an actress. And he sold that information."

I chew my thumbnail, mumbling "I guess so" around it, though when she puts it that way . . . duh.

The quiet stretches between us, and I can tell she's waiting for me to say more, but I have nothing left to say about it.

"You haven't mentioned your dad once," Mom says. "Is that intentional?"

This actually makes me laugh. Twenty whole minutes I haven't stressed about shooting a movie with Dad. Maybe the one blessing of Sam's reemergence is that Dad is suddenly the least of my worries.

"He has a girlfriend on set," I tell her. "I haven't interacted with him yet at all."

Mom exhales slowly. "I'm sorry, honey."

"Why are *you* sorry?"

"Because I know what you wanted this to be."

I feel my chest grow too-tight. "What did I want it to be?"

It's her turn to laugh, but it isn't mocking. "Tate."

I lift a hand to my lips, chew my thumbnail again, letting her gentle pressure unknot my thoughts.

"I don't want to put words in your mouth," she says gently, "but I think you were hoping this would be a turning point in your relationship with Ian."

For a flash, I let the daydream seep back in: sitting with Dad between takes, heads bent close, going through scenes, notes, ideas. The fantasy feels well-worn, a book read over and over. So I know Mom is right: I did want this to be a turning point for us. I wanted to be his peer for once. I wanted him to finally feel knowable, reachable.

"I need to get over it," I say.

"You just need to protect your heart."

I'm aware how the fallout from my relationship with Sam in London changed not only my outlook, but hers, too. She used to be such an optimist; now she's the voice of caution.

"What I actually need is to crush it tomorrow," I tell her.

"You will." I hear the fridge opening and shutting again. "Every time you look at your dad, just remember, the best thing he ever did was make you."

★ ★

The Community House is empty by the time I step out of the office. My footsteps echo down the long wooden staircase. With the anticipatory stress of the table read behind me, I'm able to actually take it all in this time. The main room is cavernous, with beautiful vaulted ceilings and wooden floors polished to a shine. Windows line the entire space; at the far end is a stage that looks like it's held some great bands and shows, but right now is a temporary storage spot for audio equipment.

The quiet lets me imagine the space in a different context—when the farm is rented out for a family reunion with familiar bodies dancing jubilantly up and down the floor, or when it is packed full of strangers from all over the area eating after long hours out helping with the fall apple harvest.

Voices rise up from outside, just beyond the hill in a small grassy clearing. I wander down, finding that a tent has been erected, with strings of lights, some tables, a makeshift bar. It looks like the scene of a wedding reception, and I register that they've turned the set of an upcoming town dance scene into a bar for the cast and crew for the time being. The flaps are folded up over the roof and air drifts through. Although the night sky is a deep cobalt blue, Indian summer winds still blow in from the east, warm and dry.

I don't see Gwen or Sam or Dad and his mystery girl-friend, but Devon is there, sitting at a table with Liz and Deb, each with a bottle of beer in their hand.

"Hey, lady," Liz says, lifting her chin to me. "You doing okay?"

The question sinks in sharply. It's fair, too—her wanting to know if there's something going on with me they should know about.

"I'm good!" I give them a bright smile. The wink may be overboard. "Totally overwhelmed by how amazing this place is."

"Right?" Deb points to the bar. "They've set up some drinks over there. Go grab yourself something."

They look genuinely relaxed and happy—and easily return to their conversation when I walk past. Liz tilts her
head back, cackling at something Devon has just said—
which tells me that whatever fears anyone has about my
ability to channel Ellen, they aren't saturating every one of
their moments the way my fears are saturating every one
of mine.

Over Liz's shoulder, I see that Nick is here, too, at a
table in the far corner, reading a book. He glances up when
he catches sight of me, setting his book facedown on the
table.

"There she is." He reaches for his beer, tilting it to his
smiling lips. "Was wondering where you went off to after
the read."

"After the terrible read," I amend.

He laughs. "I wasn't going to say it."

"I went to call my mom." Off his look, I add, "Don't
worry. I'll have my shit together tomorrow."

Nick nods and lifts his chin in acknowledgment to
someone over my shoulder. "I know you will," he says, turning his attention back to me. "I was there when you saw
him, you know."

A surprised laugh bursts out of me. In all of my
post-Sam-conversation processing about this, I'd forgotten
that Nick—and Dad—were standing on the path when I
had my run-in. I must have looked like a lunatic.

"You forgot I was there," he guesses.

I start to answer but startle a little when someone places
two beers on the table between us and then disappears.

"So who is he?"

"He's the screenwriter," I say evenly.

Nick grins, Cheshire-like. "I know *that*. I mean, who is he to you?"

I take a sip of my drink and study Nick's mouth, the way he slides his teeth over his lip. The flirty, possessive gleam to his eye reminds me, *You're mine on this shoot*. Whether that glint is about our characters, or about real life, I'm not sure. But whatever it is, chemistry crackles between us, and I cling to it, grateful that it wasn't a fluke back in LA, that whatever sparked during casting is still here out in the wide-open farm.

"I knew him when I was younger," I admit, trying to be honest without being too specific. "I haven't seen him in a long time, and it threw me."

His eyebrows rise in a skeptical lift as if the words *It threw me* are a dramatic understatement. "You two date?"

"Not date, exactly. We had a fling on a vacation once."

"Your reaction was bigger than seeing an old fling."

Shrugging, I tell him, "You know how everything feels more intense when you're young."

Nick nods at this, smiling. He takes a long, slow sip and then puts his bottle down, propping his elbows on the table so he can lean in confidentially. "I know you were stressed today. But it wasn't as bad as you think it was. The vibe in the room was weird, with every person in there who could fit just dying to see you and your dad together. It didn't matter what anyone did in there, performance-wise. It was going to be a circus regardless."

"Thanks for saying that," I say quietly.

Nick runs his finger over the back of my hand. It's not a sexual gesture, it's a gentle attention grabber, a gesture of redirection. "I think this tension is good," he says. "You and Sam. Use it. He's your Daniel, the boy you fell in love with, who hurt you." He looks up over my shoulder again.

This time, I turn to follow his attention and notice that it isn't someone on the crew bringing us beer again; this time it's the appearance of Sam, standing with Gwen and the studio executive Jonathan over by the table serving as a bar. My stomach flips, tightening. I turn back around, working to appear unfazed.

"I'm your Richard," Nick reminds me. "You don't want to fall in love again; you think you don't need it. Last time someone came to your farm he coaxed you away at sixteen, took you to Minneapolis, then turned out to be a liar and a cheat." Nick studies me, seeing too much, I think. "So I get it: when I come around you aren't going to touch another man again. Do I about have that right?"

"Right," I say, smiling with easy calm. Just two actors, talking out how I can use my feelings of anger and vulnerability to better channel my character. It's all craft, in the end. "Maybe it isn't a bad thing that he's here."

"None of it is bad. Use that resentment, resist me." He picks up his beer again and winks. "I'll win you over."

sixteen

CHARLIE HOVERS TO THE side, ready for a quick touch-up between takes. Fanned between her knuckles, her makeup brushes look like throwing stars . . . or maybe it's the effect of her tight jaw, the eyes that scream, *Stay fifty feet back at all times* whenever Sam is within star-throwing distance.

The first day on set is going . . . eh, fine. I'm not great, I'm not terrible, but I'm nowhere near where I wanted to be. I'm trying to capture Ellen's wariness, her strength, and also the way she can't resist Richard, no matter how hard she tries. It's a lot to balance with only pregnant pauses, long looks, the shift of an expression. *This is acting, Tate. You're getting paid a lot to do it,* I remind myself.

We set up for a take, and silence falls across the set. In the expectant hush, Nick blinks, narrowing his eyes at me. Under his breath, he growls, "You ready for me to seduce the shit out of you?"

I bite back a laugh and focus on the intensity of his eyes. He's got just as much on the line as I do. Nick could break out of the action-role loop. The scripts we would both start getting if *Milkweed* is as good as it can be are miles beyond the types of projects that come across my email every day. Not that I don't love fluffier movies too—but I know I can do paranormal tropes and comedies. I know who I am in those roles. I've never had to stretch as much as I do now. I remind myself it's supposed to be hard. It's *okay* for it to be hard.

A guy approaches with the clapboard, and Feng, our director of photography, calls out a "Gentle clap." When it clicks near my face, and then Nick's, we're rolling on scene fourteen . . . take seven.

EXT. MEYER FAMILY FARM, BACKYARD — DAY

Ellen ducks out of the chicken coop, cradling half a dozen eggs in her apron. Rounding the corner to the porch, she comes up short at the sight of Richard there, his hat in his hands.

ELLEN
You nearly made me drop my eggs.

RICHARD
Now that would have been a shame.

The two stand there, silence swallowing them. Ellen waits for him to get to the point. He clearly put himself together for this. Finally:

> ELLEN
>
> You here to sell me some feed, Richard Donnelly?
>
> RICHARD
>
> I'm here to ask you to dinner, Ellen Meyer.

With a short laugh Ellen walks past him, up the porch steps. He watches her go, and smiles when she turns to face him.

> ELLEN
>
> It takes a lot to come up here and ask that, and I appreciate your courage, and your energy, because Lord knows it's a long walk from town. This isn't because of the color of your skin or mine. But the last thing my life needs is another man in it.

"Cut." Gwen pulls her headphones off, walking toward us. She jogs up the steps to me, as Trey approaches Nick, powdering the tip of his nose, his forehead. Gwen turns her back to the crew and focuses entirely on me. Her eyes are this watery ice-blue; her hair has gone from platinum blond to white with barely any transition. Although I'm taller than she is, she's so intimidating; I can feel my palms sweat.

In the distance, I see the looming shadow of Sam. Near the panel of video screens, I see Dad pacing, his arms crossed tightly across his chest. I'm not sure why he's here since he isn't on the call sheet today, but I can only assume that he's either worried about my performance, or trying to play the role of the Involved Superdad. Blinking back to Gwen, I put on a smile.

"Hey."

"It's a lot," she says. "I know it is."

"It's okay. I'm just finding Ellen's voice." And trying to ignore two very distracting men in the audience.

She nods, squinting out into the distance. "It's only day one. You have time to get there." A pause. "For what it's worth," she says quietly, "he needs this more than you do. You're not the one I'm worried about."

She's talking about Dad, but it's still heartening. "I needed to hear that." On its own volition, my head turns, my eyes find Sam in the crowd. He's watching us, eyes narrowed, like he's trying to read our lips.

Never one for much sentimentality, Gwen claps me on the shoulder. "You good?"

"I'm good." I close my eyes as her footsteps hammer back down the steps and take a deep breath. I know I can do this, and there are so many people out there waiting for me to step up and just *own* it.

But only one of those people haunted my sleep last night. I look back to where Sam stands at the edge of the tree line, the boundary of Ellen's "backyard." Our eyes meet and a piece of me falls backward in time, locking onto the solid reassurance of him the way I used to, feeling that strange awareness that he's my beacon, a safe harbor.

But then he gives me a single, sharp nod. It's definitely a *Don't fuck this up*—which dissolves any of my nostalgic tenderness and sends me directly to pissed off. My adrenaline spikes, and I turn, catching my reflection in the farmhouse window with the movement.

The sight of it pulls me up short.

For actors, there's something about being in costume that transports us into the heart of the character we're playing. I certainly felt that shift earlier when I saw myself in Ellen's clothing, in full makeup, with my wig on. But here, on the back porch of the farmhouse, with the wind moving my dress and my mouth set in the hard, determined line I imagined Ellen's would make a hundred times a day, I feel possessed by someone else.

Look at her, I tell myself. *That isn't you. That's Ellen. Be her.*

Fuck Dad and his twentysomething girlfriend. Fuck Sam and his opinion of my acting skills. And fuck anyone who thinks there's a chance I won't end up being perfect for this role.

A delirious silvery, clean energy slides into my limbs as soon as Feng yells that we're rolling. I look at Nick and can tell he's getting in the zone, too. His eyes light up when we banter; we hit every beat we need to hit, and the chemistry sparks readily between us. We sail through the scene and do it once more for the master shot before Gwen lets us go for a fifteen-minute break and the crew breaks down the cameras for the tighter shots.

Nick high-fives me before trekking up the small hill to the restrooms, and I move to a quiet place in the shade of a wide apple tree, escaping the late-summer Northern California sun.

Charlie approaches, telling me to sit on a bench nearby before carefully tidying the makeup around my eyes. "You good?"

"I'm better now. That last take was good, right?"

"That last take was fucking killer," she agrees. She glances over her shoulder, to where Sam is bent with Gwen over her copy of the script; the two are deep in conversation.

I tap her arm to turn her attention back to me. Charlie's always protective, but her inner mama bear has been on high alert since learning about Sam. "Your fierce face is pretty epic."

She growls. "That kid has no idea what he's up against if he tries to wiggle back into your good graces. Not only can I shave a full six years off your age with the power of my makeup brushes, but I also know some pretty epic fight moves."

"You do?"

"As far as Sam Brandis knows, I do."

I laugh. "It's going to be hard to keep my distance from him," I admit. "I mean, especially with him having such a clear creative relationship with Gwen. I won't be able to avoid him entirely."

She pulls a brush and some powder out of her makeup belt/apron and brushes my cheeks. "I mean, even if you could, that would look weird, right?"

I chew my lip, considering this. It's not that gossip scares me. But gossip that spins out of my control does. From my upbringing, to my relationship with Chris, to my string of "boyfriends" chosen primarily by publicists, my life to date has been a work of carefully cultivated rumors. I know Dad and Nick—maybe others, too—saw my meltdown when I ran into Sam yesterday. So I have to be strategic and figure out what narrative I'm spinning.

When I look back up, Sam and Gwen have finished talking, and he hovers only about ten yards from our shady retreat. He glances at me and then quickly away.

"He's waiting," I realize.

"To talk to you?"

"I think so."

"Do you want me to stay here and touch up your makeup for the next fifteen minutes?"

I laugh, but my stomach shrivels up in anxiety. "No, it's okay. We're going to need to interact at some point. We're here for like seven weeks."

With a small air-kiss near my cheek, Charlie heads back toward the set, shooting daggers at Sam as she passes. Almost immediately, he heads directly toward me. His eyes fix on my face as he approaches, expression hard to read. By the time he lowers his redwood body down beside me on the bench, cupping his knees in his hands, my heart has volleyed into my throat.

I smile at him as he sits, but I'm sure he doesn't miss the flat disdain I can't seem to clear from my eyes. He swallows, looking away from my face and back out to the set. "It's amazing to watch you work."

When I don't say anything to this, he adds, "It's eerie to me how good that was. You were just like her."

Against my better judgment, I look back over at him. He's wearing a blue linen button-down, worn-soft jeans, and the same well-loved brown boots. When I glance at his hands, I surmise that he doesn't spend *all* his time writing screenplays: he still has the calloused, rough-handed look of a farmer. "I was just like you imagined Ellen?"

He stares at me for a few seconds, frowning, and then nods. "Yeah."

I don't want him to see how relieved this makes me, so I turn my attention away, back down the small hill to where Nick and Devon are twerking like idiots, and Liz is laughing hysterically.

"Look," Sam says, bringing my attention back to him. "I know things are complicated between us—"

"There's no complication, Sam. There's no us."

"Okay," he concedes. "What I'm trying to explain is that I didn't want you to do the role without knowing I was involved, but the more I thought of you as her—as Ellen—the more I really wanted it. I'm sorry that you felt blindsided yesterday, but I wanted you to know that I'm also really glad that you're her. It's . . . sort of perfect."

I don't know what to make of this, or how to process the tiny, carbonated feeling that courses down my arms to my fingertips. It feels dangerous to be this close to him, and not because I want him, or want him to want me—but because my body genuinely doesn't know how to react to him at all. I'm cycling through a hundred feelings every minute. Am I angry? Indifferent? Happy to see him doing well? I think the fact that I never got to fall out of love with him—that I just had to keep moving forward, stumbling into something new and totally different—means that my brain and heart don't know the protocol here.

I keep my expression neutral. "You didn't look like you believed I could do it, though," I remind him.

"I absolutely believe you can," he says quietly. "And you looked right at me, and—look, I was just remembering—in spite of everything—how well we did as a team. I'm on your team, Tate."

The way our thoughts had aligned rocks through me.

But, "*That* was your way of being on my team? An angry nod?"

"I don't think I meant it to look angry." He lets out a long breath and seems to deflate. "This is hard for me, too, okay? Really complicated." I start to laugh, and he quickly adds, "I mean, I know it's definitely harder for you—"

Self-preservation rushes to the surface. "It isn't just having you here that's stressful. It's also having my dad."

I think saying this out loud was a mistake; I sense it in the way Sam turns to look at the side of my face. "I thought you two were close?"

Now I'm trapped between lying and offering him something real that I'm not sure I'm willing to give. I remembered last night, while lying awake, that Sam had promised to come with me to LA to find my dad. Instead, I've muddled through the farce of it alone ever since.

Wait, I realize, *Sam thinks he's the hero of this story*, by reuniting father and daughter, by enabling me to have a dream career. Parts of that are true, parts aren't, but regardless, he doesn't get to be the good guy here.

"I mean," he says, "that's how it looks from the outside."

"That's how it's supposed to look." I stand, swiping any dirt from the back of my skirt, and get back to work.

★ ★

Over the next week, we shoot the scenes leading up to the moment that Richard finally wins Ellen over—through autumn and the fake rain, to summer and the brilliant sun mimicked by a hundred intense lights aimed directly at the porch. By the time Nick stands at his mark, facing me from across the yard, the budding relationship feels hard-earned and I'm jittery in that electric, impatient kind of way to see Richard walking up my driveway, flowers in hand.

EXT. MEYER FAMILY FARM, BACKYARD — NEW DAY

Ellen looks up to see Richard rounding the house, holding flowers. Warily, she looks to her father in the porch rocking chair — his expression is vacant — and then back at the man on her lawn.

                    RICHARD
      Hello, Ellen.

                    ELLEN
      My answer is still no.

Richard nods, tipping his hat.

                    RICHARD
      Would you mind if I asked again tomorrow?

She bites her lip to stifle a smile. With a little smile of his own, Richard turns to leave. From the porch, her father looks up, and seems to come into the moment.

                    WILLIAM
You like him.

                     ELLEN
He's fine.

                    WILLIAM
Fine? I see the way you hover outside,
waiting for him to show up every day. But
I didn't think you'd much care what the
town thinks about who you choose to dine
with.

Ellen stares at William. It is the first lucid
thing her father has said in days, and it catches
her off guard.

                     ELLEN
I *don't* care what they think.

                    WILLIAM
Then why refuse a nice meal with a nice
man?

                     ELLEN
You think I have time for a nice meal *or*
a nice man?

                    WILLIAM
You have all the time you make for them.
I know you don't want another Daniel, but
I don't want you lonely.

Deeply affected by this, Ellen walks to the side porch, sees Richard halfway down the driveway: hat on, shoulders square, roses in his fist as he leaves.

              ELLEN

I don't like roses!

Richard turns, and with a grin, tosses the flowers into the field.

             RICHARD

What roses?

              ELLEN

I don't like flowers at all.

             RICHARD

That's fine.

              ELLEN

I like steak, though. Think you could find me a good steak?

Richard's radiant smile could light a dark night. Ellen grins and then tries to smother it down as she straightens and turns back to her father.

              ELLEN

Happy now?

            WILLIAM

Just find the juice, Judy. I told you already I was thirsty.

Ellen stares for another breath, and then sighs. A
light has left his eyes. He's lost to the dementia
again.

Gwen calls cut, we quickly transition into the closer shots,
and then we're done for the day, letting the younger cast
take over to close out the back porch set. Giddy with relief,
I look over at Dad as he stands from the rocking chair and
walks over to me with a smile. The feeling in my belly is
effervescent. As much as I hate his approval, I know I crave
it too.

His arms go around my waist, he lifts me up, and I feel
the eyes of the entire crew on us. I feel like I'm becoming
Ellen. I'm completely falling for Nick as Richard: obsessed
with his shy smile, his understated confidence, good heart,
and the shape of him in the suit.

And Dad was brilliant: clear, wise, then blustery; his
portrayal of beloved, lost William tugged at something
deeper in me, some realization that he will age, that he
might forget this—and me—someday. I pull him tighter, my
generosity fueled by adrenaline and relief. I wonder how
many pictures are taken of this father-daughter moment.
It may be the first genuine embrace we've ever shared, but
I know no one else hears him when he says calmly, "You're
almost there, kiddo. Keep at it."

Gasoline dumps into my bloodstream and I fear it will
ignite if I let him get another passive-aggressive word in, so
I pull back and smile warmly, turning to leave the porch. At
the bottom, I'm pulled up short by the sight of Sam there,

talking to Liz, his eyes red-rimmed. He reaches up, laughing, and swipes at his cheek.

Was he *crying*?

It's hard to imagine, frankly, but if I try to frame him in my mind the way I've seen other writers on set—deeply moved to see their work being translated—I can only imagine what this experience is like for him. A tiny fracture forms in my Hate Sam wall.

Before I can even process this, Charlie steps in front of me, blocking my view. I am so busted. "Why are we staring at Satan?"

"I wasn't."

"You were. Are you feeling nice things, Tate Jones?"

"I wasn't—I just . . ." I lean to the side to peek again. "Is he crying?"

She doesn't even turn around. "We don't care if it cries. We aren't even sure it has feelings, remember?"

"I remember," I say dutifully, straightening and grinning at her.

"We have much better choices for bad decisions in the boy-toy category: Devon, Nick, even Jonathan is still here."

"Ew." I scrunch my nose. Not only has Jonathan Marino had a good deal of plastic surgery, but he's almost as old as my father. Besides, studio execs and talent are a match made in hell. "No Jonathan."

"No *Sam*," she counters, and takes my arm, guiding me away from the set. Once we're clear of the farmhouse, the breeze hits us—a glorious burst of cool, apple-scented air. "It's only two. Trey and I are going swimming down at the lake," she says. "Wanna come?"

An entire afternoon here, free? Normally on set I'd head back to my local apartment or, when we were shooting *Evil Darlings*, home. But here the location changes from set to camp as soon as Gwen dismisses us for the day. The idea makes me giddy.

"Can we bring some beer and bad decisions?" I ask her.

Charlie's eyes light up. She looks back over her shoulder. "Nick! Lake! Swim!"

★ ★

The lake is small but deep, with a beautiful crystalline sapphire surface that reflects the trees to almost a mirror image. It's in the middle of a circle of forest, far enough away from the farmhouse clearing that we're unable to hear anything on set and, more important, they're unable to hear anything from us, either. The four of us hike out to the far end of the lake, where there's a large, smooth, sloped boulder, just big enough for all of us to lay down our towels and bask in the sun.

Nick and Trey wear board shorts slung low on hips, and I envy the obvious, shirtless ease in the male body. In my simple black one-piece, I'm slathering on sunscreen like I'm actually going to be traveling to the surface of the sun, but Charlie stretches out beside me in a minuscule bikini, her golden skin shiny with oil.

"Are you *trying* to catch cancer?" I ask her.

She opens one eye just wide enough to let me see that she's rolling it. "Shh."

From behind us, higher on the rock, Nick jogs down and takes a running leap over our prone bodies, cannon-balling into the water. When he comes up gasping, yelling that the water is cold as hell, Trey holds up both hands, giving a score of eight.

"Eight?" Nick protests. "*Eight?* I jumped over two people!"

"Point deduction for form." Trey lifts his beer, sips it delicately.

"I went in so clean!"

"I think a cannonball is about the splash," Charlie explains without opening her eyes.

"Man, that's some bullshit." Nick scrambles out of the water and lies stomach down, body dripping on the warm rock. He lets out a long, happy groan. "Oh my God. This is the best rock on the planet."

We all hum in agreement.

"That was good," Nick murmurs, and then catches my eye, squinting from the brilliant sun. "Today, I mean. That was good, Tate. Today was good. *We* were great."

I cup my hand over my eyes and look down the rock at him. "We were."

"Can you imagine?" he says, grinning. *Hopeful.*

"Don't go there," I say with deep warning. Buying into the hype before the movie is even shot is a dangerous path.

Nick waves me off. "I know, I know."

I prop my weight up on an elbow. "What made you want to do this role?"

Nick adjusts his weight on his forearms. "Is that a serious question?"

"I know it's a great role, duh," I say. "I guess I'm asking specifically what drew you to it."

"Richard is a black dude who saves a white woman in the 1960s, goes on to run for city council with her, wins over an entire community on the strength of his character alone. How could I turn that down?"

"You think Richard saves Ellen?"

"Without question, I do."

It's funny. I always thought the script was less about either of them being saved and more about each of them finding their person. I thought it was about the bravery of two people fighting bigotry and racism and becoming leaders in their community.

But I think I see what he means. "You mean that she would have been alone for the rest of her life if he hadn't come along," I say.

Nick nods. "Exactly. Ellen was so ready to be old when she was so young. Richard wouldn't let her."

For some reason, this hits me right in the chest, a direct shot. Whether Nick realizes it or not, he's just found my Achilles' heel: the sense that I stopped being young the second I left London.

Oblivious to my internal brain freeze, Nick rolls on. "So. Let's recap. We're a week in. Tate was right about Devon the walking alarm clock *and* our unpleasant, *occasionally* non-smoking production secretary. Who wants to dish on Tate and the writer?"

Charlie and I say "No" in unison.

With a little growling laugh, Nick seems to let it rest. I tilt my face to the sun and feel its heat soak into my skin. "Can we pause time right here?"

Nick turns his face to the sky, too. "I thought your dad might join us."

I know he's playfully fishing for dirt, and I am too

relaxed and happy to have my guard up too high. I point without looking over my shoulder. "He's with the girlfriend in the cabin."

"Her name's Marissa," Nick says, grinning.

"I remember," I lie. Nick laughs.

"Can I be honest?" he says.

I suspect we're still going to be on the subject of Dad, and I am immediately wary. "You can talk about anything you want, but I can't guarantee that I will respond while I'm on this nice warm rock."

"Fair enough," Nick says. "I thought this shoot might be all about Tate and Ian bonding in front of everyone."

"You're not the only one," I tell him. I'll do whatever I can to keep people from prodding into the Sam backstory; if a few Butler breadcrumbs accomplish that, so be it.

Charlie rolls onto her side to face us, and throws me a questioning *Can I speak freely?* look. I nod.

"I can absolutely guarantee that's why he brought Marissa," she says.

The suggestion stings a little, mostly because she's probably right.

Nick tries to work this out. "You mean, he doesn't want to bond?"

I hum, unsure that this is the right interpretation. "More like he doesn't know how. Marissa is a good buffer."

Nick rolls to his back, staring up at the sky. "So you didn't know him at all growing up?"

"I lived with both parents until I was eight," I tell him. "Then I didn't see him again until I was eighteen."

"That's when the story broke," Nick says, nodding.

I glance over at Charlie, who meets my eyes at the same time. Nick is getting dangerously close to where Sam comes onto the scene.

"Yeah, it was time," I tell him, going for breezy. "I was ready to start working, and so a ghost publicist dropped the scoop to the *Guardian*."

Even Dad would back up this story, because he still thinks it's true: that I wanted to reconnect with my father and was ready to begin an acting career, so Mom and Nana hired someone to break the story. In fact, Dad was initially furious with Mom for not letting his team in on the plan.

"For real, though? That's a pretty sophisticated publicity feat for an eighteen-year-old . . ." Nick says, skeptical now. I wonder what information he has, and how he's been turning it over in his mind since we got here.

"For real." Charlie moves to her stomach, adjusting the towel under her. "You realize Tate is telling you things she could sell to *People* for like a hundred grand. You better be trustworthy."

"What," Nick says, grinning, "you want some quid pro quo? I could talk about Rihanna. Or my night with Selena Gomez."

"No, it's okay," I tell him, laughing as Charlie says, "Hell yes, give me all the dirt."

He confides a little, telling us bits of things I knew, and bits I definitely did not. I'm not sure if he's this open with everyone, or if it's the obvious comfort I have with Charlie and Trey that makes Nick feel like he's among family, but he gives us a genuine glimpse of who he is: an actor like me, who wants connection, yet has a hard time knowing how to find it in the bright light of the world's stage. It's clear neither of us would be very good at a fling on set, no matter how much he wants his reputation to make me think he could pull it off.

Nick looks up, and points across the water to where Gwen walks along the lake edge with Sam and Liz, the three of them deep in conversation. I'm guessing they're done shooting for the day, and the sun is already sagging in the sky, threatening to duck below the tree line and pull the cold air over us like a blanket.

I stand, just as Nick teases, "I'm gonna find out what happened with you and the writer."

"Why do you think it's at all interesting?" I ask, keeping my tone playful. "I told you we were just kids."

"Nah. I'm going to be here with you for, what? A couple months?" he says. "I want to get in that head of yours. And that story feels like a real glimpse at you. You're an enigma, you have to know that."

Charlie and Trey go still, as if they're working to be invisible during this conversation.

"I'm an enigma?"

"Beautiful," he says, "but sort of unknowable."

Huh. That's exactly how I'd describe my father.

seventeen

EVERYONE GATHERS IN THE Community House for dinner together; tonight it's a rustic spread of roasted chicken, root vegetables grown on the farm, salad, bread, and for dessert, apple pie. I sit at a table with Dad and Marissa, Nick, Gwen, Liz, and Deb. It's fun, and definitely good to bond with all of them together, but I find myself glancing in yearning every now and then at the raucous table just beside us with Devon, the teenage versions of Ellen and Richard, some of the livelier members of the crew . . . and Sam.

Despite what my head tells me, my eyes have missed the sight of him. It's so crazy how we age but don't completely change; how I can still see the twenty-one-year-old in him. I imagined him so many times in the first few years after London, trying to remember exactly what he looked like, the way he sounded. And then I worked to forget him entirely, and mostly succeeded. It's hard to believe I'm not staring at a mirage.

My attention is jerked back to our table when I realize Dad is telling a story about me. ". . . she ran off the deck and jumped right into the river. I thought I was going to have a heart attack."

Everyone laughs knowingly—*kids, am I right?*—but I scrabble through my thoughts to place the story he's telling. The only time I remember running and jumping off a deck into the river is up in Guerneville, where Dad han't been since before I was born.

"Apparently she and Charlie did it all the time," he says, shaking his head. "They'd just never done it before during any of my visits." Dad meets my eyes and winks. My fingers tingle cold. "She probably knew I'd go insane if I saw that. Such a cute little river kid."

He's full-on telling a story about something that never happened. It's not unexpected that we'd have to share some fabricated father-daughter time—we've had to do it once or twice for magazine interviews—but I'm aware of Nick watching me closely, remembering what I said earlier. But as complicated as my feelings are about Dad, I don't want him to be exposed publicly as a liar. I'm aware of everyone else watching me, waiting for me to chime in with my side of the story.

I smile over my wineglass at him. "No one ever got hurt," I say.

"As far as *I* know," Dad teases, eyes light. Our eyes lock, and his are so full of glimmering adoration, it seems he believes the lie as much as everyone else does.

"So—wait," Gwen says, "you're talking about Charlie, from hair and makeup?" She looks at me. "Did I hear right that you've been friends for years?"

"Since elementary school, yeah," I say. "She's a trip."

"Oh, Charlie," Dad says, laughing. "Now *she* was a handful." He leans back in his chair and regales everyone with stories about some fictional version of my best friend, daredevilish in ways that feel true to Charlie's spirit but are completely fabricated. Skiing down hills on cardboard skis, climbing water towers our town didn't even have. I look around—my eyes flitting past Sam's broad form only a few feet away—and find her at a table with Trey and a few of the grips. I make a mental note to tell her about all the trouble she got up to as a kid later. Dad didn't actually meet her until she was well into her twenties.

I risk a glance at Sam as I turn back around, and he's looking directly at me, smiling at something Devon has just said, but his eyes are distant, like he's really only straining to hear what is happening at my table. He blinks away when our eyes meet, down to his plate, and spears a piece of chicken.

I tune back in to Dad, talking now about what it was like to volunteer in my classroom and try to pretend he wasn't Ian Butler. My God. I feel half of Nick's attention on me, half on my father, as if he's trying to put together what version of the story to believe. Does he see me as the bitter child of a Hollywood legend, trying to make him look like a deadbeat dad? Or does he see through Ian's lies and my bright smile to the facade we're trying to maintain?

"Okay, Dad," I say finally, laughing lightly. "Enough embarrassing the kid."

He grins, and stretches his arm across the back of Marissa's chair. "You know you love it."

No words. I have no words.

Liz shakes her head at us. "You two are so cute."

"She's a chip off the old block," he says.

My voice comes out clipped. "No one says that anymore."

After a long beat of silence, his head falls back and he lets out a booming laugh. The pressure is released from the moment, and everyone else finally laughs too.

The wine flows, and even Gwen starts to loosen up, telling us stories from other sets: disasters, successes, urban legends that turn out to have been true. For a short while she even keeps Dad quiet and riveted. But then it's his turn again and he dials up the charm. I'm faintly aware of the tables around us going quiet to listen to him, and my pulse picks up, worried about what he'll say, and constantly aware of Sam so nearby, hearing everything.

With a few glasses of wine in my blood, I can no longer keep such a stranglehold on my thoughts, and the itch is back, tickling my brain, making me want to know whether Sam thought of me. Whether he saw my life taking off and ever regretted shoving me away the way he did. Were his feelings at all real? Or was it always a play to get money, from that very first night?

I return my attention to Dad, seeing directly through his veneer of self-deprecation, of humility. He's telling one of his favorites, and at least this time it's true: the first time he visited me on the *Evil Darlings* set, and all the ways I had the entire cast and crew wrapped around my finger. The subtext is always clear: *My daughter has the magic touch— she got it from me.*

Out of the corner of my eye I see Sam stand, check

his phone, and then ask Devon something that makes him point over in the direction of the stairs, to the same office I had used to call Mom earlier. He straightens and crosses the room like a ship cutting through water.

He's going to make a phone call.

Before I really think it through, curiosity propels my legs back so I'm standing, pretending I have to use the restroom, following Sam across the room.

I'm not even sure what I'm expecting to happen, what information I think I'm going to glean from this. But I need to know where he's been all these years, who he calls after dinner.

Once he's out of the dining hall and past the entryway, he climbs the stairs two at a time. He's so long; maybe he's in a hurry, maybe it's just his stride. It means I have to fall back, hang in the shadows. My hands are sweating. My head is telling me to go finish dinner and stop playing Nancy Drew.

I just want to know who Sam Brandis *is*.

He ducks into the office, lifts the phone, and I hear him dial; there's the electronic beep of a landline, touch-tone phone. I lean against a wall, pressing into the darkness.

If Sam is the man who can write the script I fell in love with, how can he also be the man who threw me to the world in London? How can this sensitive, compassionate writer live inside the body of such a heartless, cold man? I feel unbalanced. Maybe a little unhinged.

"Sorry to call so late," Sam says quietly. "The service here sucks . . . No, I'm good. What's the latest?"

A pause.

"So they'll keep her overnight?" he asks. "Okay." Another pause. "Okay, that's good news at least. Shit, I'm sorry I'm not there."

Is it about his mother? Or Roberta? I'm still trying to get clues from the words I've just heard when he says quietly, rumbling: "Sounds good, Katie. Kiss the girls for me. Tell them I love them." A pause. "I will. Go get some sleep."

★ ★

With our backs on the grass and our faces to the sky, Charlie, Nick, Trey, and I proceed to finish off whatever bottles of wine were left half-empty on the various tables throughout the dining room once everyone left.

I've warned Charlie that she used to ski down the hill on cardboard boxes. I've reassured Nick that he's sworn to secrecy now that he's figured out Dad is full of shit. I've let Trey braid my hair, and the entire time I've felt like a balloon being filled, pressure increasing inside me, but with so much wine in me, I finally break.

"So I think he's married," I say. "And he's definitely got kids."

Charlie has been peeling the bark from a stick she found in the grass, but at these words, she aggressively tosses it into the bushes. "Motherfucker."

"Can you believe it?" I ask, slurring and cutting out about two syllables. "I'm here, single, lonely, with all kinds of baggage, and he's fucking married. With daughters."

She groans and passes the current bottle of wine down the row. We've given up on the pretense of glasses. I take a swig and hand it to Trey, who partakes, even though he's barely awake.

"Who's married?" Nick asks. His words are slow, voice deep and hypnotic.

I stare at his mouth for a few seconds too long and it curves up into a smile. "Sam Brandis," I say.

He nods drunkenly, the momentum keeping the nodding going for a few beats. "Your first love."

"Why do you think he's my first love?"

"Because I saw you react to him," he reminds me. "You freaked the fuck out."

"No, I was just *surprised*."

He waves a heavy hand. "No, no, also you get that look." He points to his own face and puts on a shocked expression that in no way demonstrates what a good actor he really is. He gives it up pretty quickly, too drunk to bother. "The one where it's like you're just trying to keep breathing around him. I think he's your first and *only*."

"I don't want to talk about it anymore," I say. I feel spinny, like I've had one drink too many. I *have* had one drink too many. "I don't want to talk about Sam ever again."

"I need to get this one to bed." Charlie stands, pulling Trey up. "I'll see you at five," she tells me, and I groan.

I pull back the sleeve of Nick's sweater to look at his watch. It's after midnight, and most everyone has been smart enough to go to bed early. Only a small group, some of the camera crew and sound techs, remains at a table inside the dining hall. Devon reminded us of our call time and gave us both lingering *Be good* looks before disappearing to his own cabin. We probably should have taken his nonverbal advice, but drinking wine was so much more appealing; I needed something to put out the fire in my blood after hearing Sam on the phone to what was very clearly a significant other.

Kids. How does he get to be a dad? How does he get to have his shit together?

I'm sure whenever he thinks about my life, Sam thinks everything turned out okay. I'm famous. I have my dad back. Everything is great. Except my personal life is a total mess, and it's his fault. He's the one who taught me what love looked like and felt like and then taught me it's a lie. I have never been able to come back from that.

"No shit," Nick says. "That sucks."

I groan, swinging my head to look at him. "Did I say all that out loud?"

"You did," he says, nodding.

"What parts?"

"About how he taught you what love looked like and that it's a lie." He grins. "You also said how you wanted to make out with me under this tree."

I gasp. "I said that, too?"

He laughs. "No, but now I know it's true."

"You're trouble," I tell him.

"Not really." His words are so gentle, they're almost self-deprecating. It feels like he's admitting he's a mess, too, that distraction is good for everyone. If I were less tipsy, I would press into this a little, turn the attention away from my heartache and toward his.

But I am tipsy.

We come together like we're falling forward, mouths

meeting in a sweet, messy press of breath, and tongue, and teeth. It stirs me, waking that heat in my belly for the first time in so long. I haven't loved since Sam, but I'm not dead inside, either.

Even so, it doesn't feel right. It only lasts the span of a few kisses before I'm turning my face away. Nick kisses my neck, my jaw, my ear. It's so sloppy, so loose; I have the sense that we're leaning sideways and then we are, toppling over.

Nick laughs into my neck. "What are we doing?"

"God, we are too drunk for this."

He helps me stand, and I brush off my jeans, struggling to remain steady.

"You kissed me," I say.

"I think you kissed *me*." Nick grins at me, asking again, "What are we doing?"

"Getting into the role?"

"Did I tell you I'm nervous about the sex scenes?" he drunkenly stage-whispers.

And I know as soon as he says this that I have another friend on set. A genuine, new friend.

"You'll be fine." I point a weaving finger to my chest. "I'm a *pro*."

When I straighten, I see a shape in the shadows, walking quietly past us down the trail. It's not hard to make out who it is; no one else's walk stirs in me this brand of nostalgic heartache.

I don't know where he was coming from, what he saw, or what he heard. I know Nick and I weren't kissing for more than a couple seconds—

I immediately drag the next thought forward: *It doesn't matter how long we were going at it or what he saw. What Nick and I do isn't Sam's business.*

But I hate that he saw this. Already I can tell that it didn't mean anything romantic to Nick, either, but it's messy, and I don't like to be messy. I don't want Sam to see me like this. I know the reason I kissed Nick in the first place is also the reason I don't want to name that other feeling in me, the one that Sam pushes on like a bruise. But it's too late. My truth magnet is back, and never before and never since him have I felt such acute, painful, delicious longing.

A part of me still wants him.

But he's taken.

eighteen

I'M FALLING IN LOVE with nearly everything about this shoot—other than the presence of Sam and Dad, that is. I love working with Nick. I'm enamored with Gwen. Devon, Liz, Deb—they're all masters. And as much as becoming Ellen is a complete revelation, at the end of the day there's also something cathartic about coming back to my cabin, peeling off my costume, washing the decades off my face, and turning back into Tate.

But with no Netflix or internet, no town to visit or hotel bar to take over, the evening hours sometimes seem to stretch for an eternity. We only have a few night shoots—the big barn-burning scene is toward the end of our schedule—which leaves most of our evenings free, so the craft services crew gets creative, hosting barbecues and campfires up near some of the common buildings.

Dad once told me that Hollywood was very different in the seventies and eighties, and being on location for an extended shoot was like being at a very grown-up, R-rated version of camp. Drugs were prevalent, sex was everywhere, there were no cell phones or cell phone cameras, no internet, no political correctness or Big Brother watching your every move. He described drug dealers coming right on set, with cast and crew lining up and ready to spend their per diem, and drunken parties that lasted long after the sun came up.

A lot has changed since then. Movies are more expensive, which means schedules are tight and everything is budgeted, overseen, and accounted for. There's still sex, but drugs tend to be hidden and sexual harassment and discrimination policies mean most people are on their best behavior. But it can still feel a little wild and free, especially on a set like this, with all of us essentially cut off from the rest of the world and seeing the same people day after day.

Dressed back down in jeans and a sweater, I leave the warm coziness of my cabin and begin the short, energizing trek up the hill to the Community House. The breeze tugs on the ends of my hair as I walk, carrying with it the smell of charcoal barbecue and damp grass. Up ahead, the tent for the town dance party scene is still up and glows like a star against a dark sky.

I'm not really sure what I expect to find inside. Sam or no Sam. Nick, my dad—with his girlfriend or without. Sam and I mostly keep to our own circles. He spends time with Gwen, Deb, and Liz—though I do notice he slips away every night to call his family back home. Usually, I convene with Charlie, Nick, and Trey at the end of the day. Devon floats between the groups, being generally adorable until about nine every night, when he wisely decides to go to bed—after all, if he lets me sleep as late as possible and is always at my door around four thirty, he must be getting up at the crack of hell-dawn.

And then there's Dad. Mom was absolutely right: I went into this project knowing what it could do for my career, but I'd hoped something else would come from it too. Even now, time with him is so fleeting: a holiday here, a dinner there. The one time I spent Christmas with him, we spent Christmas Eve and Christmas Day in hospitals, visiting with sick kids. It felt . . . amazing, really, and I couldn't fault him for lacking paternal sentimentality when I watched him moving from bed to bed with a gift and smile for each person. And the way he looked at them—the way he listened to what they had to say—for those few seconds, they must have felt like they were the only person in the room.

And then we just . . . went our separate ways with a quick, tight hug. There was no delayed celebration for the two of us. I went home to Mom's gentle enthusiasm and Nana's stoic *I-told-you-so*'s, and he caught a flight to Mallorca to spend a week with his then-girlfriend, who, thankfully, was at least a few years older than me.

So when I see him tonight, Marissa on one side and an empty chair on the other, I'm hit with a wave of sadness I wasn't really expecting. He really did bring her as a buffer between us.

People load their plates with fruit and salads and meat straight from the grill. I debate lingering to fill a plate of my own and avoid what is sure to be an awkward conversation—the first round of real hang-out time with the new girlfriend—but don't have much of an appetite. The Loving Daughter move here would be to seek him out, and with everyone around, that's exactly what he's expecting me to do.

With an early call tomorrow, I grab a bottle of sparkling water from a huge ice-filled tub and make my way over. I catch Sam talking to some of the crew near the bar, but I force my eyes not to linger.

Busy listening to something Marissa is saying, Dad doesn't look up when I sit. I feel like an old toy put on a shelf, waiting to be wanted again. I open my bottle and bring it up to my lips and wonder if there will ever be a time when I'll stop trying so hard and embrace the welcome void of indifference.

Finished with his conversation for the moment, Dad seems to finally notice me at his side. "There she is," he says. "I wondered if you were coming out."

"Hey, Dad; hi, Marissa." I lean forward, giving her a little wave.

I take in her perfectly contoured makeup and miles of tousled hair. She's beautiful—they all are—but she's in heels and a Gucci jacket outside at a campfire. It leaves me wondering if maybe we have more in common than I originally thought: Daughter or Girlfriend, we both always have to be *on* around Ian Butler. "How are you enjoying being on set?"

"It's been *so* amazing," she says, a little giddy, a little breathless, and looks between us. "Okay, seriously? I still can't believe how much you two look alike. I've seen pictures, obviously, but God. You must hear it all the time."

"The apple doesn't fall far from the tree, that's for sure," he says to me, eyes sparkling in the reflection of the fire.

With a pang, I register that Dad only has a handful of these parental catchphrases. His idea of being a public dad is tossing out the wink-and-ear-tug sayings:

She's a chip off the old block!

The apple doesn't fall far from the tree!

Like father, like daughter!

It's depressing, frankly, but I guess it should help me understand why he sees my career as an extension of his.

My attention returns to his girlfriend, who I barely know at all. To be fair, Dad's supporting role means that he has several days in a row without a call time, so I know he and Marissa finally left the set and took a couple day trips up and down the California coast, but still: we're three weeks in and I'm not sure we've exchanged more than a dozen words before tonight. "I don't think I ever heard how you two met," I say.

"At UCLA. I'm a grad student there, and he was a speaker at an event on campus." Her eyes shift adoringly to him. "He asked me for a drink . . . and here we are. That was six months ago."

Six months and I didn't know a thing about it. "What are you studying?"

"I'm studying how genes linked to asthma are clinically and genetically associated with acute lymphoblastic leukemia." She smiles. "I'm working on my master's in public health."

Both Dad and I are silent for a few beats. Whereas I'm

speechless because a master's in public health is a delightful shift from the usual model/actress/influencer, Dad is clearly silent from pride, like he has some important role in his girlfriend's big brain.

But really, way to hit on a student, Dad.

It's possible my judgment isn't as subtle as I think, because he shifts forward, effectively moving between us. "How do you think things are going?" he asks. I'm sure it's unrelated to any of my interpersonal drama, but I'm pretty sure Dad's eyes just went Sam's way for a brief glance. It makes me wonder what my father's reaction to the whole story would be. Would he be protective of me? Or disgusted that I let someone get so close to ruining us both? "You feeling good about it, cupcake?"

"Yeah. Absolutely." I take a sip of my sparkling water, drowning the rising voice in me that absolutely detests the nickname *cupcake*. I don't remember him ever calling me that when I was actually a little girl.

"The sets couldn't be more beautiful," I say. "The crew and the cast are amazing. It took me a minute to get into Ellen's character, but I've got her figured out now."

God, I sound so stilted.

"Good, good." Crickets chirp in a bush behind him as he slowly rocks his chair in the soft dirt. He nods slowly, in that patriarchal way he does sometimes. When I was little, showing off my latest tap dance routine, Dad would sit in the living room chair, watching me and nodding with that same benevolent calm. It used to be a sweet memory, but I've seen him act this way so many times since, I realize it's less about enjoying someone else performing and more about making sure they know they're being watched by an expert.

I search the faces around us—purposely avoiding Sam's—hoping to find Charlie or Devon for some kind of escape. Gwen is talking to the line producer. Nick is standing back a ways, having an animated conversation with the actor who plays the younger version of his character. Most people are laughing or shoveling food off paper plates, a few are staring down at their phones, after all this time still clinging to the hope they'll find a spot with a signal.

"You know what you're doing." Dad reaches to gently pat my leg, and if a leg pat can be condescending, this one is. "It's just . . ."

I bite back a sigh. Even Marissa seems to know where this is going, because she's grown engrossed in finding something—anything, from the looks of it—at the bottom of her purse before finally excusing herself to grab it in the cabin. Deserter.

"The words on the page are just the beginning," he explains with patronizing calm. "It's up to you to figure out the rest. That's your job, Tate: Show the audience all the little pieces that make up Ellen. Show us who she is with an expression, a laugh, the smallest gesture."

I nod, biting my tongue. It's a good piece of advice . . . for someone just starting out. Does he not realize I've done seven films already?

"I'll remember that. Thanks."

"You know I'm just looking out for you." He rocks in steady silence. "I wonder if it would help to have you talk to the screenwriter."

My eyes fly to his. "The screenwriter?"

He shrugs and thankfully seems oblivious. "Ask a few questions," he says. "Get some insight into the character. Might help to see where Ellen is coming from."

I press my lips together to keep from saying exactly what I'm thinking. If I did, I think my voice would come out like a dragon roar. *You mean the guy who took my virginity and sold me out all those years ago? The reason we're even acquaintances now; the guy who made you look like a deadbeat? That guy?* I've read and reread *Milkweed* a dozen times by now. I know my lines and feel like I already know Ellen. I was ready. I was *prepared.* It was seeing Sam that threw me early on, but I've recovered. Dad wants the upper hand; he won't let that early slipup go.

But of course I can't say any of that, not here.

Almost on cue, my salvation comes in the form of Charlie. Not surprisingly, and despite all of his "stories," Dad has never really warmed up to her. The Perfect Dad routine doesn't work on Charlie, and he knows it. Which is why he stands when he sees her walking toward us and immediately offers her his seat.

"I need to head to bed anyway," he says, and leans forward to press a kiss to my forehead. "Good night, kiddo. Don't stay up too late. Big day tomorrow."

We smile as we watch him disappear from the light of the fire, and Charlie slumps down into his seat. "Is it me or did he just treat you like a seven-year-old before the first day of school? Aren't we a few weeks into this shoot already?"

"It's his thing."

"I saw that you actually got to talk to the girlfriend."

"I did. I like this one. She seems smart."

She meets my gaze over the top of her beer bottle, surprised because we both know, for my dad—a dude who habitually and without any awareness walks at least two paces in front of any woman he's with—being with a smart, self-actualized woman is a big deal. "That's new."

We watch the fire, blinking at each crack and pop that sends sparks up into the air, mesmerized by the soothing twist of the flames. Outside the tent the sky stretches overhead, vast and black and blanketed with stars that seem close enough to touch. I hate how many times in my life I've looked up at a sky just like this and thought of Sam pointing out the constellations.

"I'm nervous about tomorrow," I admit quietly. "It's a big scene, and having them both there watching makes me feel like a dumb kid again."

Charlie reaches over to grab my hand, weaving her fingers through mine. "But you're not."

"I know."

EXT. FLO AND FREEZE — DAY

A beautiful summer evening. Richard and Ellen eat at an outdoor table beneath the shade of a large tree.

People nearby steal glances their way. TWO MEN stand and walk over. Richard keeps his eyes down. Ellen is scared but meets their gaze directly.

She knows what this is about.

                    ELLEN
     Can I help you?

The two men keep their eyes on Richard.

                    MAN 1
     Ma'am, is this man bothering you?

                    ELLEN
     Have I given some indication that he is?

Their eyes shift to Richard again.

                    MAN 1
     No, ma'am, but—

                    ELLEN
     But what? We're sitting here trying to
     eat our dinner, and you're interrupting
     us.

Richard reaches for her hand on the table and
speaks softly to her.

                    RICHARD
     Ellen . . .

Man 2's hand shoots out, gripping Richard by the
wrist to stop him.

                    MAN 2
     Son, you better mind those hands.

Richard freezes.

> MAN 1
>
> Don't you live up on the big farm on
> Sutter Lake Road?

> ELLEN
>
> Not that it's any of your business, but
> yes. It's my father's farm.

> MAN 1
>
> He know you're running around with one
> of them?

A tense moment of silence. Richard has kept his
eyes down, but lifts them to meet Ellen's across
the table. Richard's face is tight with controlled
anger.

> ELLEN
>
> My father doesn't get a say in who I run
> around with. And if he did he'd sure as
> hell tell me to stay away from a couple
> of ignorant fools like you.

Man 1 moves toward Ellen. Richard stands up.

> MAN 1
>
> Somebody ought to teach you—

The MANAGER of the restaurant steps up to the table.

> MANAGER
>
> Is there a problem here?

                    ELLEN
These men were just commenting on the
weather, but they're done now.

The manager looks between them. The two men
eventually leave. Alone again, Richard looks down
at the table.

                    RICHARD
I wish you wouldn't do that.

                    ELLEN
Do what? Try to eat my dinner in peace?
I paid fifteen cents for this hamburger
and now it's cold.

A soft look across the table.

                    RICHARD
You know what I mean.

                    ELLEN
I do know what you mean. I always thought
I was talked down to for being a woman,
but I'm beginning to see it pales in
comparison.

                    RICHARD
It isn't safe.

                    ELLEN
These fools run all over the county on
Friday nights tipping cows, for God's
sake, but have the nerve to think they have

some sort of genetic superiority because
of the color of their skin? (beat) I'm
not naive, Richard. I know I'm allowed to
speak up because I'm white, and you've
been made to feel like you can't because
you're black. Please don't ask me to stay
quiet. I know you worry. If I'm honest,
I worry, too.

Richard holds her gaze.

                  RICHARD
Someone should marry you, Ellen Meyer.

                  ELLEN
Someone did.

                  RICHARD
Maybe someone should do it right . . .

"Cut."

It's as if everyone on set gives one collective exhale.

Gwen moves to check the shot, and Nick grins at me from across the table.

"Holy fuck, that was good."

A breeze twists through the scattered picnic tables and I nod in agreement, unable to shake an odd sense of déjà vu. I rub my arms as goose bumps rise to the surface of my skin. "Yeah . . . it was."

Nick's smile straightens; his head tilts as he considers me. "You okay?"

"Just . . . intense, that's all."

He nods, and we're both startled when Gwen claps her hands from behind the wall of monitors. "That looks good!" she shouts to the crew, before conferring with Sam and the script supervisor. Nodding in agreement, they each make a note, Sam in his laptop and the script supervisor in her book. When Gwen turns back to us, I force myself to focus on her, not Sam.

"Nick and Tate, you guys are killing it. That was exactly what I want to see. We're losing light, so let's break it down for the tight shots and we'll start again in—" She checks her watch. "Fifteen."

Devon follows suit with the extras, and the crew scatters. Nick stands and motions over his shoulder. "I'm gonna grab something to eat. Join me?"

The offer is tempting—I've barely had anything today and should probably eat—but I can't shake this odd sense of déjà vu.

I pass on food and head toward Charlie's trailer. Aside from being our backdrop, it seems to be business as usual throughout the majority of the farm. Fields of organic vegetable gardens and small orchards, a sprawling meadow tucked low in the valley feeds grazing sheep and cows—

I stop, my mind replaying the scene we shot today.

These fools run all over the county on Friday nights tipping cows, for God's sake . . .

"*Tipping cows,*" Sam had told me, talking about his life in Eden. "*Drinking beer in the middle of nowhere. Weird races and games in cornfields. Trying to build an airplane. It's easy to be crazy on a farm.*"

It's right there, the memory of everything he told me. About growing up on the farm. About Roberta.

And then it slams into me, an echo from fourteen years ago.

"She didn't care one iota," Luther said. *"Even when they set the barn on fire."*

For just a moment the fields disappear. The chirps of birds and the tick tick tick of irrigation sprinklers in the distance are replaced by the muffled sound of traffic and the chime of Big Ben. How did I miss it before?

Rosebushes line a stone wall and there's nothing but a bright sky overhead and damp grass at my back.

nineteen

I DON'T EVEN BOTHER to knock. Sam, sitting at the small table in his cabin, jumps when the door flies open and slams behind me.

"Tate?"

"What's going on?"

He pushes himself to stand, confused. "What's going on with what?"

I throw a copy of the script down on the table. "The barn burning down? This. *Milkweed*. It's not just some random love story, is it? It's Luther and Roberta."

He frowns, waiting for me to continue, like he's not at all surprised. He's still waiting for me to get to the part where I explain why I'm mad.

He thought I knew.

"Oh my God." I sit down in one of the chairs, mouth open. "I'm Roberta."

He drops slowly onto his seat. "It's still just a love story, Tate."

"But the irony here is that I'm Roberta, in love with Luther, the man who helped you con me in London."

"Con?" He leans forward, intense now. "Wait. No. That's not true."

Shattering, I look up at him. "What isn't true? That I fell in love with a script about the couple that helped swindle me?"

I'm thirty-two now. *Fourteen years* have passed, but I don't feel a day wiser than I did when Nana and I asked the hotel to ring the Brandis room and heard the words, *They checked out yesterday.*

With a sigh, Sam runs a hand through his hair and leans back against the counter. "You didn't want to talk about it when we first got here. You didn't want me to tell you what happened."

"Tell me *now*."

He looks to the side; jaw tight, like he doesn't know where to start. "Do you remember when I told you I thought Luther was sick?"

Arms folded protectively across my chest, I give him only a curt nod.

"He was," Sam tells me. "Very sick."

"It's good to know that some of it wasn't a lie."

He takes a step forward but seems to think better of coming any closer. "None of it was a lie."

"Bullshit."

"I know I hurt you, I realize that, and—"

I stand and burst forward to get right up in his face.

"You know you *hurt* me? Is that how you think of it? Like a broken leg or a sad couple of weeks over a high school crush? I had never let anyone in the way I did with you. You took my virginity, Sam."

His eyes soften and he must see how close I am to tears. "The last night we were together," he begins, wiping at his brow.

I feel my lip curl. "The night you said you were falling in love with me."

A tiny pause and then, "Right."

"The last night we were together before you called the *Guardian*."

I've never had actual confirmation of this, but it was the only explanation that made sense. Still, his quiet "Yes" makes the floor tilt beneath me. "Roberta called around three in the morning, after I left you at your door." He inhales deeply. "Apparently Luther had a necklace made for her, nothing too extravagant, but more than they could normally afford. On the day it was delivered out of the blue—that last day we—"

My stomach dissolves just at the moment he closes his eyes, stopping just short of saying *made love in the garden*.

"She got an inkling what was going on," he says, voice rough. "She called their doctor. Found out Luther's prognosis was shit. Taking me to England and getting Roberta a gift like that was his way of saying goodbye. He didn't want . . . they didn't have much. Not enough for a lengthy treatment. They would have lost the farm, literally."

Richard is Luther. Ellen is Roberta. The truth feels so obvious, it slots into place with a quiet, unobtrusive click. I think about the script I fell in love with; I think about

Ellen's strength and their bottomless devotion. It didn't convince me that love like that was waiting for me, but it gave me hope that it could exist. After feeling nothing for years, it was enough.

"So you sold me to save him," I say numbly.

Sam opens his eyes, and I can tell from his expression that he hates the way I've put it. But he gives another quiet "Yes" anyway.

"Would you do it again?" I ask. "Knowing that it hurt me, knowing how much my life would change?"

Sam tilts his face to the ceiling, and I watch as he blinks quickly, his cheeks growing red with emotion. "I don't know how to answer that."

"You answer with a yes," I say, "or a no."

"We got another ten years with him." He looks me squarely in the eye. His are red-rimmed. "So, yes. I would do it again."

I don't know where we can go from here. I turn to leave, but he stops me with a hand around my arm. "Tate. Don't walk out after that."

"We have to get back on set."

"Devon will come get us. Just—" He gestures to the chair again. "Sit, please?"

I lower myself back in the chair, still feeling shell-shocked. We sit in tense silence for several long moments.

"I didn't lie about anything I felt in London," he says, and a painful spasm turns something over in me. "Leaving you the way I did really wrecked me, and it's okay if you don't believe it. But I loved Luther and Roberta with everything I have. They'd given me everything." He pauses, and in the silence I can practically feel his turmoil. "I tried to give them back all the love that they gave me. I had to choose between you and my family, and at that point it wasn't even a question: I owed them everything. But when they died, I could say that I did everything I could to make their lives better, and when I love someone, that matters to me. I want you to know that."

The truth is, I do know that. It's evident in every word of his screenplay, in every nuance of the dialogue. Their voices come through so authentically; it could only have been written by someone who loved them beyond measure.

It makes it really hard to hate him, but anger isn't so quick to diffuse in my blood. The relief that it hadn't been planned from the moment I spilled my secret expands, taking up space before I've really made room for it. It makes it hard to breathe, like the air in my lungs is under pressure.

"Is there anything else you need to know?" he asks.

Through the chaos of my thoughts, the only questions that press forward with any clarity are ones that sound so young and selfish. *Did you ever think of trying to find me? Was it easy for you to just disappear?*

But I'm also wrestling with feeling obtuse for not seeing the truth from the second I knew Sam wrote the script. Even if it's set in Iowa not Vermont, the story is so clearly Sam's. I'm fighting the fear that I'm no more than a stepping-stone to every man who has ever meant anything to me. I feel small, and silly, and strangled by the realization that the longer I stay angry, the pettier I seem.

"I'm just trying to figure out how to feel," I admit.

"I'm sure." He clasps his hands, pins them between his

knees. "I guess I assumed you figured it out—about Roberta and Luther—once you saw me on set."

"I probably should have."

"Maybe not," he reasons. "You never met Roberta."

Our attention turns as we hear Nick yelling something down the trail. I have a fondness for Nick—especially for Nick as Richard—that is starting to feel the way I might for an old lover, for someone I want to forever keep in my life. I think about Nick's eyes when he's staring at me, as Ellen. His hand when it engulfs mine. It feels so real, so intense. Was this what it felt like for Sam to grow up around Luther and Roberta? Witnessing a love like this all the time?

I know my love for this script has always been fierce, even for someone who's been looking her whole adult life for the perfect role, but I get now that it's not only about being Ellen. It's about wanting to know, for certain, that this kind of love exists.

But then it occurs to me . . . where is Sam in this film?

"You never come live with them," I say. "There's no character that's your dad, either, when Ellen is younger. The script ends when they're in their sixties, but you're not in it."

"The story is about how they fell in love in the middle of one of the most tumultuous times in our country's history. They didn't need me or Michael for that."

I study him, trying to puzzle it out. Finally, he shrugs, and his smile is boyish. "It didn't make them any more heroic at that point to have her be a single mom or bring in a three-year-old kid when they were empty nesters."

Despite everything, this makes me laugh. "Artistic license means you cut yourself out of the story?"

He nods, and his shoulders seem to ease at the sight of my smile. "Can you believe me, though?" he asks quietly. "That the worst thing I ever did was for the best reason I ever had?"

His words spear through me, stabbing into a tender spot. Only for Sam Brandis have I felt such a complicated ache—devotion, desire, hurt, and envy of the wife who gets to puzzle out the man who, if what he says is true, would sacrifice his own heart to save someone he loves. Who could see true love so clearly in front of him and translate it into words on a page.

She gets to curl up against this man and be his best friend, his lover.

I push to stand, needing a few minutes alone to clear my head before Devon comes for me. At the door, I turn back. He's watching me go with a tight expression I find unreadable.

"Actually," I tell him quietly, "I think *Milkweed* is the best thing you ever did. And if that's the best thing you ever did, I'm okay being the worst."

twenty

MY CABIN'S SCREEN DOOR slams behind me, and the sound seems to hang in the fog of the early morning air. The farm has turned cold so fast. Indian summer left and abandoned us in the chilly vacuum of Northern California fall.

I don't ever want to leave Ruby Farm. It's more than just a quiet retreat; it's like a warming of my bones, some settling of the frenetic beat that seems to always course through me. My house in LA feels sterile and uninhabited, doing little to calm me down between projects. But I'm so seldom there that it's never felt worth the effort to make it into a homey place. And then when I *am* there, I regret not making the effort. The prospect just feels so overwhelming.

Here, each morning, I wake up in my cabin and try to pretend this is where I live now. I've put my clothes in the dresser and closet, stocked the small kitchen with a few staples. I go for long runs. I keep flowers on the table and had

Mom ship me a few blankets. Up here, I can pretend the chaos and exhaust and clatter of LA not only isn't my home anymore, but doesn't even exist.

The birds in the tree beside my door let out a cacophony of sound when I emerge, squawking and rustling overhead. Down the hill, in the pasture, the cows yell to be milked and fed. But there's no human sound. Everyone is taking this day off to sleep in. I hope I'm not the only one up early, unable to turn off my brain.

I stretch before heading down the trail in an easy jog. Leaves crunch beneath my shoes, and the sound must echo down the path because Sam is already looking up as I pass his cabin. He's sitting outside, clearly more accustomed to the cold than I am, because he's only wearing a thick cream sweater, jeans, and socks.

"Tate." He puts a notebook down on the small table, picks up a steaming mug of coffee. "You're up early."

"So are you."

He takes in my leggings, long-sleeved layers, and gloves. "Going for a run?" When I nod, he motions to the abandoned journal. "Was just writing some things down."

"For another screenplay?" I hike up the small incline, stopping at the foot of the stairs leading to his porch. It's the first time we've spoken since our blowup yesterday, and the part of me that will always be eighteen and infatuated with him wants to climb the steps and curl up on his lap.

"Maybe," he says. "Don't know yet." Sam studies me over the lip of his mug as he takes a sip.

"You writing yourself into this one? Maybe it's about the

heart you broke in London." The words are out before I've weighed whether or not they're a good idea.

Sam blinks a few times before smiling gently. "I don't think that's my story to tell." An awkward pause. "This time, at least."

We face each other in strained silence.

"Want some coffee?" he finally asks. "The stuff they brew in the Community House is awful."

I really need to keep moving, but he's not wrong. "Sure."

"Come on up." He stands and tilts his chin for me to follow him inside the cabin.

Trudging up the stairs, I feel so anxious and excited that it makes me nauseous. It isn't just the proximity of Sam, now it's the proximity of Ellen's, well, Roberta's, grandson. He *knew* her. She raised him. I marinated in that reality all night, skipping dinner at the Community House, skipping the campfire I could hear all the way down the trail. I curled up in bed and reread the script with new eyes. His formidable, brave grandmother. His tenderhearted, fun-loving grandfather. Was it even a question that he would do anything he could do to save them?

I didn't take much time to look around yesterday, but it wouldn't have taken much to absorb everything here. Sam's cabin is one big room, almost like a loft, with a bed in the far corner, a little kitchen to the left of the door with the table and chairs, and a small sitting area in between. It's cozy from the country decor, and he's got a fire going in the fireplace. I make a beeline toward it, holding my hands out to get them moving again.

"You're such a Californian," he says, laughing.

"It's cold!"

"It's probably fifty-five degrees out," he says, opening a cabinet and reaching for a mug.

"Exactly."

Sam laughs again as he sets a pot of water to boil and scoops some fresh grounds into a French press. Something has eased since he told me the truth yesterday; it feels like there's so much more air in here.

But with that space, it means I'm not working to ignore him, which in turn means I *notice* him again. As he goes about the business of brewing me a cup of coffee, I start to zone out a little on the shape of his broad back beneath his sweater, his enormous hand reaching for the whistling teakettle, his ass in soft, faded jeans.

Wife.

I'm not my father. I'd never cheat, or be with a cheater. I blink away, back to the fire, letting the brilliant orange and red burn into my retinas and clear my mind. I can't think of him like that.

He crosses the room, hands me the mug, and gestures for me to sit wherever I want in the living room area. When I choose the sofa, he follows suit, folding himself into the corner at the opposite end.

"You okay? After yesterday?" As always, Sam cuts to the chase.

"I'm getting there. It helps," I say, adding, "to know."

"It drove me crazy, wondering what you thought all those years."

"I thought about it a lot for the first few," I tell him.

"And then time passed and it stopped factoring into every decision I made. I stopped worrying about what Nana would think, what Dad would think, what Mom would think." I pause, then add quietly, "What Sam would think. The last seven years or so have been really good, and all mine."

He's quiet in response to this, but gives me a muted "I'm so sorry, Tate," after a few deep breaths.

Nodding, I blink down to the rug. "I don't actually want to talk about us anymore." A glance at him gives me a response I wasn't expecting to see: disappointment. "But maybe you could tell me more about Roberta."

I wonder if this surprises him a little. His eyebrow twitches, and he reaches up to scratch it. "Oh. Yeah, I'd be happy to." He pauses, waiting for me to ask more, I guess, to be more specific.

"I'd like to know more about her," I admit. "And about Richard. I mean—Luther."

Sam grins at me. "Roberta was something else. They both were."

I stretch my legs out, warming, and stop just short of pressing my feet against his thick thigh. He looks down and smiles a little, stretching his arms out along the back of the sofa. "We getting comfy?"

"I'm defrosting."

He laughs, and his mossy eyes shine with understanding at the double meaning. "I see that."

Taking a sip of my coffee, I say, "We don't get to see her as a mom. I mean, I get that it simplifies the story somewhat, but I imagine it would only make her more amazing.

Juggling all that? How come you took your dad out of the story?"

"Because my father turned out to be such a dick." Sam shrugs, crossing his ankle over his knee. "I only know how tender she was with me, but I can't imagine she was like that with Michael and he still turned out the way he did. Even though I know she was—a good mom, I mean."

"Does he know you've written this?"

"Probably not. Haven't spoken to him in years."

I make a sympathetically mad face, and this makes him laugh. "I'm fine. Better off, trust me. Though I am in regular touch with my mom. Ironically, she lives in London now."

I let out a sharp laugh. "Do you visit her?"

"A couple times a year."

I want to ask whether being there ever brings up old memories, but I'm sure I'm the only one of the two of us who is so fixated on our brief affair. It was the single most defining moment in my life; no doubt it's just one of many in his. I need to move on.

"What kinds of books did Roberta read?" I ask instead.

"Mostly history," he says. "Nonfiction. Luther loved crime novels—she'd tease him about those, but she loved reading together. She'd read these giant, boring nonfiction books about Napoleon or Catherine the Great."

I exhale a dreamy sigh. "She sounds wonderful."

"She was. She wasn't perfect, but she was about as close as you can get. It's why you're the best person to play her."

This is such an inflated compliment, it makes me laugh. "I'm nothing like Ellen. Not really."

"Are you kidding?" he asks me. "The girl I knew was every bit as brave and brassy."

I wonder if Sam has any idea how much this compliment warms me from the inside out. I know it isn't true; maybe it used to be—I like to think I was brave and brassy when I was younger, but I'm undeniably soft now. My life is made easy for me by a handful of people, and every time I'm required to be truly brave—letting new people into my life, for example—I flee.

I think about everything I could learn from Roberta now. Just to have a day in her company would feel like a gift. It was such a waste, in a way, for me to have met Luther when I was eighteen and had no idea how to get to know him, how to ask him the questions that would unlock all of his stories. I feel like I missed an opportunity to talk to someone whose life had been hard and wonderful in equal measure, and who had a wisdom I can't even fathom. But at least I laid eyes on him, can still remember his laugh, his teasing eyes, the way he could ask probing questions without ever sounding nosy. I never had the chance to meet her.

"Why didn't she like to travel?" I ask him, recalling parts of our conversations. "It seems so . . . out of character."

He nods, swallowing a sip of coffee. "Because she was so fearless otherwise?"

"Exactly."

Sam sets his mug down and reaches up to scratch his jaw. It's a small movement, such a casual gesture, but it sends a bolt of heat through me anyway. I'd forgotten how easy he is in his body.

"She hated planes," he tells me. "I think it was probably the one thing that scared her—the idea of flying across an ocean. I remember when Luther and I left, how she tried to look calm and put together, but she was a wreck."

"Do you think she would have had fun in London?" It's amazing what context can do, like I can see my past through someone else's eyes. What I've been holding on to was actually about something so much bigger than just me.

The thought blows through me, unsettling: *If Sam had asked me, would I have agreed to expose myself to help Luther?* The truth is, I had loved Sam enough to say yes. I would have. And the fact that he didn't even talk to me about it dampens the relieved, floaty feeling I've had since yesterday.

I've missed half his answer and have to mentally shake myself to catch the rest of it.

". . . couple days. She liked to keep busy. She wasn't really one for vacations." He stops, and his gaze flickers all over my face. "What?" he asks warily.

I'm not sure what he sees in my expression. "What what?"

"Your cheeks are red." He pauses again, narrowing his eyes, reading me perfectly. "Are you embarrassed about something, or mad at me?"

His comfort with honesty, with gentle confrontation, makes my irritation boil over. "Track change, but I was wondering why you didn't include me in the decision to go to the *Guardian*."

Now I know *this* question catches him by surprise. He takes in a sharp breath, leans back, and tilts his face up to the ceiling as he thinks about it. "You think you would have agreed?" he asks, finally.

"I think there's a good chance. I was pretty infatuated with you."

I see the way this word hits him sharply, that I said *infatuated*, not *in love*. Sam looks back at me. "I didn't include you because I was panicking." He leans forward, resting his elbows on his thighs and staring at the area rug beneath his feet. "It wasn't exactly a well-laid plan. I wasn't even sure it was going to work."

"Tell me how it happened," I say. "I never understood why there was a day between when you left and when the paparazzi showed up." That piece of it always felt so calculated.

He rubs a hand over his beard, squeezing his eyes closed. "Like I said, I was panicking after talking to Roberta. She told him we had to come home that instant. He fought her a bit, but finally agreed. We left, but couldn't get a flight out until the following day."

"So you wanted to be clear of the country before blowing up my life?"

"No, Tate." He frowns at the floor. "*No*. Look, I booked us at a hotel near the airport, and was up all night again, thinking on it. While Luther was showering the next morning, that's when I went to the lobby and called the paper." His voice is so flat, it's like he's reading instructions. "I said I had information on Ian Butler's daughter. They said they'd have a reporter call me back, and I thought it would take a while, but it was like two minutes. I told them they'd have to buy the story. They got some preliminary information from me so they knew I was credible—I think I told them where you lived and the name you went by, so they could look it up. When they wired money to my account, I called them back. I told them everything you'd told me."

Sam looks up, meeting my eyes. "Whatever you think—and I know it was a terrible thing to do—I don't want you to think it was easy for me. I didn't relish any of it."

"You didn't even say goodbye." I feel too exposed after saying this, so I look away. "Even if I didn't know it was goodbye, there wasn't a last, nice moment between us."

"I saw you in the lobby when I was checking us out. You and Jude were walking out for the day. You looked . . . sad. I almost went over to you then."

"But you didn't."

He looks pale, like he's not feeling well. "No, I didn't." He pushes the rest of the story out. "Anyway. We flew home and Luther got his treatment."

"And then it was just—what?" I ask. "Business as usual? Back to your regular life?"

"I mean, there were a lot of doctor appointments and hospitalizations. It wasn't exactly regular life, but yeah. I took on more at the farm. Luther was weak for a while, but then he was better." He licks his lips and takes a deep breath. "I never told Roberta or Luther what I did."

I stare at him, shocked by this. I don't know why I assumed they would have been in on it. "How did they think you got the money?"

"I said Michael sent it from New York."

"And they believed you?"

He shrugs. "I think at that point they didn't want to look

too closely. They just wanted Luther to get better. But that meant when I got home," Sam says, turning to me, "I was the only one who knew what I did." He quickly holds up his hands. "I'm not saying it was as hard on me as it was on you, okay, not even close. But I was relieved for Luther, and then at the same time I was being eaten alive by guilt." He looks over my shoulder, remembering. "You had that interview with Barbara Walters, and then pretty soon after that you were cast in *Evil Darlings*. When I got that news, I went out to the bar and got so drunk that my friend had to drive me home in his tractor."

"What?" I ask, confused. Was he upset that I went into the industry? "Why?"

"Because I'd been crazy about you. Completely fucking obsessed. And for the first time it occurred to me how stupid I'd been," he says. "How reckless with you. My life went on the way it always had, for the most part. I assumed you'd get a flash of attention and then your life would go back to the way it was before too—college, living in Northern California, whatever—it never occurred to me that it might not. That your life might have been totally ruined by what I did. How dumb was I? You turned the exposure into something good, but you could have just as easily gone the other way. How would I have felt if I'd heard about you using drugs, or—worse? What if what I did had caused real damage in your life?" He blinks into focus and looks back at me. "I really could have fucked things up."

I laugh dryly, sipping my coffee. "You *did* fuck things up."

"But look at you. You're doing okay," he says, and then very quietly adds, "right?"

"I'm doing okay." I chew my lip, debating how much to admit, and why the desire to tell him I'm not always thriving has risen to the surface. Is it because I want him to still feel a little bad? Or is it something else in me, something kinder that wants to tell him because I want him to know me better? "I'm still not great with relationships. I haven't been since."

Sam's brow pulls low, and he blinks down to his hands. "I read about lots of them."

"Most of them have been coordinated," I say. "Publicity only."

"Chris?" he asks, and there's a vibration in his voice, a layer beneath casual that feels darker, a little gravelly.

"We were real for a while, but he was a mess." Self-conscious now, I lift my thumb to my lips, chew my nail. "For a long time, we weren't together anymore but we kept up the facade."

"I saw you with Nick," he says. "That night."

The night we got drunk and kissed. Idiots. "I know."

"Are you two . . . ?"

I shake my head, embarrassed all over again. "I was messy that night. Over all this." I wave between us, but then widen it to include everything this set has contained—the pressure of a high-profile, character-driven role, the presence of a world-renowned director, and of course my dad.

He makes a little sound, a tiny "Ah" in acknowledgment, but it makes me crazy, wanting to dig a little deeper to know what he's thinking. I mean, how much can this really bother him? He's with someone else, after all. He goes upstairs to call her almost every night after dinner. And he chose our current circumstances. It's not like he gets to play jealous ex here.

"Anyway," I say, wishing I hadn't brought up any of this now. "I hate sometimes that I haven't fallen in love since London." It feels like too much as soon as I've said it, and I quickly add, "But I know I will someday."

I feel exposed in a way that he isn't—he's settled, with children, healthy. But I don't want to be the broken bird anymore. I'm tired of suffering from an emotional limp through every relationship I have, even this new friendship—is that what this is?—I'm trying to forge with Sam. Honesty, clarity, and closure. That's what I need here.

He smiles, and I can imagine the comma scar there beneath the beard. Just the thought of it pulls a band of nostalgia tight in my chest. "Well, I guess that's why I had to write *Milkweed*," he says.

I narrow my eyes, trying to puzzle out his meaning. "I don't follow."

"To remind myself that they were worth it." He laughs. "They were pretty ornery at the end."

I'm still lost. "Worth what?"

Sam looks at me as if I'm being exceptionally slow, and a half smile curves his mouth. "Worth losing you."

twenty-one

"WHY AM I SO terrible with men?"

The sun is dipping below the tree line, and Charlie's dark hair is a wild halo in the breeze. "I don't think you're *bad* with men—"

She stops when she catches my *Come ON* face. My *You have got to be kidding* face. Charlie knows my track record better than anyone: I am terrible with men.

"I'm serious," she says, eyes back across the field again, to where the set crew is putting the finishing touches on the barn for tonight's shoot. "And even if you were, who could blame you? It's not like you've had the best examples to follow. Your parents were a mess when they were together. Your mom's never dated, and your dad needs to just . . . stop. Nana never remarried. My parents were a hot mess, too, so I'm not winning any awards in the romance department either. If you suck at this, it's because you've never actually seen what a normal relationship is supposed to look like."

I consider this as I look out over the landscape. I'm nervous about tonight's shoot because it's going to be intense, even if things go exactly the way they should. The farm might be over two hundred acres, but with my dad around it feels entirely too small. With Sam there it feels even smaller. I thought settling into some kind of quasi-friendship would make things easier between us, but instead it's only made things more confusing.

Anger was easier, and it was *definitely* safer.

The thought that I've played a woman in a healthy relationship more times than I've actually been one is depressing.

"I'm thirty-two, Charlie. Thirty-two and eternally single, with crippling daddy and abandonment issues. I thought Dad and I would finally connect, and that's all gone to shit. I thought I'd finally moved on from Sam, but now all of that is a lie, too. At least you were engaged."

"For six months," she reminds me.

"Yeah, but you got that far. The farthest I got was Chris saying 'I love you,' and me replying with 'You're the best.'"

She laughs. "Maybe that's what drove him to drink."

"Charlie Zhao, you are the fucking devil."

"Didn't you get to the I-love-you's with Pete?"

"Nope."

"Evan?"

Ah, Evan. Sweet Evan only bothered with me for five months. "Nope again. Well," I correct, "he said it. And I think I tried to improve on my 'You're the best' and came up with 'That makes me so happy to hear.'"

Charlie leans between her knees, cracking up.

"I keep reading the script and thinking, 'Wow, Sam wrote

this.'" I draw a circle in the soil with a scraggly twig. "The terrible person I built up in my head wrote this beautiful thing. That has to mean something, right? That he understands women, or that he's good enough inside to have done this? Or maybe it's that Ellen"—I shake my head and correct myself—"*Roberta* was just that great? I think of everything she went through: pregnant at sixteen, put her husband through law school only to have him leave her *and* their son and run off with someone else. Her dad is sick. She falls in love with a man the whole town is against and yet she still puts the work in to build up their community and help the very same people who would have turned her away. She didn't close herself off. She didn't move from one pointless, meaningless relationship to another. She's just this wonderful person who made mistakes and learned from them and kept going."

Charlie appraises me with a small tilt of her head. "You're pretty great yourself, you know."

I try to laugh but it sounds hollow and cynical. "Do you remember those art projects we helped the kids with at YMCA camp? You fill in the entire paper with different colors, and then go over it with black crayon? You think it's just a black picture, but when you scratch at the surface there's all this . . . stuff underneath. That's a terrible analogy, but it's sort of how I feel about my love life right now. I thought it would be one thing, but it's just been covered up with this boring black crayon and I don't have the tools to scratch it."

Charlie gives me a sad smile and reaches over to squeeze my hand. "But what's under there is *still* all bright and rainbow colored. I know it's scary to learn how to scrape all of it off, but I think what's under there could be pretty great too."

We look up as Devon stomps through the tall grass. His blue button-down Patagonia shirt seems to glow in the fading sunlight. "What are you two up to?"

"Discussing why my love life is a mess," I tell him, laughing.

Devon pauses, surprised, and then gives us a knee-buckling smile. "Well, okay then."

Apparently we aren't in a huge hurry, because he settles down on the grass at my side. "We're getting ready to roll, Tate. How're you feeling about tonight's shoot?"

I weigh my response. Admittedly, the most stressful part of the filming has come toward the end of our time here: the barn fire and the love scenes. I know why we had to put them later on the schedule—the barn fire shouldn't be destructive, but in case it does cause some damage to the landscape, we needed to be done with all the other outdoor shots first, and the love scenes, well, Gwen is smart enough to know that those require a real depth of comfort between co-stars. But while I'm apprehensive about the love scenes, I'm downright *afraid* of the barn fire tonight. We've rehearsed it over and over again, but like—we are going to *set the barn set on fire*. It's not being done with special effects; it's a controlled burn and they'll be shooting with a long lens to compress the distance between the actors and the flames, but it's still being done with a newly constructed barn set, some fancy chemicals, and a lighter.

"I'm nervous," I admit.

"I know you've been told this, but I want to reassure you," Devon says. "We have—"

"Over a hundred firefighters on location to put it out,"

I finish for him. "Infrared viewers to find hot spots. I am never actually going to be in danger. I know."

He smiles again. Devon is so perfectly sweet, I experience a beat of disappointment that I'm not nearly as attracted to him as I should be. The Sam Brandis Proximity effect.

"All set, then?" Devon tilts his head up the hill, making his meaning clear.

Up the hill, that is, where nearly everyone who has ever been involved in this movie has gathered to watch this enormously important scene being shot. Even Plastic Jonathan has returned and will be seated a safe distance from the barn, in a posh area of executive seating.

Sam, as usual, hovers at the edge of the action. Dad and Marissa are sipping cocktails in the executive galley. Nick stands with Gwen, at a set built to resemble the entryway of the cabin, poring over our marks, our path of movement. I join them, and when Nick meets my eyes, I swear I can hear his heartbeat.

The barn, which has slowly been built since we first got here, looks suddenly enormous. I wonder whether it'll be thrilling or devastating to the set designers to watch it burn down.

Everyone gets into position; Nick looks at me and then takes my hand. "You good?"

"Yeah. You?"

He shrugs and only then do I notice that his hand is shaking in mine. I lean forward, kissing his cheek, and then Gwen calls for quiet on the set.

The fire crew gives the okay, the pyrotechnic specialist hits the trigger, and we're rolling.

I swear my heart has never beat like this. Not just fast, but thundering. We burst from the farmhouse in our pajamas, racing together across the lawn. Nick has to duck into the barn for buckets; he scrambles through a safe zone and back out, completing the shot. But the fire hasn't stopped, and we're still rolling.

It's such a tightly choreographed scene; the stunt coordinators having organized everything between the principal actors, the stunt doubles, the extras, and the crew, down to the most meticulous detail. Extras as townsfolk come in, in staggered waves, and we're all throwing bucket after ineffectual bucket on the roaring flames. I know it's all a set, that we're safe—it isn't real—but panic fills me like a rising tide. The fire isn't just hot, it's loud. It pops, whines, and cracks; the first wall of the barn screams before it collapses, right on cue, and the sound is deafening; the dust is real. So, too, is the feeling that we are battling this thing that we are never going to beat.

It is *hot*, unlike anything I've ever felt before. Even beneath the protective gel, my face feels dry and crackling. I know we're acting, but with Nick—*Richard*—at my side, doing everything he can to save our barn, I feel for the first time how genuinely terrifying it would be to have someone you know and see around town, who smiles to your face, try to burn down your home. I can't fathom what it had to have been like for Luther, or the bond that must have existed between the two of them to press on, continue to fight against such bigotry and evil, and in the end truly live such vibrant, optimistic lives.

After, Nick and I sit in the grass, staring at the hissing

steam that rises from the wreckage as the firefighters ensure that every ember is gone. I think we're both a little out of words, lost in our thoughts about our lives now set against the backdrop of what Richard and Ellen's lives were then.

"You okay?" I ask finally. Our faces are sooty, our limbs shaking from exertion.

He lets out a low, quiet whistle. "That was *intense*."

"I know."

"That wasn't even fiction, is the thing." He wipes a trembling hand down his face. "It blows my fucking mind that someone would have burned down that barn—someone's livelihood—just because some white folks didn't agree with what kind of love was going on behind closed doors. It's a miracle they both made it." He pauses. "So many don't."

I bend, resting my forehead on my arms. With the acrid smell of smoke still lingering on my skin I'm reminded all over again that this is bigger than a movie and the people who inspired it, and how the color of my skin means that I can empathize, but I'll never *truly* understand. "I'm sorry," I say, but the words feel insignificant. "It's sickening."

When I look up, he points at the smoldering remains of the replica barn. "You asked me why I wanted this role? It's amazing, okay, but I feel like people forget: shit like that *happened* and, honestly, still does. I want them to remember."

"They will." I lean my head against his shoulder. I truly adore this man. "This fire, in particular, actually did happen," I tell him. "The screenplay is about Sam's grandparents."

He turns to look at me. "For real?"

I nod. "I put it together a few weeks ago. His grandfather mentioned something about a barn fire when we first met. When we were shooting the scene with the men at the restaurant, it just felt so familiar. I confronted him and, yeah, it's based on real events."

"You met his grandfather?"

An uneasy wiggle takes up in my stomach, but I want him to know. Keep it simple, Tate. "Yeah. His name was Luther and he was pretty great. You're a lot like him, you know. Both constantly up to no good."

He laughs and wraps an arm around my shoulders. "See? I knew there was something bigger there. You knew his family."

"I didn't, really," I insist. "Just while we were in London."

Nick absorbs this, and then gives me a sly grin. "How old did you say you were?"

I think he's making the connection, or maybe I'm just being paranoid. "I *didn't* say."

A shadow looms over us both, and then I feel the warm presence of Sam settling into the grass on my other side. "How's everyone doing?"

It's the first time he's approached me and Nick together, the first time he's approached me at all as a friend. The realization makes me glow inside.

"I'm hot," I groan, and lie back in the grass. In a breath, I realize what I've done: lying down beside Sam in the grass, looking up at the sky. For a few tense beats, I'm begging him to not lie down beside me.

Thankfully, he doesn't.

"Man, I didn't know this story was a biography," Nick says.

"Loose," Sam says, "but yeah."

"Loose how?"

"They raised me," Sam explains, "but I left all that out."

"So this all happened before you came along?" Nick asks, and I assume he's gesturing to the site of the barn fire, but my eyes are closed now as I half listen to the two of them talk. Their conversation wanders from Luther and Roberta, to growing up on a farm, to Nick growing up in Houston, to how cold the night is turning.

"You think she's asleep?" Nick asks after a while.

I feel the heat of Sam's body as he leans over me, getting a better look. "Maybe."

I am, but I'm not. I'm drifting, half-aware, comfortably buffeted from the wind by Sam's body. It's a return to childhood and listening to adults I trust talk in those meandering, easy ways while I can dip in and out of consciousness. On top of it, the sensation of grass at my back and the night sky on my face pulls me back years to that easy sensation of being absolutely blissed out in love with Sam, and feeling safe and *known*. I want to live in that space just a little longer.

"I can carry her," Sam says.

A sharp ache slices through my sternum, and I sit up. "I'm awake. I'm good."

We stand up with quiet groans: sore joints from sitting on the ground too long out in the cold after an intense amount of physical exertion. Nick wraps his arms around my shoulders, kissing the top of my head. "You were good today, Tates."

I band my arms around his waist. "So were you."

"You were both perfect," Sam says, behind me. Tonight the three of us skipped steps, shot up the secret friendship path in Candyland. I have the sense that the bond of this shoot will keep for years.

"Come on." Nick breaks the silence. "I gotta be fresh for tomorrow."

I gently chuck his chin. "You'll be fine. Piece of cake."

Sam watches us, confused. "What's tomorrow again?"

"The sex scene," I tell him, and without waiting for his reply, I turn, calling out over my shoulder, "We're gonna be amazing again, Nicky. Good night, you two."

twenty-two

INT. MEYER FAMILY FARM, ELLEN BEDROOM — DAY

Ellen is in her room. The late-afternoon sun
filters through the window and washes the walls
in gold. Ellen is changing clothes. Her shirt is
unbuttoned. She's soaked and dirty from a hard
day's work. She's also angry.

She looks up at a knock at the door.

> ELLEN
> Come in.

Hat in hand, Richard starts to step inside but
stops when he sees that she's changing. He's
clearly flustered.

> RICHARD
> Oh—I'm—I'll come back—

With an impatient huff, Ellen pulls him into the room and closes the door behind them.

> ELLEN
>
> Don't be ridiculous. I have to get these off and get back out there. Just . . . turn around.

Richard turns to face the wall.

> RICHARD
>
> I see you've been running the tractor. I told you I could help.

Behind him, we see Ellen slip off her shirt. Her bare back is exposed, and we hear the fabric flutter to the floor.

> ELLEN
>
> I have, but I'm sure that isn't why you came up here.

> RICHARD
>
> I was in town and heard some people talking. They said your dad's worse. That nobody's seen him for a few weeks.

Ellen slips off her pants, the fabric sliding slowly down her legs. In the window Richard sees her reflection, all curves and strong, capable muscle. He bows his head, looking away.

> ELLEN
>
> I don't know why everyone can't mind

their own business. Jacob Hadley was
up here yesterday and had the nerve to
suggest I need a husband to take care of
things.

She steps into a pair of jeans.

RICHARD
I think people are just worried about you
being alone up here taking care of him.

ELLEN
Where were all these worried people when
Dad first got sick? When I had to take
care of him and everything else. Where
were they then?

RICHARD
Well *I* was in North Carolina . . .

ELLEN
You know I'm not talking about you.

RICHARD
But why not?

ELLEN
Why not what?

RICHARD
Why aren't we talking about me? I worry
about you too.

                          ELLEN
          I don't need you to worry about me.

                         RICHARD
          I know that. I know you don't need
          anything from me. I don't need anything
          from you, either. Doesn't mean I don't
          want you.

She stops buttoning her shirt. She turns to face
him.

                    RICHARD (cont'd)
          I want to give you everything.

                          ELLEN
          Look at me.

Richard slowly turns around. He takes in her
unbuttoned shirt and slowly meets her eyes.

                    ELLEN (cont'd)
          You sure I'm what you want? This? Here?
          You willing to take that on? I can't fall
          again and pick up my own pieces. I don't
          have it in me.

He takes a step forward. Slips her shirt off her
shoulders and lets it fall to the floor. We see
her naked back as she leans in and kisses him.

                        ★ ★

Two hours later, the knock that I've been dreading sounds at the hair and makeup trailer door.

Charlie tilts her head as she swipes a touch of powder under my eyes. "She's decent," she calls out.

I'm not sure *decent* is the right word, considering that under this robe I'm in nothing more than pasties and the world's smallest nude thong. I've been waxed and moisturized and airbrushed. Every scar and freckle has been painstakingly concealed, and this particular wig has been tousled just enough to look like I've spent the day in someone's bed. Which is unfortunately what I'm about to do.

The trailer opens and Devon's dimpled smile appears in the doorway. "You ready to do this?"

"Ready to roll around naked in front of a camera?" I ask. No point in putting it off. "Sure. Just your average Tuesday."

I once read that sex scenes in movies are just like actual sex, but with none of the pleasure and all of the awkward, fear, anxiety, and stress that come with it. They were not wrong. The good thing—if I had to pick a good thing—is that when done right, a sex scene can completely change a love story. It's when we're at our most vulnerable; when we let down walls and let another person see who we truly are. A lot of that rests on the actors' shoulders, but the director and crew factor in as well. They set the tone for the shoot and the scene, determine how close the shots are, and let us know when it's working and when it's not.

As a director, Gwen is known for being meticulous. The love scenes are no different. We know exactly how the scene will be blocked, how we'll move and what we want to come across on camera. I'm not looking forward to this, but at least we'll all be prepared.

On days like today, only essential crew members are present. As we return to the room that's designed to look like Ellen's bedroom in the farmhouse, I see Gwen, Liz, Feng, the camera operator, the assistant camera operator, the boom operator, script supervisor . . . and Sam. It never occurred to me that he'd be here.

I stop short but I needn't have bothered, because he's already headed my way. "I tried to grab you before you left earlier," he says immediately, expression tight with what I can only assume is panic.

I'm feeling a little panicked myself. Today will be hard enough, but knowing Sam will be here too? I mean, shit, we've just found some easy, solid ground. I'm not ready to be naked in front of him all day. "Sorry, I went for a run and then had hair and makeup." I bite my lip.

Why am I explaining myself?

"So, if you look at your contract you'll see I'm supposed to be here," he says. "But since my name wouldn't have meant anything to you before, you probably wouldn't have noticed. I tried to tell Gwen I wasn't needed but she said she'd prefer if I stay." He runs a nervous hand through his hair and then looks around before lowering his voice. "I didn't know what else to say without telling her too much . . ."

"No . . . it's fine," I say, exhaling a slow, steady stream. "Really. We're all professionals, and I mean . . . it's not like you haven't seen it all before. Though fourteen years of gravity takes its toll . . ." The joke lands harshly and creates a dead zone of uncomfortable silence.

"Right," Sam says finally.

Thankfully, we're rescued when Charlie comes over to check my makeup.

Her glare follows Sam as he steps away and takes his seat just behind Gwen. "What is he doing here?"

"His job." I close my eyes as she runs a brush over each of my lids.

"Well he better do his job in the dark corner over there. Behind a thick wall."

I look at her. "Charlie. Come on. He's not Satan anymore."

"Tater, you're going to be *naked* all day."

"Uh, yeah, I'm aware."

"You can't blame me for being protective. It's like when a friend breaks up with someone and tells you all the terrible things about them. They get back together but you're just supposed to forget about it all?"

"We're not— You know that's not what's happening here."

"Fine. But if I see him looking at your boobs, I'm going to beat his ass. I'm ride or die Team Tate here. That's *my* job."

When I turn back, Nick is watching us.

"Everything okay?" he asks, tilting his head as Trey makes some last-minute checks on his makeup.

"Just ready to get this over with."

Trey barks out a laugh and Nick reaches over to pinch my arm. "I can assure you that is the only time I've ever heard a woman say that to me."

★ ★

In the middle of some passionate thrusting, Gwen cuts and I have no choice but to stare up to where Nick is hovering—naked—above me. He's not really naked, of course. He's wearing a modesty pouch (a glorified penis sock) and has enough glycerin and rose water on his back to make it look like we've been at this for a long, long time. Which, frankly, it feels like we have.

A sheet covers my right breast, and Nick's arm blocks any view of the other. I'm at a place in my career where I can stipulate what I will and will not show. By contrast, Nick's entire ass is on display.

"Do you know what time it is?" I ask.

"I left my watch in my pocket and, as you may have noticed, I'm not wearing pants." For as awkward as it must be to have your junk in a sock and a pillow between you and the parts you're supposed to be convincingly fucking, Nick is still as easy to be with as ever.

"I meant, can you see a clock or a sun dial or something. All I can see from this angle is your gleaming chest."

He shifts slightly. "I can't see a clock, but I *can* see our screenwriter. And he does not look happy."

This piques my interest, and without thinking, I try to crane my neck and get a look for myself. Nick stops me with a gentle hand to my shoulder. If I move, the shots won't line up, and we'll have to do the scene all over again. I know this, but the idea of Sam's frowny reaction is throwing me.

"Oh?"

"Yeah, 'Oh,'" he says with a shake of his head. "You ever going to tell me what really happened between you two or should I continue with the most lurid version I can imagine?"

I'm saved for a few moments when Gwen calls for us to

pick up where we left off, for me to bend my leg and slide it up toward Nick's side, for him to kiss down my neck.

"That's right, that's right," Gwen calls out; her voice will be cut out later. "Arch your neck a little more, Tate."

"Yeah, give her what she's looking for, Tate," Nick whispers against my throat, his face hidden from view. "And tell me why Mr. Intense over there looks like someone just canceled his birthday."

The moan I give for the camera might be fake, but the way his words snag and hold my attention is completely real.

"I mean, I am playing his grandmother in this scene. I'm sure he's not *enjoying* watching this."

"Yeah, I don't think that's what this is."

I hate the jolt of adrenaline this gives me, because in what world does Sam have the right to be upset about any of this? And why do I care? *I'm working.*

We stop so a battery in the boom mic can be changed, and I stare up at the beams overhead. That's the way movies are: hurry up and wait. Hurry up and wait. It leaves way too much time to think.

Because there's that feeling again, the urge to break out of the box I've put myself in, the urge to rebel and tell Nick what really happened. "I told you, we had a fling when we were younger."

"And he's pissed a decade later."

"He's the one . . ." I pause, not sure how far down this track I intend to go. Nick is so easy to be with, so easy to confide in. Even now, he doesn't push, just wraps a piece of my hair around his finger and waits for me to continue—or not. Like it's my decision. Nothing about Sam has ever felt completely like my decision. But I've also been burned by spilling to a guy before and am not up for it to happen again, from lover *or* friend.

I lower my voice to barely a whisper. "Okay, complete vault here, Nick: Sam is the one who told the papers that I was Ian Butler's daughter. He sold the story and then just sort of vanished, and I didn't see him until that day on the trail."

It's a tribute to Nick's acting skills that he barely reacts. "Okay," he says, and gives the smallest tilt of his head. "That explains *a lot*. Wow." After a minute, he adds, "What a dick."

I straighten the leg that's hidden by the sheet, just to have something to do. I feel restless and uneasy. I don't exactly want to defend Sam, but a strange protectiveness builds in my chest.

"He had a really good reason for doing it," I say, "and I know that now, but it doesn't really erase the habitual rage from all the years I *didn't* know it."

"Makes sense." He glances up. "He's always looking at you. The man has *longing* in his eyes."

"No he doesn't. He has a wife. You've seen him go upstairs at the Comm House to call her every night. I'm sure it's just awkward for him to watch this."

Nick shrugs, unconvinced. "Whatever. Fuck that guy if he doesn't know what he missed out on—whatever his reasons. I don't care how nice he is now. Even if he were single, no way would you go for that again. Once bitten, and all that."

I go quiet at this, and Nick looks down at me.

"You know I won't tell anyone," he says quietly. "I know

I've been hounding you for the dirt, but only because your brand of quiet makes me mad curious. You can trust me."

I don't say it, but I know he sees it in my eyes. *I hope so.*

Gwen tells us we're ready to roll, and once Nick is moving over me again, I know I'm mostly hidden from the cameras until they move in for the tighter shots. I imagine how Nick looks from above, how the shape of me looks beneath the sheets, and wonder where Sam Brandis thinks he gets off being jealous, and why there's a tiny, glowing ember in me that needed that petty consolation that this isn't easy for him, either.

twenty-three

BY THIS POINT IN the shoot, the Ruby Farm staff seems pretty used to the nightly chaos caused by an entire cast and crew crowding around a campfire or taking over the dining hall in the Community House. In fact, many of them regularly join us. It's cold out tonight, so the crowd inside is enormous. Some of the permanent staff have hauled a pool table into the main room. Someone else found an old, dusty karaoke machine. A brave—or masochistic—soul has passed around a couple bottles of Patrón, and everyone appears to be taking swigs as the amber bottles wind around the crowd.

I have an early call so I stick to a little wine, not wanting to deal with a headache in the morning on top of everything else. I listen to the conversations happening in our little circle, chiming in when I need to, all too aware of Sam on the far side of the room.

I catch him watching me a few times, always looking

away the moment our eyes meet. He's sitting with Gwen and Devon, but he doesn't seem to be listening. And then I see it on the table between the three of them: my *Vogue* cover. The issue came out today; I completely forgot. They chose the Audrey Hepburn–style photo, the one that reminded me of myself, then.

I lift my eyes from the magazine on the table to find him studying me. Did he have the same reaction to the cover photo as I did? Did he read the profile, full of the same lies about my return to Hollywood that have always been told—never any mention of the man who, for better or worse, changed my life completely? Is that a flash of pain I'm seeing in his eyes?

It's hard to deny what Nick said—I knew Sam once upon a time, and his expression isn't completely without longing. Even so, he hasn't bothered to come over, to tell me what he thought of the scenes today, to be at all social. Maybe I was wrong last night on the grass—no bond was forged. I feel perpetually wrong about that.

When he stands, he doesn't do what I expect and head upstairs to make his nightly phone call to Katie. Instead, he heads toward the exit, and I feel an electric impulse to follow and poke at him. Maybe just to find a way to tell him to stop making this emotionally complicated for me. I don't want to want him anymore. I don't like the feeling that I would kiss him in a heartbeat if I could. This is the trouble with sets like ours: It's forced proximity, intense and constant. It makes the rest of the world fall away.

I wind my way through the tables and out the door, into the chill of the lawn outside. Sam's footsteps crunch on the gravel up ahead, and I have to lengthen my strides to keep up. Once we're far enough away from the Community House, I call out to him.

"Sam! Wait."

He turns around, surprised, but his eyes immediately turn wary. "Hey. What's up?"

"I was going to ask you the same thing." I reach forward, give him a gentle punch to the shoulder. "What's going on?"

He squints at me. "What do you mean?"

"Don't do that." Inside I'm all twisty. Am I reading him wrong? Am I projecting or seeing what I want to see? I'm trying to make things easy between us, why isn't he? "You've been weird since the shoot this morning."

At this, he winces and looks away, to the side. I hate how every little thing lately reminds me of the boy in the garden: the angle of his face, the set of his shoulders, even the cold air around us.

All I get is: "I'm sorry if I was weird."

"Can you at least tell me why? I mean, if it was awkward, you could have stepped out." The truth flows out of me. "You're making me feel like I did something wrong."

"You didn't."

I laugh. "Well, I know that, I'm just trying to figure out what happened."

He takes a breath that seems to draw in for ages. Finally: "I guess I'm having a bit of a hard time with Nick and everything."

I scrunch my nose, trying to puzzle this one out. "With Nick?"

Sam looks back at me. "Yeah. You and Nick. Watching

the scene today was hard." He laughs, raking his fingers through his hair as he looks away. "I realize it was a set. I mean, I wrote the fucking movie, right? But I just had this awareness that you were naked there. That he was—" He breaks off, cursing. "Just—God, I sound insane."

"You do, but say it anyway."

Sam returns his gaze to mine. "I was jealous. It seemed so real when you were kissing. And you kissed before, though you said it was nothing. Look. I know it's unfair."

"Unfair for like a million reasons," I agree, voice tight. I'll put up with a lot, but I won't be someone's mental cat toy.

A tree branch creaks overhead, and I'm aware of every second of silence that passes between us. I expected him to deny that anything was wrong. His honesty leaves me dizzy.

"I made my choice all those years ago. I get that I have to live with it. I'll do better," he says.

"What does that even mean? 'Do better'?"

"I'll try to keep my shit under control, is what I'm saying. I'll try to manage my jealousy."

"Oh my God," I say, angry now. "Please tell me you're joking. Aren't you *married*, Sam? Don't you have children at home? You don't get to go away for a few months and pretend to be heartbroken when you look at me acting out a sex scene *you wrote*."

His brows draw together, and the shadows emphasize each year that has passed between us. "Married?"

"Your wife? On the phone? I heard you talking to Katie. About the girls?"

His expression clears. "Katie is my ex-wife, Tate. *Ex*."

The ground drops out from under me. "Oh."

"All this time you thought I was married?"

I nod.

"We've been divorced for three years, but we're still good friends," he tells me. "She met a new guy a couple years ago and they just had twins. One of them isn't doing so hot, so she had to have heart surgery."

"Oh my God. I'm sorry."

"She'll be okay," he says, waving a hand. "She's a fighter."

I don't know if what I feel is relief or terror. Relief that Sam isn't married. Terror because Sam is single. "How long—when?"

Thankfully, he knows what I'm asking. "We met when I was twenty-nine. Got married pretty fast." He wipes a hand over his beard. "In hindsight I know I just wanted Luther and Roberta to see me settled. To not worry about me. We split up after three years."

I try to fit this new information into the story I'd created—the image of him with this perfect wife, perfect life—and I can't. I've been so angry for so long, and I'm not even sure what it was about anymore. About his life, or the shortcomings in mine?

"Apparently I wasn't a great husband." He pauses, narrowing his eyes. "She's a great woman, though, and I'm lucky that she still wants to be family. But if you had just asked me any of this before, I would have told you everything. Why didn't you ask?"

"What was I supposed to ask you?"

"Anything. About this wife you think I had. The daughters. If you'd just talk to me, we could avoid at least half our problems."

"Because your track record is so great," I say, pulse picking up. "Because protecting my feelings and my truths has always been at the top of your priority list."

"You told me to stay away and, other than to tell you how good you were at the role, I did. Every time we have a blowup like this, it's you seeking me out. You want the truth?" he asks, shoving his hands deep into his front pockets and leaning forward. "I *hated* seeing you in the grass with Nick. I hated seeing you in the bed today with him. I don't have any right, but I did. Every time you're near me I can't touch you, I can't pull you closer. I have to sit in it, stew in it. You're beautiful, and hilarious, and ambitious. You're still—" He cuts off, shaking his head. "I have to see what I had and what I gave up. But feeling bad for myself isn't how this works, is it? I made the choice." He takes a step away from me. "This is me living with it." He takes another step away. "I'll apologize a million more times, I swear, but just let me have a bad fucking mood tonight."

Sam turns and starts walking away. But he isn't walking toward the cabins; he's walking in the direction of the distant parking lot, where the long tractor trailers that brought up all the equipment are parked.

"Where are you going?" I ask, tripping several paces behind him. My feet are crunching through the gravel just as loud as his are; he has to know I'm behind him.

"My truck."

I stumble over a stick on the path that I didn't see. It's black out; nothing but stars overhead. "And then what?"

"Don't know."

We continue to march in stony silence, gravel crunching, crickets making a racket in the grass all around us. I could turn and go back to my cabin, have another glass of wine and try to process the fuck out of all of this: jealous Sam, guilty Sam, brilliant Sam. And the confused, relieved, hysterical anger bubbling up inside me. But I don't feel done with this conversation tonight.

So here I am, following him into the darkness.

What kind of doormat am I? We're weeks into this shoot, in the middle of nowhere, and he tells me he's sorry and he's jealous and that's it? Fourteen years and I'm ready to pick back up where we left off?

I hate myself, but I can't stop. There's a voice inside me saying, *This is how you scratch off the black crayon. This is how you find out what's underneath. You stay with it, you become dogged, you don't back down.*

Sam slows in front of a big red truck—a rental, I assume—and presses his hands to the hood, bowing his head. His fingers are so long, palms wide and muscular. I know those hands, know those fingers and the way they curl and grab. I know those arms, and that shoulder, and that neck.

"Did you decide where you're going?" I ask.

He turns. "No."

"Going to go with your default, then, and just take off?"

He growls, taking a step forward, coming right up close to me. "What do you want me to say, Tate? What should I say? That I'm trying to figure my shit out? That I'm trying to give you some distance? That I'm losing my mind being near you? All of it, okay? Fucking all of that is true. Being near you like this is completely wrecking me, and—what am I supposed to say?"

I take a step back, finally breaking, too. My voice echoes off the trucks all around us. "What do you want *me* to say? I'm happy you're single? I'm relieved you didn't break my heart for fun? How much do you want me to debase myself here? You hurt me! You never tried to find me, not in all those years. But here I am, following you into the goddamn parking lot, trying to find my way back to you!"

The heat radiating off his chest is intoxicating. I've had two glasses of wine, but it suddenly feels like twenty. He's so huge in front of me, this wall of man, of Sam. I lift a hand, rest it just above his solar plexus. His breath jerks, his hand comes around my wrist.

"Not like this."

"Like what?" I spread my free hand out. "In the middle of nowhere?"

"Not when you're pissed off."

"*I'm* the one who's pissed?" I say, laughing sharply.

He drops my hand and tilts his face up to the sky.

"I'm not pissed, Sam. I'm conflicted."

"That's better?"

It's another match ignited—he thinks he gets the only say in when or how this happens? So I step closer, slide my hand up and around his neck. I raise up on my toes and hover there, just an inch away from his lips. He smells like water, and wine, and the strawberries of dessert, and it's like a knife to the ribs to remember that day in the park, when he tasted like berries, and we ate them under a tree and then he laid me down so carefully in the bed, sliding a towel under me.

He's shaking, shaking under my palm at the back of his neck and my other hand pressed to his chest, feeling his heart under there. It's like a treasure in a fortress, this heart. I wonder what it's felt, how many times it's beat painfully enough to make him wonder whether he's dying.

He did that to me.

Am I really the only terrible thing he's ever done?

I shove him once and he stumbles back, landing against the side of the truck. My hands come to the front of his shirt, pulling the cotton into my fists, and I want to tear it off, dig my hands into the skin underneath and pull his heart free.

His hands come slowly to my hips, steadying me. "What do you *want*, Tate?" He lets his eyes fall closed. "You want me to leave? You want me to stay? I don't know the right answer here."

I don't want to have to say it. He's smart enough to figure it out. And I'm exhausted enough that the truth pushes past any barriers of mental self-preservation: I want him to *want* me. I want it to eat him up inside, like a cancer that can't be cured. I stand there, looking at him, watching his eyes open again and his expression go from indecision, to hesitation, to that melting of relief, and he bends in jerky, halting movements, as if he wants to give me time to change my mind.

His lips meet mine, so soft, just resting there, but it feels like I've been ripped open the way everything pours from me. He lets out a hoarse sound of relief, and I remember this, how it felt to stand on my tiptoes, to reach for his neck, to pull him down to me, wanting more and deeper, wanting that slide of his tongue and the way his groan felt like it came from a fairy tale, the giant begging for something precious.

His hands grip my waist, holding my hips to his thighs, and against my stomach he stirs, his teeth brush against my lip—deliberately, a gentle tug turns into a bite, and fourteen years of anger and unresolved hurt pour out of me. I have two fists in his hair, tugging his head to the side so that I can bite his neck. He cries out, wrapping one arm around me and lifting me roughly, flinging me to the side so he can open the back door of the truck.

He all but tosses me in, watching as I scoot back and he's a predator, or maybe I am, the spider luring him in here, hoping to give him something he'll never get again.

I want every wish he ever makes to be for this. A penny in a fountain. The first star. An eyelash. Eleven eleven. Just for one more time.

The door slams shut behind him, and he's too big for the space but he doesn't seem to care. On his knees, he slides the skirt of my dress up over my hips, pulls down my underwear, and looks at me like he wants his mouth just there, right there, but there isn't room for him to lay me down, stretch out between my legs.

Instead his hand comes to his trousers, unbuttoning, unzipping, and I'm there to help pull him free; and for the first time I can't hold the sound back, that sharp cry when I remember this, too. The weight and heat of him. The noises he makes, helpless but deep.

He's there, pulling my ass farther down on the seat,

closer to him, beneath him, and he tells me not to say a word, *a fucking word please don't say a word because I can't be in you and hearing you and feeling this.*

His desperate incoherence throws me. In the barely there light, when I look up I can see the angry red bite on his neck, the conflict on his face. He presses into my thigh, and we both fall still.

I am a girl made of a million questions. Or, maybe, just two: *Do you really want this? Or is this part of your penance?*

"Are you going to regret this?" he asks.

In truth, maybe. But it would wreck me to watch him back away right now, put himself together, and climb out of the truck.

"I'd regret it more if we stopped."

He ducks his head, chin to chest, and seems to debate whether this is good enough for him. But I want to touch. I unbutton his shirt, tiny button by tiny button, and spread it open, feeling the hard, smooth expanse of his chest. He is a continent, maybe even a planet over me.

Fingertips brush across his nipples, down to his stomach, and the muscles there clench under my hands. I trail a finger across the soft hair, and find him, making the decision for both of us, bringing him to me.

Sam's hips come forward, and he adjusts his position with one leg on the floor of the backseat and one wedged on the seat. He pulls my legs around him, and when I hear his shaking exhale, it sounds like the most exhausted kind of relief. Like succumbing to sleep on a battlefield.

"Tate," he says, and rests his head on my shoulder. "You don't know what you do to me."

I try to tell my body, *Focus on this, just here, don't remember, don't compare*, but it's hard because nothing and no one has ever felt like Sam. There isn't an army of men between then and now who've been this tall, this broad, this capable of blocking out the sky overhead or the grass beneath and just giving me nothing but him. There's never been another sensation like this, and it's impossible to not feel that, somewhere deep in that ancient part of my brain that stores up these perfect experiences and brings them forward when I get even a little whiff of them again. *See?* It says. *This is what you've been waiting for.*

But I'm not getting a little whiff, I'm getting everything. Sam is giving me everything, in deep, long strokes and his mouth on my neck, his hand on my ass pulling me up to him, onto him, and then he reaches between us, his thumb finding what it wants, and he circles, and circles, and I can see him moving in the odd hazy light, and can see his stomach growing tight and that's what does it for me, that realization that this feels good to him, and it feels so good and so fast that he's close and we barely started.

My back arches away from the soft leather of his seat and he rears up, bringing his other hand there, holding me while I fall. He tells me he's coming, saying my name again and again and when he finally does come, he makes a sound I've never heard before. It's a cry, muffled by my neck.

Then I hear nothing but crickets outside and the jagged push-pull of Sam's breath and mine. He stills, and then slowly shifts us so he's sitting and I'm on top. I think he wants to look at me, for me to look at him, but it's not that easy. I think looking right at him might make me crumble, so instead, I focus on his jaw.

His hands come up, cupping my neck. "You okay?"

"I'm not sure yet."

He leans forward, resting his mouth on my shoulder. "I admit I don't love that answer."

"I don't have a better one right now." This swirl of reactions is too big to process in this small space, especially when all I can smell or feel or hear is Sam.

His mouth makes a tender path from my shoulder to my neck, to my jaw. "I'd do anything to get you back."

"You never tried to find me. Even here, you've been so careful. I don't see you fighting."

"I figured it wasn't my right to try."

I close my eyes and lean forward, resting my forehead on the bulk of his shoulder. I can't exactly argue with that. If he'd pushed me, I would have shoved him away. And when he was cautious and distant, it felt like disinterest.

"I haven't been good for anyone else," he says.

"That makes two of us."

"Tate, come on, talk to me about this. Is there even a chance here? If there isn't, I need to know. This isn't just fucking for me."

"It isn't for me, either," I tell him.

He cups my face, turning me to him and kissing me, and it gives me an excuse to close my eyes. I am both relieved almost to the point of debilitation, and mildly nauseous—I was going to get up and leave in a perfect display of love-him-and-leave-him, and here I am, melting under his touch.

I push the thought away, unwilling to trip down the road of self-flagellation. I wanted this, wanted *him*, and here I am.

I can deal with the fallout.

"We're in the backseat of a truck," he laughs into a kiss, "but I don't want to leave. Not for anything."

And with this, Sam's just reminded me that he's still inside me, still half-hard. The single kiss melts into another, and I'm lost again, dizzy from the taste of him. His hands slide down over my shoulders, around my back to the zipper of my dress, and it's like we're doing everything backward—undressing after the sex—and soon he's exposed my back and then is sliding the fabric down my arms and pressing his mouth to my collarbone.

The words spill out of me: "I *am* okay. There's your answer. I'm better than okay." I push my fingers into his hair. "I missed you."

At this, his hands go from gentle to hungry, to desperate. I hold his head to me as he pulls my breast into his mouth, gripping the other in his palm, and we go from still to moving again.

twenty-four

IT'S UNREAL TO ME that, only a day later, we're already having the wrap party. It's been a surreal time warp from the moment Marco and I drove down the gravelly path to meet Devon to now. I've been so preoccupied with what happened between Sam and me last night that I'm disoriented when I see a few crew members walking past my cabin, dressed up instead of in sweaters and jeans.

The party is so loud I can hear it before the Community House comes into view. It's the golden hour, that elusive period of perfection when the sun is still above the horizon, but just barely. Scenes shot in this light always take my breath away, but the moment is so fleeting, the sky shifting from blue to sherbet colored too quickly for anything requiring multiple takes.

In fact, it seems to get darker with each step; the shadows growing longer all but disappear by the time the Community House comes into view.

Inside, the main room is packed, drinks passed around and plates piled high. Someone's been brought in to cater and even the craft services folks get to enjoy themselves.

My eyes scan the crowd. I'd like to play coy and pretend I'm not looking for him, but even I know it'd be a lie. I haven't seen Sam since we climbed out of his truck and he left me at my cabin at the crack of dawn, early enough to avoid an awkward encounter when Devon came knocking for my call time. Sam should be easy to spot—standing at least a head above everyone else—but I don't see him anywhere.

"I can only assume you're looking for me." It's Charlie, dressed in leggings and a long sweater, makeup as camera ready as always. She loops an arm around my shoulders and I lean into her.

"I mean, obviously," I lie, and we probably both know it.

A server passes with a tray loaded with sparkling pink cocktails, and Charlie snags two, passing one to me and looking out over the crowd as she takes a small sip. "I can't believe we go home soon."

I take the glass and try not to let on how my eyes keep finding their way back to the door, hoping to catch Sam walking in. "I know. It feels like we just got here."

"This gorgeous place. That lake. The endless possibilities for skinny-dipping and rolling around in the literal hay, and neither of us got any." She raises an eyebrow at me.

I down my drink a little too fast. "Yeah. About that."

She slowly turns.

"I sort of," I say, hesitating while I try to come up with the best way to say this. There isn't one. "I had sex with Sam. Last night."

Charlie's brows disappear beneath the sharp edge of her bangs. "I know I heard that wrong because there is no way *you*, of all people"—she leans in to whisper-hiss—"would sleep with a married man."

"Apparently he's not. I mean, he was but they've been divorced for about three years. The girls I heard him mention are hers, but with her new husband. Twins."

Knocking back the rest of her drink, she eyes me shrewdly before reaching for my hand and pulling me toward the door. "Follow me, young lady."

Outside, we head down one of the trails that lead away from the Community House. The sun is gone entirely now, and the light is soft and diffused, like the world is suddenly wrapped in a blue filter. Charlie pulls her sweater tight around her body against the chill.

"So," she says. "You and Sam. Hot dates." She narrows her eyes at me. *"Lovers."*

"Not exact—"

Charlie holds up a hand. "Tate Jones, do not lie to me right now, or so help me I will throttle you. You told me you slept with him. With *Satan.*"

I take a deep breath, knowing that straightforward is best with Charlie. "He was weird yesterday during the love scene, so I confronted him and asked what his deal was."

The protective glint in her eye is visible even in the fading light. We pass one of the small cabins where smoke rises from the chimney. The little rectangular windows glow against the dark wood. "He was jealous," I say.

"Huh."

"Yep."

"Wow." She lets this sink in for a few more steps, long enough to reach where the path narrows, running beneath the overstretched branches of two apple trees. Fallen leaves are pressed into the ground beneath our feet, and crickets start to chirp from the fields across from us. "What did you say?"

"I don't even remember what I said. I was yelling and then he was yelling and then we were at the truck he rented and—"

She stops. "A *truck?*"

In hindsight, I'm not sure how to explain how it happened. The decision was more sensation than thought, a bubble of longing that expanded in my chest until I couldn't breathe, couldn't think of anything but the feeling of his hands on me again.

Charlie looks away, down the trail toward the apple orchard. I don't need to ask what she's thinking—it's written all over her face.

Turning back, she searches my expression. Her cherry-red mouth—usually open in laughter or a cutting remark—is pulled into a firm line, her eyes tight with worry. "I just want you to be happy." Her features soften. "This makes me worry."

"I know." I take a breath, attempting to form words around the feeling that's been building inside my chest. "Despite everything that's happened, whatever was there . . . it hasn't changed. It was like being back in that garden, being eighteen again."

"You know I'm always on your side. If you think this is a good idea and will make you happy . . . I'll work on it." She shakes her head. "I can't believe you had sex in a parking lot."

Footsteps sound on the trail and we glance over as Dad comes into view, hands tucked in the pockets of his jacket.

"Hey, kiddo," he says, leaning to place a kiss against my forehead. "You two headed into the party?"

With a thumb over her shoulder, Charlie motions toward the muffled sound of Top 40 behind us. "As a matter of fact, I was just heading in. Need to find Trey and make a game plan for when we get home." She turns to me. "Tater, we're not done talking about that thing."

Dad frowns. "'Thing?'"

"Nothing—" I say, just as Charlie says, "A truck. Tate's thinking about buying a truck. Took it out for a test drive last night and everything. Said the stick shift stuck a little but the ride was goo—"

"Right," I cut in. "Thanks a lot, Charlie. Your advice was very helpful. Have fun inside."

Charlie waves over her shoulder and walks away with a little bounce in her step. I decide to unscrew all her foundation bottles later.

When she's gone, I turn back to Dad. "Were you going to the party?"

"I was."

"Okay, well." I motion for him to lead the way back down the small hill, and fall into step behind him. "Is Marissa coming?"

"She left last night, actually. Couldn't miss any more class."

"I liked her. She seems smart."

"She's lovely."

"When are you leaving?"

"Friday."

Awkward awkward awkward. "Yeah," I say. "Me too."

"How's your mom doing?" he asks. "I haven't talked to her in a few months."

"She's good. You know Mom. She'd be good anywhere."

He smiles. "That's true. I remember shooting this western when you were little, and you both came on set. It was awful. This tiny little ghost town in the middle of nowhere. Nothing for you guys to do. But I'd come back at the end of the day and your mom had found this old trough or something, had cleaned it up and made you a swimming pool."

"How old was I?"

"I don't know, three, maybe? It looked ridiculous, but you two were having the time of your life."

"I don't think she ever told me about that." But it sounds exactly like something Mom would do. Turning a trough into a swimming pool. Making an old playhouse into a chicken coop, complete with a tiny beaded chandelier. Taking something forgotten and making it new again.

"Probably doesn't remember," he says. "It was a long time ago."

We walk a little ways, the silence between us growing louder with each step. "The shoot went by so fast," I say.

"It did. I'm glad we decided to do this together. You did good, kid. I'm proud of you."

"I . . ." A hundred words collide in my head, and I can't seem to put any of them together. It's not that Dad hasn't complimented me before, it's that it's usually followed by something cutting, or there's somebody else there, an audience to witness his show of fatherly encouragement. I resist looking to see if there's someone up ahead or trailing behind; I know we're alone. "Thanks."

I can hear the music up ahead and it occurs to me I don't know when we'll see each other again. "Where are you off to next?"

"Home for a while," he says. "Not sure after that. I've been waiting to hear back on a few things."

"Maybe . . ." I start, my inner cynic holding me back, the hopeful daughter urging me forward. "Maybe we could do Christmas this year? Or Thanksgiving?"

He looks almost as surprised by my question as I am. "Oh, that sounds nice, Tate. Let me check with Althea and I'll let you know, okay?"

"Of course." I'm out of my depth and don't want to push. "I'll be home for a few weeks, so give me a call. Or a text, or—whatever."

We round a corner in the trail and the Community House comes into view, light from the wide porch spilling out onto the ground below.

"I wanted to talk to Gwen before I left, did you—?" he starts, motioning toward the party.

"No," I insist. "Go ahead. I need to find Nick anyway."

He smiles and ruffles my hair before heading toward the house. Not ready to go inside just yet, I follow a trail of stone pavers set into the ground, moving from each one until I reach a greenhouse near the back.

I'm just about to look inside when I hear voices around the corner.

"Was it surreal seeing all of this? Hearing actors say lines you wrote?" someone says, and I recognize one of the boom operators and a few others from the crew, and Sam.

"Yeah," Sam says, and then pauses. "I never thought we'd get this far, so I've just tried to enjoy every second. The casting was perfect."

"But didn't I hear you had a problem with Tate at first?"

I step closer, still in the shadows but able to see them now illuminated in a small cone of yellow light.

Sam waves him away, his movements a little exaggerated, and I wonder how many of those pink cocktails he's had. "No. She was perfect. I wrote it with her in mind."

I stop, feeling my pulse drop in my throat. *He what?*

"I've got a couple of films with her in mind," one of the crew jokes.

Someone adds, "Date with Tate," and everyone but Sam laughs knowingly.

I see Sam stand to his full height, chest forward as if he's going to address this with fists. I step fully out of the shadows, clearing my throat.

They all startle, straightening and tucking their beers behind their backs as if I'm their mom and just walked in on them watching porn.

"Hey," I say quickly, looking up at Sam, trying to communicate for him to *Be cool*. After a few mumbled words of greeting—and it's awkward because it's very clear I've overheard what they were saying—they quickly make excuses and head back toward the party.

When it's just the two of us, I pull Sam into the greenhouse. It's quiet inside, and the air is damp and scented with soil. The open panels let in just enough light for me to make out his expression. He's trimmed his beard, but even with it still there, I can see how tight his jaw is. I stand across from him in one of the narrow aisles.

"Hey you. Everything okay?"

"I think you stopped me from punching Kevin."

I laugh. "I think I did."

He bends, wiping a hand over his face. "Holy shit. That would have been bad."

"You can't do that," I say quietly. "If you want to do this with me, you can't get riled up about stupid shit like that."

He steps forward, crowding me against one of the metal tables. "I do. I won't."

I start to say more but he cups my face in his hand and bends, not kissing me yet, just breathing, sharing the same air. He smells like the cherries from his drink, warm and sweet, lips stained slightly pink. When he presses forward, he tastes like cherries, too. His hand goes around the back of my neck as he opens his mouth, soft and sucking.

There's no place to go, and he lifts me, setting me on the table and stepping between my open legs. I'm surrounded by flowers; the air is sweet and bordering on too warm, a contrast to the bite of cold coming in through the open door. He kisses me again, harder now with tongue and teeth, dragging over my lip and pulling me deeper.

Something is happening beneath the surface of my skin, bubbles of carbonation rising to the surface, electricity moving along a wire and threatening to short out.

"Do you want to try doing this?" he asks quietly.

"I do." My fingers twist in the fabric of his shirt. "But

you can't get involved every time people talk about me—because they will." I look up at him, back and forth between those mossy-green eyes. "But also, Sam, we can never speak publicly about London. If we're really doing this, we have to start over, completely. A clean slate. If it ever gets out that you sold the story to the *Guardian*, it will be all anyone talks about. Even years from now, every mention of our names will include a footnote about London and what you did. We'll never be able to move past it. They'll never let *us* move past it."

His eyes are wide, and he nods once. "No, that totally makes sense. I would never betray you again."

I press a kiss to the side of his mouth. "We're almost done here, and then we can figure out what we're going to do next."

He growls, grinning into a kiss before dragging me to the edge of the table, and along his body. With my feet safely on the ground, he takes my hand, bringing it to his mouth to press another kiss to my palm. It turns into a bite, and he moves his mouth up my arm.

"Stay with me tonight?" I ask.

He pulls my hips to him, bending to suck my neck. "How long do you have to be at the party?"

"Maybe another hour?"

Sam steps back reluctantly, and we step back outside. The temperature has dropped and the air is a shock after the heat of the greenhouse. Sam closes the door behind us and we turn, stopping short when we see who's standing there.

"Dad."

He's not even coming to a stop; he's completely still, as if waiting for us just on the other side of the hazy glass wall.

"Hey, honey," he says calmly, looking between us.

I'm tempted to take a step away from Sam, but I don't want to look guilty. My heart climbs up in my throat as I try to gauge where Dad could have been coming from and what he heard and why he would just be *standing there*.

If it ever gets out that you sold the story to the Guardian, I said, *it will be all anyone talks about. Even years from now, every mention of our names will include a footnote about London and what you did. We'll never be able to move past it.*

Finally, Dad cuts the tension, blinking back up to my face. "Did you find Nick?"

Shrugging, I manage an even "Someone said they saw him come around this way with Deb, but I didn't see them."

"I think they're back at the party." With a smooth tilt of his head, Dad turns his attention to Sam. "Sam, in case I don't see you before we leave, it's been a pleasure. Thank you for writing such a beautiful script."

What a weird thing to say. Admittedly, I don't know the nuances of his moods—and he's a great actor—but I can't read Dad's tone at all. Even in the moonlight, Sam looks pale, sobered by the possibility that Dad knows he's the one who sold us both out.

Even so, he manages to reach out and shake Dad's offered hand. "It was a dream to have you play the part. Thanks for being so welcoming on set."

Dad nods, and his smile goes from friendly to faint when he looks to me again. "Tate, I was looking for you because I spoke to Althea. Looks like Christmas is wide open."

My eyes widen, pulse slowing to a steady beat. I realize a part of me never expected a real answer, assuming he'd conveniently forget or leave Althea to come up with some excuse. I certainly never expected one so quickly. "Wow. That's great."

"We can talk later, but think where you'd like to go, okay? The house in Telluride would be great, or we could go somewhere else. We could even do your place and you could spend time with your mom, too. I haven't seen her in ages."

I can only blink. Non-passive-aggressive compliments, and now this?

"I'll see if she has plans. But we can do it wherever," I add quickly. "I'm not really picky. It'd be enough to just see each other."

The smile he gives me isn't the one I've seen on the covers of magazines or at award shows. This one feels different, adoring, and just for me. He leans down and kisses my forehead.

"It'll be fun," he whispers, and then straightens. "Well, I'm headed to bed. Sam, again, it was nice to meet you. I hope we see more of each other."

Sam tilts his head, smiling, and with a wave, Dad heads off.

The quiet seems to stretch around us as we watch Dad's retreating form. Finally, I let out a long, quiet "Fuuuuuuck."

"Do you think he heard that?" Sam asks.

"I definitely got that impression." Pressing the heels of my hands to my eyes, I tell him, "I'm going to have to figure out what he heard, but I can't do it here on set."

I feel Sam turn to look down at me. "You're spending Christmas together?"

"Looks that way."

"I don't know how to read what just happened." He gives the words a few seconds to dissolve in the space between us before admitting, "I don't think I understand your relationship."

I nod, blinking up to his face. "I don't think I do, either."

twenty-five

MY LAST FULL DAY at the farm begins with a blast of an alarm before the sun is even up.

The room is dark and cold; the fire inside the wood-burning stove has burned down to flickering embers. I pull the quilt up to my nose, and Sam mumbles sleepily at my side, looping a heavy arm across my waist and pulling me closer. I turn toward him, pressing my nose to the curve of his neck and melting into the heat of his skin.

It would be so easy to stay here. To take him in my hand and my mouth and my body, to make love again until I can't remember why I ever thought I shouldn't stay. But I can't. Everyone on the farm will be up soon, and nobody can see me leaving, not yet anyway.

When I finally manage to drag myself from his bed, I feel a little like Baby kissing Johnny Castle goodbye on the porch of his tiny cabin. The sky is still inky purple, and he uses a single finger to tip my face up to his. He kisses my cheek, my temple. I rest my head on his shoulder and tighten my arms around his torso.

"I have to talk to my dad today. I'm not sure he heard us talking, but I can't shake this feeling that he did."

He exhales against the crown of my head, pressing his hands to the small of my back. "Are you going to tell him? About the current us?"

"I don't know. We've never had that sort of relationship, but him agreeing to Christmas? Complimenting me? It's like we're in the Upside Down. Plus, he saw us holding hands."

"You know I'll go with whatever you decide. Just keep me updated."

"I will." I want to climb back up his body, head back inside, and lock the door. "Will I see you later today?"

He straightens to look down at me. "I was going to go on a hike with a few guys on the crew. Maybe we can grab dinner together?"

I lean back to see his face, to gauge whether he's serious. Things are still very much on the downlow between us; I might have to tell my dad, but I can't imagine meeting for dinner just the two of us is the best way to let people know.

He reaches up, brushes the back of his knuckles against my jaw. "Somewhere quiet. I'll grab something. We can sneak off to the lake and look at the stars. Nobody will be out then."

"Because it'll be freezing."

"I'll keep you warm. Come lie in the grass with me and look at the stars."

How could I resist that offer?

★ ★

Back in my own cabin, I pack most of my things so I'm ready for the early drive tomorrow. After I'm showered and dressed for the day, I follow the familiar trail to the Community House. I take each step up the gentle hill knowing this could be last time I do this. I've grown so used to this place—the smell of mud and grass, the sound of the cows and the roosters stirring me before Devon knocks on the screen door. It's hard to imagine leaving. But I'm excited to see Mom and Nana, to tell them both about Sam, to bring him home and see how this thing between us can grow.

Craft services has been replaced by the farm kitchen staff, and I indulge this last morning before I'm home and back on my strict diet and exercise regimen. Meaning: I fill my plate with blueberry pancakes and bacon. The dining room buzzes with a dozen different conversations—so many goodbyes happening today. Nick is near the fireplace, and I make my way through the tables and slide onto the bench across from him.

"Good morning, dear husband."

"Hey, wifey," he says around a giant mouthful of food.

I take in his skintight Adidas shirt, compression leggings, and running shorts. I motion to the bowl of oatmeal, and the two empty, syrupy plates in front of him. "Fueling up?"

"It's the last day with the studio trainer and I plan to take advantage of it. I've got to keep these farmer muscles, you know?" He winks at me over his coffee mug. I envy him his twentysomething metabolism. "You want in?"

I swallow a groan. My legs, back, arms, and neck are all tender from making up for lost time last night.

"As fun as that sounds, I'm going to pass. I heard about the *Big Bad Wolf* announcement, by the way," I say, referring to an article Charlie mentioned, a big-budget period horror film Nick's just been cast in. "Congratulations. You headed there next?"

He nods as he lifts his napkin to his mouth. "Vancouver. What about you?"

I reach for the bottle of syrup and drown my pancakes. "Nothing for a few months. I wasn't sure how I'd feel at the end of the shoot, so I gave myself some breathing room until after the holidays."

"That'll be nice. I'm assuming you won't just be sitting around. At least not alone . . ." he says meaningfully. At my confused expression he adds, "I saw you and Sam the other night."

My eyes widen. "You . . . what?"

When Nick bursts out laughing, I realize I've just given myself away.

"Relax, Tate," he says, smile lingering. "*Walking*. I saw you two walking. Jesus, what did I miss?"

I shrug, grinning guiltily and trying to get my pulse under control. "Nothing. I mean—I can't imagine you'd have seen anything scandalous."

He laughs. "Sure you can't."

I feel the tips of my ears get hot, and he shakes his head, smiling. He scoops up a bite of oatmeal and looks at me over the top of it. "I assume this means you got everything straightened out?"

When I don't answer right away, he leans in, voice quieter now. "For what it's worth, he seems to genuinely like you."

"I know." I slide the bottle of syrup closer, finger where the edge of the label has started to peel away. "He's not married after all. That was me eavesdropping and jumping to conclusions. We've decided to try, you know . . ." A burst of confetti goes off in my stomach at the idea. "But it's . . . complicated."

"Your history."

"For one, yes. My dad, if he ever found out about what Sam did, might be harder to deal with."

"But if you're willing to forgive him, that's all that really matters, right? I'm assuming Ian would be pissed at first, but his relationship with you is worth more than that. Besides, if Sam was the one who talked to the press all those years ago, then he's the reason you and Ian have a relationship now. He'll get over it." With an easy shrug, he finishes off the last of his oatmeal.

But would he? I think about seeing him outside the greenhouse, the way his eyes seemed so flat, his lip curled as we stepped out together. Was it something as simple as my estranged father being jealous that there's clearly a man in my life, or did he hear? I have no idea how he'd react to that history. Would he understand Sam's motivations and why I've agreed to give him another chance? And if not, how would that make me feel? Now that things seem to be changing for the better, am I willing to risk a good relationship with Dad for a chance with Sam?

Or am I just projecting my fears that I'm making a terrible decision? No matter how good things are with Sam, I can't completely escape the nagging thought that going back to him makes me mildly spineless.

I blink back to the table when Nick stands, stacks his plates together, and sets the empty bowl on top.

"You heading out?" I ask.

He checks his phone out of habit, and laughs when he sees that—of course—there's still no signal. But our brains are already detaching from this place. His unconscious gesture reminds me that tomorrow I'll have reception and Spotify and texting again. I could weep.

Nick slips his phone back into a zippered pocket on the side of his shirt. "Listen, you have my numbers. Use them if you need someone to listen, or talk to, or hell, even if you just want to hang. I'm going to miss you, woman."

Nick rounds the table, and I stand, wrapping him in a warm hug. A pang of sadness slices through me. After weeks here, the end really seems to have snuck up on me.

"I was right about one thing," he says, looking down at me. "You were definitely fun. And if I don't see those side-kicks of yours before I head out, tell Charlie and Trey it was good, all right?"

I lean into him again. "I will. Take care of yourself, okay? I can't wait to work together again." And I mean it.

He winks and bends to pick up his things. "See you, Tate."

I watch him drop his dishes at the kitchen and say good-bye to the staff before I take my seat again. My food sits mostly untouched in front of me, but I don't have much of an appetite anymore. I feel a bit drained all of a sudden. The most intense role of my life, the bubble of this set, the turnaround of the last few days with Sam . . .

I dump my garbage and set my dishes on the counter, thank the staff for everything, and head for the door.

"Hey, kiddo."

"Hey, Dad."

Impeccably dressed and handsome as ever. His jeans are perfectly worn, his thick sweater the same whiskey color as his eyes. "I was looking for you."

Anxiety sends a flash of heat down my neck. Did he agree to Christmas plans without really thinking it through, and now he's come up with some excuse?

"Hey. Yeah, I was just headed to find Charlie," I say, pushing open the swinging door. "Wanna sit outside for a few?"

"Actually, I came to see if you wanted to have lunch."

I wince. "I just ate."

He smiles, and I try to compare it to my catalog of Ian Butler Smiles to figure out if this is one the world has never seen before. "We could drive into town first, walk around? Spend a little time together before we head home."

I glance around the dining hall. Nobody is watching us; this doesn't seem to be for show.

"Sure," I say, facing him again. "Let me go grab my purse?"

The drive to the restaurant is quiet. He suggested having the driver take us, but I talk him into letting me drive his sleek black Tesla. Dad drums his fingers on his knees, staring out the passenger window. We spend the first five minutes of the hour-long drive with a tinny country station covering the heavy silence.

But finally Dad breaks the ice. Thank God, because I had no idea how to. He talks about his house in Malibu (he's getting new windows this year), the struggle of owning two homes ("It's the maintenance that'll kill you"), and how he'd read a script for a new superhero film, but they'd decided to go with someone "edgier" (my read: younger).

Driving gives me something to do, and I think I *ooh* and *ahh* in all the appropriate places, happy to let him talk because it means that I don't have to, but also because even after all these years, I'm still needy enough to want every little piece of information I can get.

We park in the center of town, but quickly realize that strolling around in daylight is not going to be possible. We get stopped for an autograph before we've even gotten out of the car. Instead, Dad enters the address to the lunch spot in his GPS, and we navigate to a sweet white farmhouse with a red door. A wooden sign displays the name Trillium Café.

"Althea told me to take you here," he says in a way that makes me preemptively sympathetic for Althea in the event that this restaurant turns out to be only mediocre.

"It looks cute." In the distance, the sky has grown gloomy, with clouds creeping over the tips of the evergreens and resting heavily on the shingled roof.

But inside it smells like fresh bread and wood polish. A woman with a long braid swallows her reaction admirably and leads us to a booth toward the back of the main dining room. A couple turns in their seats as we pass, and I give a small wave and smile.

Our booth extends out from a window overlooking a wide yard of unruly grass and, farther back, a thick line of pine trees. It's breathtaking.

Dad frowns down at the menu. "I want gnocchi." His frown turns into a smile when he looks up at me. "I'll probably order a salad."

My laugh is too loud. "Gnocchi is my favorite too."

"Is it?" His smile flattens, and I sense that I'm trying too hard.

"Excited to get home?" I ask.

"Sure." He scans the menu one more time and flips it closed again. "I had some work done in the backyard. I'm excited to see how it turned out."

A waitress fills our water glasses, lists the specials of the day, and then makes sure to mention which of Dad's films is her favorite.

He grins brightly at her and leans in as if to confide. "That's my favorite, too."

She's beaming. Dad orders wine, we both order food, and once she's gone, he rolls his eyes. "I judge everyone who tells me *Cowboy Rising* is their favorite. If you like disjointed trash, I can't help you."

Wow. I bite my tongue and squash my inclination to remind him that most of his early career is based on "disjointed trash."

"Does Marissa live nearby?" I ask instead.

He blinks up to me over the rim of his water glass. "What?"

"Marissa," I repeat. "Does she live near you?"

He takes a sip of water. "Oh. Yeah, she has an apartment near school, but she usually stays at my place." He winks and I don't know why, but it's a little gross. "More space."

"So things are serious between you two?"

The surprise registers on his face; I've never asked about girlfriends like this before. The waitress comes with our salads and the wine, giving him time to either formulate an answer or change the subject when she leaves.

But he doesn't dodge the conversation like I expected. "I'm not sure I'd say we're serious," he says. "She's finishing her degree and . . . we're good friends."

Something snags in my thoughts, a bite of curiosity I've never given space before. "Why do you think you never remarried? You and Mom broke up so long ago."

If anything, he seems to have expected this follow-up. He answers without hesitation. "I don't think there's one specific reason. Relationships are hard in this line of work. The schedule can be hectic, and it's hard to know what someone's true intentions are." He points his fork at me. "Not that I need to explain any of that to you, of course."

What on earth does that mean? I weigh my next words carefully.

"Most of my relationships have been for PR anyway," I admit. "Always seemed easier that way."

"Yes and no." He takes a bite, chews, and holds my gaze as if he wants me to know he's not done making this point. "Both have their drawbacks, but it's probably easier when someone at least understands how the business works."

"Speaking of . . . I wanted to talk to you about something."

Dad picks up the salt and pepper, and looks at me expectantly.

"I'm seeing someone."

"Really? Do I know him?"

My palms grow sweaty, and the hair on the back of my neck stands up. Is he being coy? "It's Sam, Dad."

Despite his flawlessly administered Botox, his brows

disappear into his hair. "The screenwriter?"

Maybe he didn't hear us last night after all. Maybe it didn't strike him as odd that we came out of the greenhouse together. Maybe I've just confided in Dad unnecessarily.

I nod, bending to take a bite of my salad to avoid his eyes. The more I chew it, the more the crouton in my mouth feels like sand. When I swallow, it turns to glue.

Dad sits back in his seat and stretches an arm over the seat beside him. He really does look surprised. And if I'm not mistaken, completely tickled. "So I *did* walk in on something last night," he says with a grin. "Very interesting." He leans forward conspiratorially. "You've never talked to me about boys before."

This makes me laugh. "I'm thirty-two. He's thirty-five. He's hardly a boy."

He grins, eyes crinkling warmly. "You're my kid. It'll always be *a boy*."

"And I guess . . . I mean, we've never really talked about this kind of stuff before. Like, life stuff."

He hums quietly. "Life stuff." He leans forward, forearms propped on the table, the weight of his attention solely on me. "So tell me, to use your words, is it serious?"

"It might be, yeah. He's really . . ." I feel my cheeks warm and bite back a smile. "He's amazing, and smart, and I think I fell in love with him the moment I read *Milkweed*."

In a hot flush, I think I want to tell him everything—but I don't. Maybe one day, when things are really solid between us.

It's crazy, but for the first time I have hope.

★ ★

When the waitress stops by to check on us, Dad reaches for the bill before she's even placed it on the table. He holds up a hand when I protest. "You are not paying for your old man's lunch."

He tosses down his card, and I catch Althea's name on it. *Smart,* I think. People would be stupid enough to take a picture of Ian Butler's credit card and post it online.

We're stopped three times on our way to the door, by people who've clearly been patiently waiting for us to pass back through the room.

I knew you were filming something, but I had no idea you were so close!

I have loved you since Cowboy Rising.

How are you even better looking in person?

Dad is eating it up.

I take one last look at the menu, wondering if I should pick up something for my picnic with Sam tonight. I imagine the two of us stretched out on a blanket, looking up at the stars, curled into each other's arms to stay warm.

A flash of movement catches my eye and I lean to the side to see out the window, immediately wary. A photographer. Not unexpected, since we aren't exactly trying to stay hidden. I'm sure Dad will be annoyed that I talked him into letting me drive instead of taking a car and driver, but there's nothing to be done about it now.

He finishes signing an autograph, and I place a hand on his arm. "Just a heads-up that there's a photographer outside."

"Not a problem," he says. "Was bound to happen sooner or later, right?"

"Guess that's what I get for traveling with Ian Butler. It's like you're even better looking in person," I tease.

With my head down, I take Dad's offered arm and step outside. Voices call out to us, and it's not just one photographer, it's two now, calling for us to look up, to give a couple words, a smile. I can feel Dad beside me, standing straight, and a quick glance at him tells me he's grinning happily.

But the glance at him also shows a group of photographers jogging around the side of the building.

There's no longer just two of them; there are at least twenty.

Time shifts. I'm eighteen again instead of thirty-two, and we aren't in front of the quaint farm-to-table restaurant, we're in the circular courtyard of the London Marriott County Hall. Faces are hidden behind giant cameras and zoom lenses; microphones are hoisted up and shoved toward me. The questions seem to come from everywhere.

Tate, is S. B. Hill Sam Brandis, the author and screenwriter?

Is Sam Brandis the same boy you met in London?

What does it feel like to be reunited with the man who sold you out all those years ago?

"Tate! Tate! Over here!"

Ian, what is your relationship with Sam? Are you aware of their past?

Tate!

We've only been here for an hour—how did they get here so fast?

Their voices call out, sharp and bright, and the single

question is bulleted at me again and again from a dozen places: *"Tate, who is Sam Brandis?"*

I'm frozen, staring at the mob in complete shock.

Dad wraps an arm around my shoulders. "She doesn't have any comment, but you all enjoy the rest of your day. Stay safe."

Cameras flash in a manic staccato and Dad ushers me toward his car, helping me in the passenger side. He strolls around, waving amiably, shaking his head to indicate he's not answering either. "You know how this works, guys," Dad says, opening the driver's-side door. "We know you're just doing your job, but this isn't how you get answers."

He gets in beside me, behind the wheel.

"Tate!" someone shouts. "Is S. B. Hill the same person who sold your story when you were eighteen? Is it true that you were lovers and he betrayed you?"

It takes everything I have to stare straight ahead, not give a single reaction that can be used on the cover of a tabloid.

Dad pushes the button to start the car and then looks over at me. "You okay, cupcake?"

I am not okay. I am stunned to the point of numbness.

None of this makes sense. "How in the world did they know about Sam?"

"You know how these guys are," he says, pulling away from the curb slowly, careful to not hit any of the reporters still leaning in, hammering questions through the windshield. "They know everything."

"I know but—" Once we are half a block away, I bend, putting my head in my hands. My mind races, inundated with the static of voices, the clicking of cameras and bodies chasing after the car, angling for the perfect shot or sound bite that will get the highest price, the most clicks.

Did Nick do this?

Nick.

I feel like I'm going to throw up. I trusted him.

When am I going to learn?

I groan, leaning my head back against the seat. "This is such a fucking mess."

"It'll be okay."

I glance over at him. "I'm so sorry. I . . . I should have told you. I just don't know how they found out. I think it was Nick who—"

My words dissolve away. Dad hasn't asked me what this is about. He hasn't registered a bit of surprise.

"Tate, it's going to be fine." He reaches across the seat to squeeze my leg, before returning his hand to the wheel. "You've been doing this a long time. You know how the press is."

A mile or so flies by and he sings quietly along with the radio. My mind spins, trying to piece this together, to figure out what is happening. I can't imagine Nick calling the press and sharing this. He has nothing to gain and so much to lose by betraying me.

I look at my father again; he's so calm.

"Did you hear me last night?" I ask, trying to mask the tremor in my voice.

"You know I saw you, we already talked about that at the restaurant."

"Yes, but did you *hear* me? Me and Sam. Were you listening to us talk about London?"

He tightens his grip on the steering wheel. "Kiddo, I

told you, it's fine. No press is bad press. This will bring Sam more attention and will be great exposure, not only for the film, but for all of us." When I don't immediately reply, he glances quickly at me, then back at the road. "Imagine the headlines. People are going to be fighting in the streets to hear this story." Another glance. "Can you imagine the buzz when they see the three of us together?"

There's a hint of glee to his voice that actually makes me nauseous. Everything he said, every bit of progress I thought we were making, it was all a lie.

"Dad, that's all anyone is going to be able to talk about," I say quietly. "With me and Sam, forever."

He laughs, and it's a genuine burst of sound; true amusement. "Honey, seriously? Forever? Please don't tell me you're that naive. What you should be thinking about is how to make it last as long as it can." He holds a finger in the air, emphasizing his point. "Listen to me on this. The only sure thing in this business is that you'll have to fight harder every goddamn year and you can only count on yourself. If you want to stay relevant, you have to make opportunities wherever you can, and this is a gold mine, Tate." He takes a deep breath and lets it out slowly. "A gold mine."

In a way he's right: Tonight, Ian Butler's name will be on every gossip show and probably trending on Twitter.

I finally did something right in his eyes, and he only had to sell me out to get it.

twenty-six

WE SLOW AND ARC around the final curve leading to the farm, and my throat constricts. For the last quarter mile of the narrow two-lane highway leading to the humble gates of Ruby Farm there is a cluster of vans, cars, and photographers parked along the side of the road.

Dad sits up straighter in the driver's seat, eyes focused. "Ready?"

I gape at him. This is déjà vu all over again. Only this time we're not pulling up to Nana's house on the river with reporters and paparazzi cluttering the tiny pothole-strewn street. And it's not Marco beside me, it's Dad.

Dad's car is mobbed as he slows to make the left turn into the farm. Cameras are swiveled and aimed, mics extended. Putting on a pleasant smile, Dad turns up the radio as we pass, trying to block out the shouts, but it just makes everything feel more chaotic: the shouting of photographers mixes with the blasted, raspy voice of Lucinda Williams fittingly telling all these people she's changed the locks on her front door.

Photographers press up against the car. Dad can only go about two miles an hour because the one thing that could make this scandal worse is hitting a photographer. I put my head down against the flash of cameras, breathing deeply between my knees and trying to anticipate what will face us inside the gates. Is it possible that Sam hasn't even heard yet? Could I be so lucky to walk into a sweetly oblivious scene on the farm, with everyone still blissfully cut off from Wi-Fi?

Someone bangs on the window, startling me enough that I look up. The flash lingers in my eyes long after they've taken the photo, but I know it's the money shot: Me, eyes wide, mouth agape, looking directly into the camera and appearing as frazzled by all this as they want me to be. In general, I'm used to this: the mania of photographers at premieres, catching me running errands, at any publicized event. But I'm not used to *this*. This is a true invasion of my life, not the coordinated response to a bit of intel dropped by Marco or his contacts. This bloodthirst is completely beyond my control; my heart jackhammers inside my rib cage.

Next to me Dad offers the occasional awkward wave, but his friendly smile has slipped into more of a grimace. Maybe he's worried they'll scratch his paint. Maybe it's that here in the car he can't charm the photographers into getting his good side—an angle that makes him look younger and taller. I'd like to think that he's having second thoughts about whatever it is that he's done, but know that's not the case.

We manage to get through the gate, it swings shut behind us, and I barely get a deep breath in before my stomach sinks along with the fantasy of an oblivious crew: Marco is already here, waiting in front of the Community House. He jogs down the front steps as soon as he sees us and hovers beside my door before we've even come to a full stop.

"Would it kill you to take your phone?" He helps me up, already in rescue mode, and begins leading me toward a black SUV parked a few yards ahead, the engine idling quietly. "Charlie is packing your things. I've—"

"Slow down. Marco, what is *happening*?"

He glances over my shoulder at Dad. "You tell me."

Dad squints against the bright gray sky. A tense moment of silence passes between the two men and I look away, trying not to freak out too much. A few members of the crew loiter on the steps, watching us without trying to look like they're watching us. I don't see any sign of Sam.

"We were having lunch in town," Dad explains, "and when we came out, the parking lot was full of photographers. They were asking us about Sam, and Tate, and her trip to London when she was a teenager. No idea how they found us."

Marco nods slowly. "A mystery."

I quickly jump in, nodding at Dad as if we're telling the same story. "They came out of nowhere."

Marco's gaze swings to me, and I blink over to him,

hoping he catches on that we need to just play it cool here. Marco doesn't have to get along with Dad, but I do. The press *loves* my father. I mean, shit, he weathered the scandal of cheating on his wife and abandoning his only child with barely a scratch. And now he's slipped this story to the press, deciding when and how it's going to break. He has all the information; he has every single one of the cards in his hands.

Regardless of what he's done to me, I can't alienate him.

I need him on my side, at least until I can come up with a plan.

"We're going to need to brainstorm some damage control in the car," I say. I look back at my father. "It sounds like we'll all be heading out soon, so I'll reach out to Althea about Christmas."

Dad's confident smile returns. "Sounds good, cupcake." He leans in to kiss my cheek and then offers his hand to Marco.

Out of nowhere, hot, betrayed tears prick at my eyes, but I quickly blink them away.

"Marco," Dad says, "it was nice seeing you, as always."

"Likewise." Marco and I watch as Dad makes his way back to his Tesla, small puffs of dust kicked up by his feet. I assume he'll just send someone to the farm to pack up his things; he has more important things to do than take care of a suitcase full of clothes. With a final wave and his trademark smile, he pulls the car around and drives back down toward the gate.

The subsequent silence is heavy.

"I'm sorry, Tate," Marco says finally.

"It's just business," I tell him. "I should be used to it."

"No, you shouldn't be."

Shoulders sagging, I feel the enormous weight of everything happening. "I know you want to jet, but I need to talk to Sam."

He stops me with a hand around my arm when I've only taken one step down the path. "Tate . . ."

The swell of dread rises higher and higher in my throat. Not again. Please. "He's gone, isn't he?"

Marco looks ten years older. "Gwen put him on a plane."

"Did he leave a note or say anything?"

Sensing my impending panic, Marco takes a step forward. "He didn't, Tate, but honey, I need you to listen to me."

"I don't," I say, beginning to feel light-headed. "I don't understand what's happening. He just left?"

Marco places a hand on each of my shoulders, and bends to meet my eyes. "We'll go over everything once we're on the road, but here's what I know right now. I got a call from one of my guys this morning saying he'd received an anonymous tip, and a few others were already headed here. They're also staked outside your place, Nana's house . . ." He pauses, swallowing. "And Sam's farm."

My eyes snap up to his. "In Vermont?"

"I'm sure they're already talking to his neighbors, his ex-wife—"

"Her baby just got out of the hospital," I tell him.

Marco nods. "Tate, I had to call Gwen. This is a multi-million-dollar film, and one of the biggest scandals in Hollywood has just been dropped in the middle of it. This shit is like candy to these guys"—he lifts his chin toward the front gate where the photographers are undoubtedly still waiting—"and the studio needs to be ahead of it. I'm sure you have at least a dozen messages by now—something you'd know if you had your damn phone with you." Frowning, he tells me, "Sam was gone before I got here."

"Marco," I say, and the idea that hits me feels so terrible, it makes my hands grow immediately cold. "You don't think Sam had anything to do with it, right? Calling the press? Like, we agree this was all Ian."

"We agree it was all Ian." His mouth turns down into a grim line. "I know that doesn't make it any easier. From what Gwen told me, Sam was as shocked about all this as any of us. He's going to go retreat to his support system, and you need to go home to yours. Your mom flew down about an hour ago. She'll be at your place when you get to LA."

I take a few seconds to press the heels of my hands to my eyes. I don't know what his support system looks like. His ex-wife is going to have her hands full. Roberta and Luther are gone. Does Sam even have a manager? This is going to be a pain in the ass for me, but it is going to be brutal for him, and he's going to need all the help he can get.

I know this, and I keep repeating it over and over, but when we reach the Oakland airport almost three hours later and I still haven't heard from him, my stomach feels like a hard, sour pit. Everything's a mess. Between the last-minute flight, the stress of knowing this story is out there and the message is careening out of control, and the chaos of the press—there's so much happening. Maybe his phone is being inundated. Maybe he just turned it off. Maybe he doesn't have my number—why would he?

Maybe it's going to take a few calls to find me, and maybe he assumed, like I should, that we'll figure it all out when the dust settles.

★ ★

After the cabin at the farm, my house feels enormous and sterile. The art I used to see as minimalist and clean just looks lonely on the expansive white walls. My living room— filled with white furniture I once thought of as inviting and cloud-like—just seems overly precious; not anything some- one could actually collapse on at the end of a day.

Even my bedroom is too big, too empty, too impersonal.

Oddly, just imagining Sam here with me—stretching out long and muscular on my bed, reading on my couch in socks and sweats, whistling while he cooks dinner at my massive stove—makes this house feel incrementally warmer. For the first time in my life I get it: home isn't always a space; it can be a person.

I turn and stare out the window while Mom folds laun- dry on my bed.

"Will you still see your dad for Christmas?" She smooths one of my shirts on the bedspread, folds it into perfect thirds, and places it on top of the stack.

I pick at the hem of my sweatpants. "We left the farm as if everything was okay but . . . I don't think so."

She gives me a sad smile. "I'm sorry, hon."

With a groan, I fall back against one of the pillows. The cotton is cool against the back of my neck. "I don't really know why I'm surprised."

"Because he's your dad. He should be better than that."

I shrug, feeling oddly numb. "Yeah, but he's always shown me exactly who he is, and I just never want to believe it." I give myself to the count of ten to feel sorry for myself before I sit up, crossing my legs. "I might have a shitty dad, but I have a fantastic freaking mom. Some people don't even get that. I'm not complaining."

Mom gives me a sweet little grin and leans forward to press a quick kiss to my forehead. "If I hadn't met him, there wouldn't be a *you*. It's hard to regret it, but I'm sorry that you have to deal with the same egotistical jackass I left all those years ago. Heaven forbid he grow up a little." Straightening again, she reaches for another shirt. "Have you talked to Nana?"

Oof. Guilt shimmers through me, and I shake my head. "I'm worried she's going to give me a mountain of I-told-you-so's and a prolonged silent treatment."

"I don't think so. I think she's worried about you, but in typical Mom fashion, she hasn't wanted to talk much about it because you know as well as I do that she isn't one to relish the I-told-you-so's."

I know Mom is right that Nana doesn't *relish* it, per se, but it would still be first thing on her tongue. She barely forgave me for London. Her disapproval was as quiet as Nana herself, but it's always been there—in the slight angle away from me when my career comes up or the long exhale and slowly raised coffee cup to her lips when a trailer for one of Dad's films comes on the television.

"This is going to make a mess for her, too," I say, and then groan, falling back against the pillow again. "People are going to come into the café again and ask her for pictures.

There's nothing Nana hates more than covert selfies people take with her in the café."

Mom laughs at the image of this. "Well, she needs to retire anyway." She nudges me off the bed. "She came down here to see you, so go talk to her. And go eat something," she calls after me. "Life goes on."

★ ★

Charlie is sitting on my kitchen counter, eating a piece of the blackberry pie Nana brought down from Guerneville. Other than the iPhone near Charlie's hip, it is an image so immediately familiar it's almost easy to forget that we're thirty-two and not sixteen.

I look out the window with a view of the long, immaculate driveway. The entrance is blocked by a fifteen-foot-tall iron gate, and surrounded by trees and shrubbery, but I can still see a few photographers pacing just on the other side. I count four of them. One looks like he's eating an apple. Another is telling a story, gesticulating wildly. They're chatting so casually; they're more like coworkers hanging out in a break room than paparazzi stalking me.

"They still out there?" Nana asks from the kitchen table. I glance over just as she straightens the already-neat rows of playing cards in front of her.

"They'll hover for days." Charlie groans around a bite of pie.

I shake my head, wanting to refute this, but my words come out thin and reedy. "I bet they'll get bored and leave soon."

Nana peers at me over the tops of thick glasses as if to say, *Do you think I was born yesterday?*

Sensing the tension, Charlie hops off the counter. "I'm gonna shower." She plugs in her phone, flipping it facedown. It occurs to me she's been glaring at it off and on. Whatever she's seeing, I'm pretty sure I don't want to know. "Let me know if something happens," she says on her way out.

Reaching for the kettle, I fill it with water and turn on the stove. "Nana, do you want some tea?"

"I'll have tea if you'll stay away from that window and come sit down."

I take the seat next to her.

"Where's your mom?" she asks.

"She was doing laundry," I say. "Most of it's already washed, but you know how she is."

Nana scoops the cards together and shuffles them between her hands. These are the hands that taught me how to make pies, that put on Band-Aids after I fell and helped me learn to tie my shoes. They look so different now than they did then. Her hands used to be smooth, strong, and capable. Now her joints are swollen with arthritis, her skin marked by age.

"She does like her laundry," Nana says, "but mostly I think she likes to keep busy."

I grin at her. "Sounds like someone else I know."

She laughs as she continues to shuffle the cards. "I don't know. I've learned to enjoy the quiet times. Definitely not up making pies at four in the morning like I used to be."

I'm grateful that Nana and Mom have apprentices of sorts—a younger woman named Kathy and her cousin Sissy—taking over much of the responsibility of the café. But mention of the Nana I grew up with knocks the words loose inside me. "I'm sorry about all this," I say. "About what's happening outside . . . and before."

She splits the deck in half, gives me one stack, and then turns over her first card. Nana motions for me to do the same. I laugh when it registers that, for all of her card expertise, she's set us up to play the simplest game ever: War.

"You think I can't handle cribbage or gin, Nana?"

"I think you should give that brain of yours a little break."

I can't exactly argue with that.

When I reveal a four, she slides it with her seven into her pile and flips her next card. "I haven't talked about your grandpa in a while," she says. "Do you remember anything I've told you about him?"

The air in the room seems to go still. Nana and I have always communicated primarily about practicalities: What needs to be done before the breakfast rush. How I need to use colder water for the pie crust. When is it a good time to come down for the holidays. When are my breaks this year.

We don't talk about her past, her feelings, and certainly not about her husband, who died decades ago. In fact, he died long before I was even born. It wasn't until Grandpa passed away that Nana decided to open the café, had the freedom to do it.

"I know he was in the army and fought in the war," I say. "Mom said he loved blackberries and fishing in the river, and she has his eyes. But you and Mom don't talk much about him."

"That's probably because he was a hard man to love," she says. "And when he died, I think I figured, if I found a difficult man when I was young and pretty, there was no hope for me finding an easy one when I was older, tired, and had a kid."

I'm so focused on what she's saying that she has to tap my stack of cards as a reminder to take my turn. I flip over my card—a seven to her ten. She takes them both.

"I know she had her own reasons, but your mom never tried again either." She flips over a card, a two. It is not at all satisfying to take it with an ace. "She loved your dad. They were genuinely happy for a while, but afterward, she didn't want to bother with men either."

"Must be the Houriet women curse," I say darkly. I finally turned my phone off a couple hours ago. I'd been looking at it every few minutes, waiting for Sam to call. A watched pot never boils, and a watched phone never rings.

Nana pauses with her next card midair. "Tate. I never wanted that for you. I never wanted you to be closed off like that." She leans in, catching my eyes. "No matter what happens this time with Sam, I'm glad you tried again."

Hot tears pool in my eyes, and Nana waves the sentiment away to quickly change the subject. "Have you had anything to eat?"

Before I answer, there's a commotion outside—a chorus of shouting voices followed by the purr of an engine rolling up the drive. I move to the window; relief is a warm flush through my limbs when I see Marco's car.

But once we all meet him at the door, he steps inside, expression grim. "How's everything here?"

"Have you talked to Sam?" I ask immediately, a little taken aback when he ignores my question and heads straight to the scotch I keep stocked on a bar cart in the living room.

We wait in tense silence while he pours himself a glass and takes a long drink. "Have you seen any of the headlines?" he asks me finally.

A blend of anxiety and irritation simmer in my gut. Gwen has some powerful connections in this town, and I've been optimistic in thinking that she'll be able to pull some strings and get this handled quickly.

"I haven't looked because I know you're just starting damage control and I don't want to freak out," I say. "Isn't that what you told me to do? Keep my head down, hang tight until you got here?"

His eyes swing to Charlie. "What about you?"

The moment stretches as they hold each other's gaze. Finally she gives a small nod.

"Do you want to show her?" he asks.

"Show me what?" I ask, looking between them. "Marco, how bad is it? What the hell is going on?"

Charlie's shoulders slump in resignation before she walks to the kitchen and returns with her phone in her hand.

"Just scroll," she says, and tries to hand it to me.

"No," I say, pushing it away. "I'm not on social media because I don't want to see people's shitty opinions."

Marco sighs. "Tate."

Finally, I take her phone and look at the stories in the Twitter column under the hashtag #TateButler. A link to a TMZ article is right up top, and I open it.

We've all read the story: Tate Butler—daughter of superstar Ian Butler—was kept out of the limelight until she was eighteen and ready for her star to shine. Or so we thought. In a blockbuster exclusive this week, we report that Tate and her team weren't the ones who engineered Tate's launch back into the public eye, it was a scheming teenage lover, set on cashing in, and eighteen-year-old Tate was blindsided.

And it looks like he's back in the picture. S. B. Hill—the pen name for a Vermont native named Sam Brandis—is the screenwriter of Milkweed *(which just wrapped shooting this week in Mendocino, starring— you guessed it—Tate and Ian Butler). He's also the man who sold Tate Butler out all those years ago. Is their reunion a romantic twist of fate, or is he back for another publicity grab?*

Article after article says the same general thing.

"This is insane!" I toss Charlie's phone down on the couch. "Come on."

"I agree it's ridiculous," Marco says. "But it's also the current narrative, and everyone—and I do mean everyone— is running with it."

"What are you doing to fix this?" I feel my voice thinning out, growing hysterical. One look at Marco and I'm reassured that my demands aren't bothering him; he knows I've hit a proverbial wall.

"I've reached out to my contacts at AP and most of the networks." Marco takes a deep breath. "But Sam isn't refuting it, and neither is Ian."

"Then get me an interview. I'll explain it."

Marco is already shaking his head.

"What about a statement?" Mom asks.

"We'll issue a statement," Marco explains patiently, "but we have to coordinate with Gwen and the studio, and that is not a fast-moving machine. Ultimately, this is on Sam, too. If he doesn't get out in front of this and face the music, he looks like an opportunistic monster."

"So we get out in front of this now and tell them the truth," I say.

"And what's that exactly?" Marco says quietly. "That he did exactly what everyone is saying he did?"

"You know that's not true," I practically shout. "They're twisting everything. If we explain—"

"Tate, I need you to listen. You said you trust me, right?"

My heart is racing in my chest, adrenaline pumping. I manage a short nod.

"Then trust me to do my job. All these people care about is a sound bite. Something titillating enough to get people to click. They don't care about excuses or extenuating circumstances because nobody has the attention span to read more than a headline or a tweet. In this version you come off looking like the victim, yeah, but also weak and gullible. That is not who you are or the brand we've created. Let Sam worry about Sam's brand. We need to get out of here for a while and let the studio come up with a message. *Then* we talk about an interview."

"I need to talk to Sam. I need to find him."

"He doesn't want to be found, Tate. I've tried. Nobody can get ahold of him."

I let that sink in. Was I wrong about him again?

Did I get tricked again?

"Okay." I let out a long, slow breath. I've done this before—picked up my pieces and carried on. I can do it again. "When do we leave?"

twenty-seven

MARCO MAKES ARRANGEMENTS FOR us to stay somewhere sequestered from the press. Before sending us out the back way, with a few security guys leaving in decoy cars, he also suggests I get in touch with some of my friends in the media or with big online followings. Not to give an official statement, but a quick call to convey that I know what's happening, my team is on top of it, and I'll reach out as soon as I'm able to say something concrete.

As usual, it was the perfect move. Now there are a handful of tweets along the lines of:

I know Tate and this story isn't accurate.

Don't believe everything you read.

Everyone needs to calm the hell down and wait for the real story to come out.

The tide changes, as it so often does online. My friends' tweets are retweeted with confident commentary:

The knee-jerk reaction is never right

You fools jumped on that too fast
Get outta here with your drama shit

The rebuttals may not be entirely fair, but they're enough to allow me to take a breath.

★ ★

The house Marco finds for us is a breath of fresh air. I didn't want a city, and I didn't want the country or a cabin in the woods where I'd be reminded of Ruby Farm. Instead we drive to San Diego, take a flight to South Carolina, drive to Murrells Inlet, and pull up in front of a two-story, gray-sided house that's surrounded by beach and ocean. The clock reads 6:30 a.m. when I finally collapse into my bed with the Atlantic Ocean just outside my window.

I pull the blankets over my head, blocking out the burgeoning sunlight and wishing I could shut out the static in my brain just as easily. My mind is going haywire. The relationship I wanted with my dad is never going to happen. I let Sam back in, ignoring the voice in my head telling me to be careful this time. Regardless of how he feels or whatever circumstances are keeping him from reaching out, it doesn't change that I am in the exact same position now I was then: alone, embarrassed, duped.

I want to put a name to this feeling and call it love. I've never felt before or since what I feel for Sam, and it's a devotion so intense it makes me feel carved out and filled up with something warm and pliable. It's like having a hundred hummingbirds in my blood, thrumming. Even thinking about him now is distraction enough from the madness of the gossip machine.

But he hasn't called, hasn't tried to get in touch with me. It doesn't take that long to fly from California to Vermont. Has he decided what we have isn't worth it? And am I really lying here wondering if I'm good enough for Sam Brandis *again*?

I close my curtains, turn out the lights, but it still takes three episodes of *Schitt's Creek* on the small television to distract me from this spiral and to pull my ego back up above water. *Remember?* I tell myself, *You never wanted to feel this way again. The bliss is not worth the anguish.*

There's a knock just as I start to drift off.

A slice of light stretches across the carpet, and I crack open an eye to see Mom standing in the open doorway.

"Sweetie, your phone was ringing." She pauses, and then brings it across the room to me.

I look down. Only a handful of people have this number. A notification on the screen tells me I've got a voice mail, but I don't recognize the caller.

Mom slips out at some point while I'm staring down at the screen, half hoping it's Sam, and half hoping it isn't. *The bliss is not worth the anguish.*

Holding the phone to my ear, I listen to the voice, even more gravelly through the line.

"Hey, Tate. It's me." A long pause—during which my ribs begin to tightly constrict my lungs—and then a dry laugh. "This is nuts. There are guys with cameras outside my window right now. I just wanted to make sure you knew it wasn't me this time."

He falls quiet again, and then clears his throat. "I don't even know what to say. I wish I'd been able to say goodbye. I don't know what you need from me—hell, I don't know what you even want from me at this point, but I'm here. This is my number. Call me when and if you're ever ready."

★ ★

There's not another house for almost a half mile. The nearest neighbor, a woman Nana's age named Shirley, seems to have no idea who I am and admits to us when she brings a welcome casserole that her favorite show is and will always be *Hill Street Blues*. I don't think we need to worry about Shirley calling up the paper and giving away our location.

Nana takes to baking pies with local ingredients and hand-delivering them to the handful of people within walking distance. Mom sets up an easel on the back deck and tries to capture the sunrise every morning. I walk up and down the beach, searching for intact seashells and hoping that this is the day I wake up and know what to do.

By the time we've been here a week, it hasn't happened yet.

Sam hasn't called again, but—as far as I know—he hasn't made a statement yet, either.

But on day eight, Marco comes to town with a stack of scripts and the news that in an unrelated interview, Gwen finally addressed the S. B. Hill scandal.

"'Gwen Tippett confirmed that Tate Butler and Sam Brandis had a relationship in the past, and reconnected while shooting the feature film *Milkweed*,'" Marco reads, squinting down at his phone. He came directly from a meeting in

New York and is sitting barefoot in the sand wearing what has to be an eight-hundred-dollar suit.

"'When the director was asked if the relationship affected Tate's performance on-screen, Tippett cheekily hinted that audiences would just have to wait and see.'" Marco rolls his eyes. "Very subtle, Gwen."

I tuck my legs to my chest and pull my sweater around them to keep warm. "So the circus has died down."

He tosses his phone to the sand beside him, and looks out over the waves. "For the most part. At least until the press junket. Or until someone gets a glimpse of you and Sam together." When I don't say anything, I feel him turn to look at me. "Any chance we'll see that happen?"

"I don't know." I chew my thumbnail, thinking. "Was it you who gave him my number?"

"Yes."

I let out a long, slow breath. "Okay."

"Tell me what you're feeling, Tate."

"I miss him. I want to call but then my brain pipes up, reminding me that I did everything too fast last time." I frown. "And the time before that. I figure this is the time to really think it through and be sure."

"My parents moved in together after a week," he says, and shrugs. "They've been married for fifty-two years. What's fast to some isn't fast to everyone."

I consider that, wanting it to be true. I think about the first day of filming, seeing Sam on the trail, and the way it all came back in a rush. Sometimes I'm glad I didn't have any warning. Would I have still accepted the part? Looking back, it almost seems like fate that—

I stop, my mind snagging on that detail. Something must change in my posture or my expression, because Marco is suddenly leaning toward me.

"Tate?"

His emails.

I reach for my phone in the pocket of my sweater, and start searching through the emails that Terri archived. I scroll through months and months and then there, Tuesday, January 8.

Thursday, March 14.

Wednesday, July 24.

Thursday, July 25.

My head is spinning. I hold my breath, and I read.

To: Tate Butler <tate@tatebutler.com>
From: S. B. Hill <sam@sbhill.com>
Subject: Milkweed
Date: Tuesday, January 8

Dear Tate,

I'm not sure how to start this email. In fact, I've spent years thinking how to start an email to you, but given the news I've just heard, I can't afford to linger too much on the wording.

First, in case you didn't put the pen name to the person, it's Sam, from London. I realize I have no right writing you. I fully intended to leave you alone after what I did, but this particular situation warrants a heads-up.

You see, I am the writer of Milkweed, and as I understand it, you've just signed on for the role of Ellen.

From the looks of things, we will be shooting on a small farm in Northern California. The cast and crew are going to be housed together on the farm for the duration of the shoot.

I believe it's early enough for you to back out if you wish; no announcements have been made yet, and Gwen tells me we are still a few weeks out from making one.

I'm sitting here, wondering if it's worth saying all of the things I've stored up for the past fourteen years, but in truth I'd be crazy to think you'd want to hear any of it.

As much as I'd love for you to play Ellen, I understand if you back out.

I wish you nothing but the best in life, Tate.
All my love,
Sam

To: Tate Butler <tate@tatebutler.com>
From: S. B. Hill <sam@sbhill.com>
Subject: RE: Milkweed
Date: Thursday, March 14

Hi Tate,

Things have gone along in the development of the film; the cast is coming together, the crew and location are being finalized. For all I knew, you were still involved. But when I saw the announcement in *Variety* today, I panicked, wondering whether you'd seen my first email. I'm not sure if it's too late for you to back out; contractually, I don't know how these things work. But the idea that you wouldn't know about the film, and the backstory, before coming on set makes me feel nauseated.

I need to tell you a little bit about Luther and Roberta. My life with them was good. Better than good, it was the best kind of life. Free-range, bottomless love. Wisdom and commitment to community. Anyone who crossed paths with them was lucky to have known them—I was by far the luckiest for having been raised by them.

I think of this sometimes and wonder whether my decision made your life better or worse in the long run. It's impossible for me to know. I carry the weight of my guilt with me every day, every step. I don't say that to mean it should be a concern on your end; more that we've both had these inflection points in our lives where, unbeknownst to us, someone is making an enormous decision that will impact us forever. I've thought about this in hindsight quite often. What an arrogant kid I was.

It's important to me that you know that none of it was premeditated. What I felt for you—to be honest, what I still feel for you—was genuine. I made the call on impulse, in a panic.

That phone call got me ten more years with Luther. I've examined it from every angle, but I wouldn't trade those years for anything.

When we see each other on set, I'm sure it will be strange at first. If I am especially strange, I'm sorry for that, too. I'll do everything I can to respect your wishes, whatever they may be. If you'd like to have your manager or publicist send along a note to me with a response from you, I'd appreciate knowing that you've seen this email.

With love,
Sam

———————————

To: Tate Butler <tate@tatebutler.com>
From: S. B. Hill <sam@sbhill.com>
Subject: RE: Milkweed
Date: Wednesday, July 24

Dear Tate,

We are two months out from filming, and I haven't heard from your manager or your PR representative (Marco?). I still have no idea if you've even seen these. Should I tell Gwen? Should I contact Marco? I don't want to betray your privacy. I don't want to mess up your official PR story. You have a right to control the narrative, and I don't know who knows.

I am an absolute fucking mess over this. I can't wait to see you but am terrified that it's going to be awful for you to see me.

I want to crawl out of my skin thinking about it.

If I could move past this, it would be easier. But I

can't. It looks like you have, and I'm glad for that, Tate, I really am.

I'm still in love with you (the real you, not the television version, not the magazine version. I'm in love with the girl who wanted to take charge of her life—fuck, the irony—who wanted to grab the world by the balls). You're the reason I still feel like my life hasn't started yet. It's like I'm waiting for you to release me.

I can't wait to be near you, and I just need to know that you're seeing these.

I've loved you for so long, and I just need to know that you know.

Sam

To: Tate Butler <tate@tatebutler.com>
From: S. B. Hill <sam@sbhill.com>
Subject: RE: Milkweed
Date: Thursday, July 25

Dear Tate,

I'm sorry about that last email. I'd been out late with some friends, had one too many drinks. It won't happen again. I promise that I will be nothing but professional on set.

I am, as I've always been, yours,
Sam Brandis

It's really only when I look up that I feel the tears running down my face. Marco is on the phone, pacing a few feet away. Mom is standing on the back porch with her arm around Nana's shoulders; they're both watching me intently.

"Two?" Marco says, pulling my attention back up to him. "That works. Business or better."

"Two what?" I mouth when he looks at me.

"Thank you." He hangs up and ignores me, looking up at the house. "Emma," he calls. "Can you get some clothes packed for—"

"They're all clean and folded," Mom interrupts with a laugh, turning to head back inside. "I'll put them in a bag."

"Marco?" I ask, confused.

He looks down at me, blue eyes softening. "You don't even need to say it, Tate. It's written all over your face." He grins. "But don't worry. I just booked your ticket."

★ ★

There's a no trespassing sign posted at the bottom of the long road, so the taxi stops near a white wooden gate.

"There were a bunch of reporters here last week," the driver says, waiting while I run my card. "Whole road was blocked. Couldn't even get up this way."

I look up past the fence. Trees hide the house and most of the property. "Can you wait down here in case he isn't home?"

He shakes his head. "That's a ten-minute walk. I can give you a number to call if you need another ride, but it's too long to just wait."

Because Eden, Vermont, is bursting at the seams with

cab fares waiting for rides? I give him a tight smile and sign my receipt. "Thanks anyway."

He gives me a questioning look in the rearview mirror. "Why didn't you just call the house?"

"Don't have the number," I lie. That's not exactly true. Sam had to change his number when the news broke, but the studio has it. I'm sure Marco does as well. It's just that this is something I needed to do in person. I'm not a writer like Sam is; I couldn't put what I want to say in an email or a text message. But I know how to love him in person. I don't think I needed to know Roberta and Luther's story in order to know that love like that can exist, but if it hadn't been for Ellen, I'd never have figured it out.

I climb out of the car and reach for my bag. "Thanks."

The driver waves in reply and pulls away, and I'm left staring down the long dirt road, framed by white split-rail fences on either side. I step forward, my bag heavy on my shoulder, the road damp beneath my feet.

It's uncanny, really. Although *Milkweed* ostensibly takes place in Iowa, the set was designed to look like Luther and Roberta's farm. It was beautiful, but it doesn't hold a candle to the real thing. Staring down the lane is a little like looking in a fun house mirror: the pieces are all where they should be, but everything here seems at once bigger, smaller, brighter, older. The apple orchard on Ruby Farm was too big; this one is maybe only two dozen trees. The replica barn was too small and weathered; in reality, the barn here is massive and painted a fresh, brilliant red.

Behind me, hills stretch as far as you can see, and the grass is dotted with grazing cattle and sheep.

My stomach twists a little tighter with every step. What if he isn't here? What if he isn't happy to see me? What if he is? I haven't exactly worked out what I need to tell him, how to take the feelings inside me and turn them into words. But I want to take back control of this story. I don't want Dad or Sam leading the way on this. Not even Marco. I want to be the one to tell the world the truth, but it's terrifying to imagine doing that: putting my feelings out in the world for everyone to read. It's occurred to me more than once lately that I've always been better at living someone else's life than living my own. But here I am, walking down this long road the same way Luther did all those times, all those years ago.

As the road curves, the beautiful two-story farmhouse stands proudly in the distance. A wide porch wraps around the yellow building, and I half expect to see Ellen Meyer fixing her washing machine on the back lawn.

My heart knocks against my chest as I near the house and my feet crunch over the dirt road. The November evening is cold—it's probably forty degrees out—and the sun has just dipped below the tree line, turning the sky a flirtatious cornflower blue. I can barely make out two black rocking chairs looking out over the orchard. Did Roberta and Luther ever sit outside there together, talking, rocking, making each other laugh?

A small dog bounds off the porch as I approach. He barks, at first in warning and then happily as, I guess, I am determined to not be threatening. I drop my bag and kneel, holding out a hand to see if he'll come closer.

The screen door squeaks open and then falls closed again with an echoing slap.

"Rick!" a deep voice calls, and when I look up I see Sam moving down the steps. I straighten, pushing my knit cap higher up on my forehead, and he stops cold in his tracks.

He's wearing worn jeans and old brown boots. The sleeves of his blue flannel are rolled up his forearms, and a dark beanie is covering his head. My eyes never tire of looking at him.

"Tate?" he asks, squinting as if I might be some kind of a mirage.

I don't know what the right thing to say is right now, but the words that come out first—"Your dog's name is *Rick?*"— are probably not it.

He tilts his head, reaching up to scratch his jaw. "Yeah. Rick Deckard." He doesn't add more; he just stares like he's not sure what to do with me.

"From *Blade Runner?* That is fucking *delightful.*"

There's no warning when he jogs the few steps to reach me and scoops me up into his arms. He's trembling, arms wrapped tightly around my waist as he buries his face in my neck. "Oh my God. You're here."

I let myself breathe him in, and my arms find their way around his neck. "Hey."

He walks in a small circle, around and around, and then presses his mouth to my neck before setting me down. But he doesn't back away; I have to tilt my chin to look up at him.

We stare at each other for a good ten seconds, just taking it all in. "I got back from lunch with my dad," I say finally, "and you'd already left the farm."

"Gwen hustled me out of there."

I shrug. "Still. It sucked. I felt like you ditched me again."

He winces at this, and then bends, pressing his mouth to mine for two perfect seconds. "I don't like that."

"I didn't either."

"I assumed they'd tell you that I was worried about you. That they'd sent me home to get away from the madness and not make things worse, I suspect."

"Only a few crew members were left on the farm when we got back. I had no idea whether you were worried or not."

"I realize," he says, and his gaze is level, totally calm, "how easy it was for me to disappear last time. No one knew I was involved. I made you take all the heat. This time, it was my name dragged through mud, and I had to reckon with that." He looks down, kicking a stick away, onto the lawn. "I figured if you called or wanted to talk, I'd be up for that. But if you didn't, I'd understand." He looks at me and grins. "Then I got impatient, but you wouldn't return my call."

"You took a long time to call me that first time," I reply. The truth was always so easy when it was just us like this. "And I let it get in my head."

He wipes his mouth, laughing. "This is some mess we made."

"This is some mess my *dad* made."

Sam's eyes go wide. "No shit?"

"He's eating it up, I bet."

"You haven't talked to him?"

I shake my head. "I still can't believe he sold me out like that. Marco has us—me, Mom, Nana—sequestered away in South Carolina."

"You all're pretty good at hiding."

I can't read his tone. It doesn't sound chastising exactly, but it worms under my skin, making me uncomfortable anyway.

"I don't want to hide," I admit. "I don't want this story to die out because we've disappeared. I want to face it head on."

He tilts his chin up, grinning. "Do you, now?"

"I mean, me and you." I swallow past a lump in my throat. "I want to take over the narrative. If you want that."

Sam takes a small step closer and it brings his body right up against mine. "I want that."

"I found your emails."

His brow rises. "Yeah?"

"And I want *that*," I tell him, adding at his small, confused frown, "I want free-range, bottomless love."

His grin sneaks in from the side. "You know what they say about this farm?"

"What's that?"

He bends, and inhales just behind my ear, smelling my hair. "That anyone who walks down that road in search of love finds it."

"Is that right?"

Sam's mouth is on my neck now, gently biting his way up. He hums in confirmation.

I stretch against him; he's so warm. "Well, that's pretty handy."

"How so?"

"I was just wandering down the road, hoping to find it and—lucky me—you stepped out. You'll do just fine."

With a laugh, Sam picks me up, hauling me over his shoulder, and carries me toward the farmhouse. The sky has settled into a deep starlit canvas overhead.

"Have you ever seen the stars from this exact spot on Earth?" he asks me.

My heart squeezes and then stretches into a thunder. "No, sir."

He slowly sets me down on a thick patch of lawn, dragging my body along his, and then lowers himself, patting the grass beside his hip.

"Come on," he whispers, patting the ground again. The moon is high and full, the sky is an explosion of stars. I settle down next to him, drugged by the heat of his body curved around mine.

"Come right on down here with me, honey," he says, "and let's look at the sky."

Acknowledgments

Writing a book is a lot like giving birth: it's painful, you're sweaty and probably swearing for a lot of it, and just when you think you'll never do it again, you cross the finish line and have this brand-new thing in your arms.

Just like having kids, putting a book out into the world takes a village. We rewrote this book at least three times, and our former editor, Adam Wilson, saw it when it was something else entirely. Thank you for pushing us to make each book better than the last, Adam. Kate Dresser held our hands through the rewrite and helped make this book into what you're holding today. We're so happy with how it turned out.

Our agent, Holly Root, is simply amazing. Thank you for guiding us through the ups and down of publishing, for knowing when to cheer us on and when we need perspective.

Kristin Dwyer isn't just our PR rep, she's our third Musketeer. You work so hard to get our books into the hands of people who will shout about them, and we are so grateful.

Dirty martinis, dry, with extra olives all around (no blue cheese). We love you, Precious.

Have we mentioned how much we love Simon & Schuster and our entire Gallery family? Thank you to Carolyn Reidy, Jen Bergstrom, Kate Dresser, Adam Wilson, Jen Long, Aimée Bell, Molly Gregory, Rachel Brenner, Abby Zidle, Diana Velasquez (we miss you), Mackenzie Hickey, Anabel Jimenez, Tara Schlesinger, John Vairo, Lisa Litwack, Laura Cherkas, Sarah Lieberman, Stacey Sakal, and last but absolutely not least the Gallery sales force who attend meeting after meeting and fight to get our books on shelves and into readers' hands.

Erin Service always happily reads our books when they are messy, when they are less messy, when they are polished, and just before they go to print. She's very good at finding typos even at the end of this whole process, which is a particularly impressive talent. Thanks for being the best pre-reader and sister ever.

Betsy Sullenger took hours of her own time to help us make the film shoot feel realistic—though we must say we did take some artistic license so anything that doesn't feel authentic is totally on us. You were also very kind for not laughing at us when we asked the most basic film questions . . . and there were a lot of those. We adore you, woman.

Candice Montgomery is one of our cherished friends, fellow writers, and—in this case—sensitivity readers. Thank you for helping us carve Luther and Nick out of the most precious of stones, but also helping us see where we fell short in our writing of them. We hope we captured your feedback, but if we missed the mark, it's on us. We love you, and will listen forever. Everyone please read Candice's beautiful books, *Home and Away* and *By Any Means Necessary*.

The librarians and booksellers of the world are true heroes. Thank you for what you do! And to every blogger, reviewer, Booktuber, Instagrammer, and podcaster: we know you do what you do because you love books, but we also know that it is a lot of work. Thank you for reading our words, and for taking your time and talents and voice to tell others about them. We see you and we are grateful.

To our families: we love you the most. Our babies have grown a lot in the time since CLo first began a decade ago—from nine to nineteen, from three to twelve, and from birth to nine years old. We of course, haven't aged a day. (Our husbands have, but they're still pretty fantastic and, more than just putting up with us, somehow seem to still find us charming.)

Thank you to BTS—Nam-joon, Jin, Yoon-gi, Hobi, Jimin, Tae, Jungkook, and ARMY—for being Christina's happy place.

Lo, these pages are full of thank-yous, but my biggest has to be saved for you. People are always asking about our friendship, and how this works. To put it simply: you're my person. Thank you for sharing your beautiful words with me, for helping me become a better writer, for always ALWAYS being supportive, and letting me be annoying in your text box all day. You're my best friend. I love you.

PQ, thanks for pulling my head out of the sand with this book. I guess I should be glad that we made it to twenty-four books before one of them nearly drove me insane. Even if that had happened, though, you'd still be stuck with me forever. ILY.

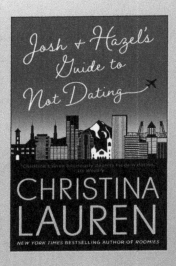
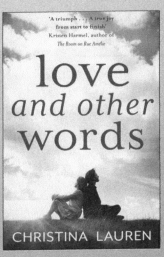
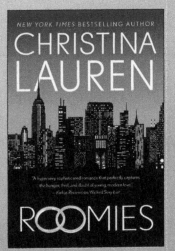
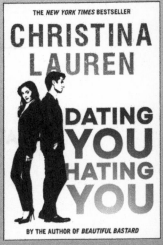

Don't miss Christina Lauren's next
"heartfelt and funny" (*Kirkus Reviews*) novel.

THE HONEY-DON'T LIST

**AVAILABLE FROM PIATKUS
IN SPRING 2020!**

piatkus

PRAISE FOR THE NOVELS OF
Christina Lauren

"What a joyful, warm, touching book! I laughed so hard I cried more than once, I felt the embrace of Olive's huge, loving, complicated, hilarious family, and my heart soared at the ending. This is the book to read if you want to smile so hard your face hurts."

—Jasmine Guillory, *New York Times* bestselling author of *The Proposal*, on *The Unhoneymooners*

"Witty and downright hilarious, with just the right amount of heart, *The Unhoneymooners* is a perfect feel-good romantic comedy. Prepare to laugh and smile from cover to cover."

—Helen Hoang, author of *The Bride Test*, on *The Unhoneymooners*

"Sassy and appealing, writing duo Lauren's (*My Favorite Half-Night Stand*) latest endeavor is sure to please. A perfect read for the beach or poolside, this is one hot summer story not to miss!"

—*Library Journal* on *The Unhoneymooners* (starred review)

"A funny, sexy page-turner that warns: Keep your friends close and their avatars closer."

—*Kirkus Reviews* on *My Favorite Half-Night Stand*

"This is a messy and sexy look at digital dating that feels fresh and exciting."

—*Publishers Weekly* on *My Favorite Half-Night Stand* (starred review)

"You can never go wrong with a Christina Lauren novel . . . a delectable, moving take on modern dating reminding us all that when it comes to intoxicating, sexy, playful romance that has its finger on the pulse of contemporary love, this duo always swipes right."

—*Entertainment Weekly* on *My Favorite Half-Night Stand*

"With exuberant humor and unforgettable characters, this romantic comedy is a standout."

— *Kirkus Reviews* on *Josh and Hazel's Guide to Not Dating* (starred review)

"The story skips along . . . propelled by rom-com momentum and charm."

— *The New York Times Book Review* on *Josh and Hazel's Guide to Not Dating*

"Lauren has penned a hilariously zany and heartfelt novel . . . the story is sure to please readers looking for a fun-filled novel to escape everyday life with."

— *Booklist* on *Josh and Hazel's Guide to Not Dating*

"From Lauren's wit to her love of wordplay and literature, to swoony love scenes [and] heroines who learn to set aside their own self-doubts . . . Lauren writes of the bittersweet pangs of love and loss with piercing clarity."

— *Entertainment Weekly* on *Love and Other Words*

"A triumph . . . a true joy from start to finish."

— Kristin Harmel, internationally bestselling author of *The Room on Rue Amélie*, on *Love and Other Words*

"Lauren's standalone brims with authentic characters and a captivating plot."

— *Publishers Weekly* on *Roomies* (starred review)

"Delightful."

— *People* on *Roomies*

"At turns hilarious and gut-wrenching, this is a tremendously fun slow burn."

— *The Washington Post* on *Dating You / Hating You* (a Best Romance of 2017 selection)

"Truly a romance for the twenty-first century. . . . A smart, sexy romance for readers who thrive on girl power."

— *Kirkus Reviews* on *Dating You / Hating You* (starred review)

"Christina Lauren hilariously depicts modern dating."

— *Us Weekly* on *Dating You / Hating You*